THE TRYST

THE RED THREAD SAGA

BOOK ONE

L. MARIE WOOD

CONTENTS

COPYRIGHT NOTICE

2nd Edition

Paperback ISBN: 978-1-962353-31-1

E-book ISBN: 978-1-962353-32-8

Cover Art by Maya Preisler

Editor: Lucy Blue

Publisher: Mocha Memoirs Press

OTHER L. MARIE WOOD TITLES

The Realm Trilogy

The Realm

Cacophony-The Realm, Book 2

Accursed-The Realm, Book 3

Other Titles

Unworthy

The Unholy Trinity

12 Hours

Mars, The Band Man, and Sara Sue

Crescendo

Telecommuting

The Black Hole

The Open Book

Tales of Time

The Promise Keeper

NON-FICTION TITLES

The Horror Aesthetic: Essays from the Dark Corner of the Genre

About Horror: The Study and Craft

PRAISE FOR THE TRYST

"L. Marie Wood's haunting vision of the human journey through life/death and everything in between delivers riveting work that fascinates and thrills."

- Linda D. Addison, HWA Lifetime Achievement Award recipient and SFPA Grand Master

"L. Marie Wood crafts psychological horror you can't put down."

- John Edward Lawson

"*The Tryst* has such a powerful undertone of not only romance, but it blended so well with the horror elements of the story that you were drawn in completely. L. Marie Wood weaves a tale of three people who drawn together to form something so powerful that the love and loss was palpable. Fate, a journey of self discovery, more? Each reader will take away some element from The Tryst that is different and memorable. But one thing is clear, L. Marie Wood leaves you breathless until the very last page is turned...."

– Dahlia Rose, USA Today Bestselling Author

"This book has it all. Love, suspense, mystery, and it's a thriller of a story. Through everything, the love between Nicole, Mark, and Eric finds its way. L. Marie Wood is truly an artist at crafting an intriguing story, adding just the right amount of

romance and horror.

- Cindy O'Quinn – four-time HWA Bram Stoker nominated writer. Rhysling and Dwarf Star nominated poet.

"The Tryst might be the weirdest book I ever read, and that's absolutely a compliment. This heartfelt and intelligent three-way romance engages exactly the conversations we're all having about technology and humanity in 2025. The characters are relatable and specific, and they react to one another and their situation the way real people with healthy self-esteem and empathy would react. We fall in love with them as they fall for one another. Then the science fiction twist kicks in and makes this story something more and better and completely new—Blade Runner meets Anais Nin. The same insight that makes horror writer, poet, and critic L. Marie Wood able to put characters through the most horrific events imaginable and describe their reactions in a realistic way serves her well in creating a romantic and sexual relationship between three fascinating equals, even when their world turns into something neither they nor we the reader could ever have expected."

– Lucy Blue, Author of *The Devil Makes Three*

ACKNOWLEDGMENTS

Thanks for the unexpected beta reads, GBL and KB, and for the Canadian slang tutorial, MG. Thanks, JH, for the exchange of energy–helping you helped me in ways I didn't expect. As always, LF, thanks for your perspective and real talk.

For SAW, BKW, and MDW... always

PROLOGUE

Early.

For one of the first times in her adult life, she was deliberately early. And like the last time she was early on purpose, he was already there... waiting for her. Only this time...

The flowers were beautiful. They always were at those things and that made everything sadder somehow. Their scent permeated the air, sweet, aromatic, subtle, deceptive—subliminal as it inundated, permeated, overwhelmed... serene, like fresh water from a spring, as it cascaded lies over the surfaces that it touched and left its residue behind. Lies about life, about rebirth, about continuation and the happiness it should bring. White lilies on stands, on the floor, everywhere—brilliant, vibrant, alive. But he's not.

He's not.

She closed the door behind herself quietly, sneaking into the room unseen. It was a small funeral home, one of the last mom-and-pop shops that ran their operations out of a house in the middle of town. Their home? Who knows? If big business hadn't gotten to them yet, it might be. Or maybe this was just a façade to mask the machine. A way to tap into the boutique funeral market if there was such a thing. But none of that mattered to her. A small funeral home meant fewer people on staff. Apparently it also meant an unlocked front door and easy access to the room where he lay waiting.

Dead.

She had her lie ready should she have to use it. It was there on the tip of her tongue. Old colleague, heard about his passing when in town for a meeting, had time to come by and pay her respects before flying out again. It sounded good enough in her head, anyway. She hadn't planned to stay long, wouldn't be there after the ceremony should someone want to inquire more, look deeper, if she even stayed that long.

She couldn't let them see.

There he was. His wife had chosen a handsome suit for him, that much she could see from where she stood. But she found that her body didn't want to get any closer. To do that would bring him into view. She wouldn't be able to escape his still, unnatural face. To get closer would mean that he was really lying there, out of reach... gone.

How long had she been standing there, her back nearly touching the closed door? A minute? Ten? It felt like forever and only a second at the same time.

There he was.

She took a step forward but found that she was unsteady. She stopped, taking a deep breath, trying to calm herself down, her nerves getting the best of her. But she couldn't. Because he was right there, right there in that box where he would lie forever, right there where he wouldn't be able to touch her, smile at her, laugh with her ever again.

Right there.

But not.

Tears stung the corners of her eyes again, and she leaned into the feeling. The sensation was an old friend now.

She took one, two, three more steps until she reached him, walking toward the man she would have to learn to live without, for the last time. A shuddering breath escaped her lips as her eyes avoided his face to land on his hands. She didn't want to see his face yet, didn't want to have that image burn itself into her head. She did not want to remember him like that, the face she loved to stare at now waxen and sculpted, the last lines of his story smoothed to placidity. She *could* not. She did not want to see, for once and for all, that he was indeed gone.

His hands.

Large palms with proportioned fingers. Manicured nails. Prominent veins. Strong. She remembered those hands, how they engulfed hers, how they interlaced with his, how warm, so warm they were.

How cold they felt under her own now.

She never heard the door open and close, never heard footsteps approach where she stood in front of his casket, but when he spoke she didn't flinch. It was as if he were speaking to her from within a dream, another dimension, a place where he had always been, a place where they would live together and she would feel his hands holding her again and she would see him touching his face, and the white lilies wouldn't make her think of the earth, of death, of rot.

His hand.

It touched the small of her back, resting there as though that was where it belonged, and she supposed it did.

"Felt like I was dead too, but then..."

"You touched me," she said, finishing his sentence, the words holding as much truth for her as they did for him.

The pause was heavy between them.

"I knew you'd be here," he said, his voice thick with emotion.

"I made it early, for once," she replied, her voice sounding hollow, lost.

The chuckle that emanated from low in his throat was quiet, almost airy. It would have been misconstrued by anyone else except...

"Hoped you'd make it—" she started, but he cut her off with gentle words she knew almost broke him to speak.

"Nothing could have stopped me from..." His voice was warm even as it trailed off, the rest of his thought left unsaid, given over to heartbreak.

"I know."

They hadn't looked at each other yet. They didn't have to.

"I feel it," she said, her voice wavering, cracking around the edges, breaking.

"Me too. It's... cold... I'm... cold."

She nodded, felt how close he was behind her and wanted to lay her head on his shoulder, but if someone walked in, there would be no explaining that.

"I never thought—in London, I never thought that would be our last..."

His breathing hitched. She could feel it against her neck, feel it reverberate through her own body.

"I never thought it would end." She said it, but they were

both thinking it, incredulity mixing pitifully with resignation to color their thoughts.

One of his hands snaked around her waist, and she placed her free hand on top of it.

Warm.

Familiar.

She fought the urge to bring his hand to her lips, to kiss his fingers as she did the last time they were together. Because nothing was like the last time they were together. Nothing would ever be like that again.

His other hand came into view slowly, passing by her body to rest on his hands.

His thumb grazed hers as he touched him, held on to him desperately.

Her eyes brimmed with tears as their hands met over his.

"He's gone," she said, a sob catching in her throat.

He didn't realize he was trembling, but he could see how unstable his hand was against his stillness.

"Hurts s-so bad, baby," he said in a whisper that she wasn't sure was intended for her or for him.

They leaned into each other then, unable to stop themselves, unable to maintain the distance that they should have to keep the questions at bay. But how could they now? It was over. Everything was over. Because he was dead.

The funeral director saw the couple inside and thought about approaching them. They were early—too early. He would have to talk with his assistant—just a kid really, working his way through school—about locking the front door for reasons just like this. These two seemed ok; they weren't wailing, screaming, thrashing around. But he had seen his share of mourners whose emotions got the best of them, and they started pulling at the body, at the casket, at the flowers. One person even tried to climb into the casket with the deceased. That had really been a scene. Ruined all his work, suit wrinkled, hands unclasped and arms askew, looking more like doll's limbs than a human's. The makeup held, though, and he thanked his lucky stars again for that online course he took on updated corpse makeup application methods. He looked at the couple again. At least they weren't doing that. He'd have to talk to the boy about leaving the door open for sure—he was thinking when he opened the door to the viewing room. The door unlatched soundlessly, and he couldn't suppress the prideful smile that tickled the inside of his mouth. Discrete. Unobtrusive. Just the way a funeral home should be.

The couple was mourning, holding each other in front of the body of Mark Lewis. The mortician ran through the details, couldn't help but do it—it came with the territory. Mr. Lewis was aged 48 at the time of his passing. Brain tumor, and it took him quick, poor guy. Or maybe that was a good thing—he didn't know. He never knew how to think about things like that, didn't know what he would think if someone asked him that same question about his own mortality. One might think that a long illness allowed people to prepare for what was to come, and that was true, but knowing a thing was going to happen was never the same as the thing actually coming to pass. There was no getting ready for someone to die, he had learned over the years, even if the death was a relief. But fast... fast might be even harder on the family, he thought as he watched the two people before the casket supporting each other as best they could. Fast didn't give you any time to prepare, to make your peace, maybe not even to say goodbye. Fast might be hardest of all.

The couple with Mr. Lewis was crying.

The mortician closed the door quietly, deciding to let them have their moment. In an hour, the place would be filled with mourners for the man they were standing in front of and they wouldn't get the chance to be alone with him again. They needed the time with him, he could see that: being perceptive was as important in his world as it was in a psychiatrist's. He also knew that they wouldn't be here when the family came, would probably not show up in the crowd when the funeral began or at the cemetery either. The woman, who wore a stylish yet muted suit with her hair pulled back into an understated bun that did nothing to tone down her natural beauty, indeed only managed to showcase her long, delicate neck, and the man who looked uncomfortable in his suit, off the rack and so new the mortician thought he could see the tags tucked into his sleeve, but gifted with a masculine jaw and a considerate brow... handsome in spite of himself—they would be long gone. He didn't allow his thoughts to linger on why that might be.

After all, it wasn't his place to.

The mortician closed the door quietly and turned to survey the foyer.

Gardenias and eucalyptus in a vase on the round entry table that subtly directed the flow of traffic.

Fountain pen in its holder next to the funeral registry book.

Brass polished; wood waxed.

Neat.

Clean.

Everything in place.

Maybe he would only tell the boy how good of a job he had done with the foyer and setting up Mr. Lewis' room. Just that.

Maybe he would leave the door locking conversation for another day.

Ryan made sure everything was working the way it should, that energy levels were maxed and temperature was optimal. This run was important – he was running out of time, and he knew it. The Galactic Collaborative expected results, and Ryan had missed his deadline by weeks. He had to show proficiency in at least half of the elements to secure funds to continue the trial. He was close... so close... but the program hitched at the same point every single time.

Who would they send to shut him down? Maureen? She'd been in liaison for years, so that made sense. For her it would be business only—the numbers didn't lie. Ryan hadn't produced the product he said he would, hadn't been able to provide any assurances that he ever would. It would just be part of the job if Maureen was the one to pull the plug. If it was his brother, that would be different. There would be a special kind of glee in Jason's eyes if he was the one to tell him to pack it up, to take his pods offline and watch the specimens begin to decline, to deteriorate... to rot. Ryan didn't want to give him that satisfaction.

He'd started the simulation before anyone could stop him.

He hoped he wouldn't regret it.

CHAPTER 1

This was just not her scene.

Lots of people crammed into comparatively small spaces, moving from booth to booth in clumps. She wondered if the feet of the people in the middle of the group even touched the ground at all or if they were just being carried along, floating above the floor, hoisted by the press of bodies, strangers' bodies... so many bodies.

Excited people.

Bored people.

Hyper people.

Pensive people.

Too many people.

Nicole's mind wandered as she manned the booth, looking at the featureless faces of the newest batch of visitors. She heard herself beginning to speak, launching into her presentation for the 300th time without thinking, her mind blissfully slipping into autopilot as some small part of her being wondered how the hell she had gotten there.

Low man on the totem pole at 40.

Empty smiles, robotic nods, aggrandizing, posturing...

Bullshit, bullshit, bullshit.

And it was only day two of a four-day event.

Fan-fucking-tastic.

Nicole's mind wandered as she waited for the next batch of people to make their way to her booth, musing over things she'd just as soon forget.

'Great idea, Nicole. Let's discuss it after you put together the slide deck for so-and-so's meeting.'

'Check my calendar and set up a meeting, Nicole.'

'Man the booth, Nicole, while the big boys play with gadgets upstairs.'

Switching careers had seemed like such a good idea at the time...

And it was—it really was. Being able to see the kids off to school then do the work that actually spoke to her soul instead of pushing papers and making excuses was better than she could have ever imagined it would be. But entry level sucks—always has and always will, no matter how enthusiastic one is about being there.

At least no one had asked her to get their coffee... yet.

"... if you want."

Nicole looked at the man in front of her, hoping she didn't look like she wasn't paying attention. She *hadn't* been paying attention, but she hoped she had kept her face straight anyway. He was a wiry man in his early thirties with a lot of dark hair casually styled and splaying across the shoulders of his industry-specific t-shirt.

This is someone I know, not a booth visitor.

"Do you?" He kept talking.

What is his name? It's unique... it's on the tip of my tongue...

"Or I could go grab it...?

Wait... he didn't just ask me to get him something, did he?

"Hmm?" Nicole replied, sounding dazed and hating it.

Good answer, genius...

... but it better not have been coffee.

"I said," the man replied, stepping behind the booth to put something on the shelf, encroaching her personal space in a way that didn't seem to matter as much to the Millennials as it did to the Gen Xers, "I can run and grab the extra pens Joe forgot to pack or you can."

Nicole's face was blank. This time she knew it was. She could feel the way her cheeks fought to stay still as she tried her best not to assume because, damnit, if her picking up coffee for them was part of this little errand, she might just scream.

"I saw a bookstore near that copy place when I was looking for parking. It was right next to the coffee shop," he continued, and Nicole's blood started to boil. Because there *was* a coffee shop right next to the bookstore—she noticed it too—and Nicole did *not* leave middle management to start memorizing how some thirty-something-year-old exec took his latte, and she'd be damned if—

"You said you wanted to write a romance novel, right? Figure you'd probably kill for a few minutes alone in a bookstore away from," he gestured at their surroundings, all blues and grays and greasy hair and glasses. "... all this. Unless you don't want—"

He *remembered.*

It had been just an offhanded conversation in the break room on her second or third day. They had stood on either side of a table, chitchatting about nothing the way you do in an office when someone new meanders into the common area, and life aspirations had come up. He had said something about writing code if she remembered correctly—something that sounded like he was speaking another language and made her eyes cross for a second. She remembered how dreamily she had confessed that she wanted to write a romance novel, probably looking every bit the sap she was when it came to that subject. It was a nothing—a throwaway conversation buried under dozens of more important work-related back and forths that they'd had since, yet still, he remembered.

Curious. But there at the trade show booth was neither the place nor the time to unpack that.

"No, that sounds perfect," Nicole said, sure the relief she was feeling for not being marginalized resounded in her voice. But now she knew. It was good. The change she had made, as scary as it was, was very good.

"Thanks, Ananda."

Mercifully, his name came to her in the moment she was expected to speak it. A Thai name for an American man. Go figure.

"Yeah, sure thing. I'll take over here for a while. You go read some Dickens,"

No.

"...or Poe,"

Really?

"or, I don't know, Zane,"

Hmm...

"...or somebody."

His smile was infectious even if it was self-deprecating.

She smiled her thanks back at him and left before overthinking it, the cutthroat business model that had made up her first career trying to browbeat her, guilt her into staying, chastise her for thinking she could do anything else. But no, she admonished in a voice that sounded stronger than she had expected it to, no more of that.

Nicole fought the crowd in search of the door, finding it only after a throng of people had left the hall where her company had set up shop in favor of the main conference room, clammy flesh and stale breath spilling into the triple-wide space with padded walls and the oddly ornate facade that mid-range hotels do so well.

She couldn't believe how fresh the air outside smelled.

Nicole cinched the belt on her Rabato coat and turned in the direction of the bookstore, trying not to form a mental picture of herself doing so. It was new. Everything about her was new right then, and she didn't want to over-analyze any of it or talk herself out of anything. She just wanted to let it happen, but that was hard, to say the least. Before, when attending events like these, she would have worn a suit and heels, would have made sure her hair was a modest length, and would have kept her makeup neutral. But there she was wearing a black mock turtleneck over black jeggings with black suede knee-high boots and a coat that looked like an elaborately tied bandana when closed. Her lipstick was anything but subtle—earth red perfectly following the contour of her lips. And her hair? An undercut that might be a little shorter than she was expecting on the exposed side, but that was a whole other conversation. She either looked like a chic modern woman whose clothes looked as if they were made especially for her or an aging goth who didn't know when it was time to tone it down a little.

She hoped for the former.

Boy, did she.

If there was anywhere to try out a new style it was in a

little micro city like this one, close enough to Toronto to be redeemed by it, where no one knew her.

The wind tousled the little bit of hair she had left. It cascaded prettily in front of one of her eyes. Canada was chilly. She couldn't believe the forecast; it was going to be between 9-15º C while was she was there (something like 48 º F, which she had to look up to understand that it was going to be much colder than her American self expected it to be in May—thank you Google), but after seeing the snow that fell that morning as she sipped coffee in the hotel lobby restaurant, she'd buy anything. At least now the snow had stopped; none of it had stuck, and the sun was warming up the air.

What time was it, anyway?

The wind whipped.

Her cheeks were cold.

Her mind was confused—*weren't we already out of winter?* The air felt like the opposite—the very beginning of winter's chill wrapped up in a neat little bow.

A man nodded, smiled. And not a man who might have been her father's age, closer to his seventies than his sixties, the gray in his hair more prominent than the brown. He was a younger man, mid-thirties at the oldest, not a speck of gray in his dark hair, at least not that she could see.

Maybe she didn't look like she was playing dress up in somebody else's clothes.

The jury was still out.

Nicole spotted the bookstore and quickened her pace, spurred on by the prospect of a warm cup of coffee and a book in her hand. A gust of wind reached in from between buildings to place a cold hand on the small of her back, inching her forward even faster. She entered the bookstore, which was the closest door offering shelter from the cold, at almost a jog, shaking the cold from her shoulders as the warm air caressed her face.

Ahh, hazelnut.

Hazelnut and maybe vanilla.

Bless the gods who came up with combo stores. The coffee shop had an entrance inside the bookstore for those who wanted to read while they drank. The people who preferred to keep their book browsing and their coffee drinking separate could do that, though in that instant Nicole couldn't imagine anyone ever wanting such a thing. The smell from the coffee shop permeated the bookstore, kissed the pages as it danced in the air, making the place feel homey and comfortable: the only kind of real she ever wanted to feel.

She needed a cup of whatever had created that tantalizing smell, and she needed it right away.

Nicole walked into the bookstore and made a beeline to the break in the wall where the two businesses converged, taking stock of the book displays lining the way and making a mental note to peruse each and every one of them once she had a cup of that goodness in hand. There was a line, as would be expected for something that smelled so good. Nicole stepped into the queue, taking her place behind a middle-aged woman who obviously loved floral prints and whose favorite color was probably purple considering the prevalence of both in her outfit. Nicole almost felt compelled to lean in and smell the large lavender bush on the back panel of the woman's shirt, was almost sure she could smell its scent warring with that of the coffee. Memories of Yardley London English Lavender soap in her mother's bathroom sprang up, filling her head with that fuzzy, warm tingle that only comes when snippets and flashbacks of the past came from out of nowhere. Yardley's lavender soap. Only she and her mother called it Yardley's *of* London, not Yardley London as she came to know it years later...or had they been right when they called it Yardley's of London and Yardley *London* was wrong? It was on the tip of her tongue—she remembered calling her mother and telling her something about the name years later, when she had already graduated college and was living on her own with a bottle of the stuff gracing her own bathroom sink. What was it that she had said? 'Hey Mom, you'll never guess, but we've been calling the lavender soap by the wrong name the whole time! Aunt Chris was right after all,' or had it been, 'Mom, you'll never guess, but Aunt Chris was dead wrong about the name of our soap.'

I should find some and send it to her.

Do they even make that soap anymore?

I need to look it u-

"Miss?"

Lavender lady was gone, long gone, by the look of it, and Nicole had been left standing there, staring into space, the smell of English lavender filling her head.

"Oh, yes," she stumbled, recovering gracelessly.

The man behind the counter smiled at her kindly enough. There was no urgency in his voice, no flitting eyes and impatient shifting of his feet. Because things were different here. She was in a city, sure, but it wasn't New York, or Los Angeles, or Washington DC. There people understood that relaxing was a real thing and that, of all places, a bookstore with a coffee shop on its side was the perfect place to do just that.

Nicole took a deep breath, and the scent of that amazing

coffee took over her thoughts again, showed her what was important. The barista smiled again. Laughing at herself, she asked what the coffee was, knowing that it didn't really matter what he said. She would have that drink, regardless of its name or what was in it—it smelled way too good to leave on the counter. She was reflecting on that as she drifted over to the waiting area, lined with bagged coffee beans, specialty mugs, and other coffee paraphernalia, and filled with people waiting patiently for their drink du jour. She was lost in her head again, but this time without discernable thought, the sound of the coffee brewing, the chatter between people sharing space as they waited for their purchases, the visual onslaught of brightly colored travel cup sleeves and cocktail stirrers lulling her into a comfortable haze... so much so that she didn't notice the man coming toward her, nor his foot—the one that she mashed with her boot.

"Oof," the man breathed as he turned toward her with surprise on his face as his drink sloshed around in the covered to-go cup.

"Oh! I'm so sorry," Nicole said, ripped from her reverie in the most embarrassing of ways.

They jostled a bit, both with shoulders raised in surprise and doing that strange touching but not touching, first her reaching for him then him reaching for her but neither of them ever quite getting there, engaging in the dance that strangers do when they collide unexpectedly.

Furrowed brows.

Chagrined smiles.

Nervous laughter.

Talking at the same time, looking nowhere and everywhere at once, not really seeing.

Until...

Nicole looked at the man whose foot she had stepped on. He was regaining his composure from the stumble he took after she lost her balance and fell into him, adding insult to injury. She had apologized, but he hadn't said anything, hadn't done the usual blow-off she was expecting, no 'It's ok,' or 'No harm, no foul.' Oof is what he had said. *Oof.* She wondered... wasn't that more like a sound effect? Like the reaction you'd have if something heavy knocked into you and took the breath right out of your lungs? Wait, does that mean he's hurt? Maybe a rib was cracked in the clumsy exchange and he didn't say anything because he *couldn't* say anything?

Nicole started to speak, but looked closer instead, taking in his face, the set of his jawline, how sharp it was.

And his eyes...ice blue and clear as glass.

"...zelnut Raf?"

The barista gave her look that people who worked in fast food the world over had mastered, that practiced patience that was really nothing more than veiled frustration; Nicole didn't need to see his expression to know what it was - she could feel his eyes boring into the back of her head. She blinked but was still there, lost in the man's eyes and... dear god, was he holding her up?

"I'm—I'm so sorry," she said again, removing herself from the arms that had braced her when she stumbled, more embarrassed by this mishap than ever. She was sure her face was red—her skin was too hot not to be. She was sure he was sufficiently done with her, the little mistake nothing but water under the bridge now, but there she was, still leaning on him... touching him.

She was sure she could see the galaxy in his eyes.

"It's fine—" he started, but she prattled on, missing how smooth his voice was in her nervous rambling.

"You're not hurt, are you?"

"No, not at all."

He smiled.

She smiled.

They smiled.

"Are you...?" he started again, but felt himself shut down, thrown off course by the woman in front of him, the beautiful woman he was standing incredibly close to.

He stared, the rise of her eyebrow doing something to him that he didn't expect. He couldn't look away from it, from her. Her eyes, chestnut brown and rich, perfectly oval and adorned with long lashes, were hypnotic. They squinted when she smiled, the lids coming into each other to meet in the middle and almost close. He looked at her eye smile in awe, watched as she blinked, as she realized he was still looking, then as she smiled again, her eyes nearly closing from the intensity of it.

Wow.

"Hurt, I mean. Did I hurt you?" he said, recovering. He looked away, a feat in and of itself, and forced his legs to take a step back... a step he regretted immediately.

"Me? I should be asking you that," Nicole said, missing the warmth of his closeness more than she was willing to admit. "Well, I guess I *did* ask you that."

She felt the heat rising in her cheeks.

"I'm so clumsy," she continued, with effort. "I should have been looking where I was going."

"With so many things around, how could you?"

Brilliant comeback, guy, Eric chastised himself inwardly.

He wished he could rewind the moment and say something wittier, cooler... just better. Then he worried that his embarrassment was showing on his face.

Quiet.

Too quiet.

It had only been a few seconds, but they felt like minutes, hours, time that should have been filled with something—a laugh, words of agreement... anything at all. He started to laugh self-deprecatingly, hoping that would salvage the moment, wipe the egg from his face and allow him to look aloof, indifferent, or at minimum, unassuming again. Because that was how he looked before, right? His interest, the fact that he was downright besotted in the span of a minute, hadn't shown on his face already, had it? Part of him was sure it had, that his eyes had grown soft and unfocused, revealing his thoughts, as unorganized and caught unaware as they were. But maybe his eyes hadn't given him away or maybe, just maybe she had been too caught up in her own world and almost knocking him over to notice...?

She dipped her head and smiled at the floor. He thought he should turn away because he knew that if she glanced up to look at him from under the fringe of hair that was so artfully cascading over one eye that he might not ever be able to turn away again. But he couldn't. Something inside him wanted her to do exactly that.

She snickered, a simple *tsh* escaping her lips.

Don't do it.

She pulled her bottom lip into her mouth to bite one corner.

Please, please do it.

And then she did.

Those oval chestnut eyes regarded him with a look that

was both embarrassed and playful at the same time. He knew then that he was done, finished, ruined... hers.

"Hazelnut Raf?"

A different barista this time, searching for the elusive 'Nicole', this one less patient than the last.

They both jumped at the sound of the woman's voice.

They were both secretly happy to see the other so affected.

"I think that's me," Nicole said, finding her voice, trying to clear her throat discreetly, trying to make it even out without having to engage in that loud, unladylike barking thing she might have done into her hand at any other time, in any other place.

"Only if you're Nicole," he said, hoping his smile came off as disarming because his comment surely hadn't. He couldn't help but wonder exactly when he had stopped being cool.

"I am," she said shyly, and he had to bite back the urge to follow it with, 'Duh.'

She first leaned toward then took a step toward the coffee counter, which is exactly what you would expect someone to do when they heard their named called to pick up their beverage, but still he couldn't help but feel jealous, maybe even irritated by the shift in attention. The barista was still there, her eyes landing on the woman, this Nicole that was taking over his senses, and looking at her expectantly, if not a little urgently. She should go pick up her drink—of course she should go—but, god, he didn't want the moment to end.

"R-right," he stuttered, leaning toward her, stepping forward even, bridging the gap created when she had moved away. "Of course you are."

He watched as she turned look at the barista, no doubt with an apology etched on her face, but then she turned to regard him again, this man leaning clumsily toward her, gesturing abstractly with his hands, the motions meaning nothing decipherable. She hesitated. Then she smiled.

His heart stopped.

He felt it happening, could envision his awkward pause as if he were looking at it from outside himself. His mouth was working like a fish, flopping open to speak but remaining soundless. But yet she still smiled. How did the people in her life handle it when she smiled like that? Were they able to keep on doing whatever they were doing or did they feel compelled to turn to her, to revel in the way that she lit up the world, to blush at how those dimples, barely there but ever so slightly indenting her cheeks, winked at them? Did they feel breathless when they saw the way her smile encompassed her whole face, all attempts at hiding her true self gone in favor of raw emotion? Did they feel like they might have died and gone to heaven too?

It was difficult, but he closed his mouth, swallowed, then opened it again, this time to speak actual words.

"Because why else... would you, you know, claim Nicole's drink?"

He pointed at the drink but she kept looking at him instead of turning her head like probably any other human being would have done.

Did he notice?

Nicole was afraid he had, that he saw her standing there unsure of what to do with her hands, staring at him like he was the most amazing thing she had ever seen in her life, with the silliest look on her face to prove it. How could he *not* have seen the way she was staring at him? Her eyes felt like they were open too wide to look normal. Her smile felt too big for her face. She must have looked like some love-struck teenage girl standing in front of her favorite celebrity, nothing but stars in her eyes and air between her ears. She wanted to close her mouth, bring down the wattage on that smile just a little bit, actually told her mind to get a grip and rein it back in, but she couldn't tell if she had actually followed those instructions. Her mind was preoccupied with other things, things like how broad he was, his shoulders reaching to opposite sides of the room in the most distracting of ways, how much taller he was than her, making her feel small, like she could tuck herself into his arms and be safe there, how his hair was styled just so—the perfect messy, textured low fade hairstyle that made you wonder how anyone could look so good after the wind had had its way. Tinged pink, that hair.

Interesting.

Blink.

Blink!

You're staring.

"Hazelnut. Raf. For. Nicole."

This time the barista was done.

The sound of her voice, laced with resignation over the fact that she might be asked to remake a drink that had been perfectly fine when served but was growing colder by the minute, snapped Nicole out of her weird reverie like pressing an on/off switch.

Thank God for small favors.

Nicole turned toward the barista, whipping her head harder than she meant to, feeling herself lose the precarious balance she had just reclaimed because of it. She took a step forward, hoping she had hidden how off balance she was by moving, and took two wide steps to reach the counter where her neglected drink stood waiting.

The barista smiled when she surrendered the drink, a knowing smile that was more like a judgmental smirk when you got right down to it, one that made Nicole giddy and nervous at the same time. Was it that obvious that something was going on there between her and that handsome stranger or, worse, had the barista issued that half there, half not corner of the mouth lift in disdain for the woman before her who was so out of her element she almost reeked of insecurity?

Nicole's heart dropped as she wondered exactly what she must look like that in that ridiculous get up she was wearing with her silly haircut and way too eager eyes. But then the barista gave her the slightest of winks, cast an enraptured glance at the man with the curiously pink hair, and feigned fluster. Now Nicole knew. Sometimes you *can* believe what you read online. Canadians really *are* nice.

Nicole nearly whispered her thanks, not trusting her voice enough to speak just yet. She turned back around, half expecting the man's interest to be pulled in some other direction, the casual interaction nothing more than that to him, just a little banter with the woman who nearly severed his toes from his foot with the heft of her boot. Nothing earth-shattering, nothing particularly special. But he was still there, looking at her but trying not to, letting the woman behind him go around him because wait, what was he doing?

He was approaching her.

She didn't know whose turn it was to speak, hoped she didn't look every bit as out of sorts as she felt.

Nicole opened her mouth to say something, calling up a

witty quip that teased her, staying just outside her reach when, thankfully, he spoke.

"I'm sorry, you must think I'm, what's the word you use here... daft? Or wait, no, maybe that's an English thing. I mean, a UK thing, because you speak English, right, you're not speaking French, but you might—"

He gestured wildly, trying to quell any misunderstanding that might arise from his ramble.

He was nervous.

Her heart flipped.

"I-I'm not from here," she said, cutting in when his hands started waving off the prospect of offense at not being bilingual. "I'm from America."

"Ain't we all, hun?" a man interjected with a smile that contrasted with the sharp edge of his words. "Would you mind moving this discussion over to the seats so I can pick up my double-double?"

It was then that Nicole noticed that the man had ended up half in and half out of the line which was stretching closer to the door with every passing second and people kept having to maneuver around him to reach the counter. She almost reached out to guide him out of the man's way. It was instinctual, that motion, so natural despite the fact that she didn't even know his name.

Hi name... what was his name?

Yes was on his lips, the unspoken answer to whatever she might have asked next, whether it was, 'Do you want to join me over there on the sofa?', 'Does it suddenly feel hot in here?, or 'Do you want to stay with me forever?' But he bit it back. He didn't want to come on too strong. He was sure he had already made an ass of himself. Why would a woman like her want to spend time with someone who behaved the way he did, like he didn't have a clue where he was or what he was doing?

They were stuck for a moment, lost in suspended animation, staring openly at each other without an inkling of what to do next. He knew that all she needed to do was tell him what she wanted, and he would do that for as long as she would allow. At the same time he wondered what the hell was happening to him, how he could be so absolutely sprung so fast.

Her skin was smooth, unblemished. It did things to him.

"Do you want to...?"

She let the question hang, gesturing toward the seats in a flash of courage that caught her off guard, and thank the stars above, he nodded yes. She started walking toward the seating area replete with leather loveseats, oversized armchairs, and coffee tables—homey, just the way she liked it. The seating area straddled the break where the two stores met; shoppers in both the bookstore and the coffee shop had to navigate around it through the wide entryway. This further solidified the thought that Nicole had been considering from the moment she walked into the place: these people understand what a bookstore is supposed to be—a refuge, an escape, an oasis.

He caught pace with her easily and walked next to her, side by side, the placement familiar in ways he didn't understand. He tried to remain neutral, only concerning himself with taking one step after another, but it was hard to do. He didn't want to ogle, couldn't allow her to think that's the type of man he was, but she was so stunning that he was afraid he wouldn't be able to stop himself. Classy. Naturally stylish in an understated way. Poised without trying.

Gorgeous.

He almost left her as she slowed, so caught up in the energy she put out that he nearly overshot her.

She hadn't noticed.

With growing dread, he realized that she hadn't noticed that he almost kept walking, would have walked right out the door the way his head was in the clouds. Did she care? He felt a chill snake its way up the back of his neck to tickle the short hairs as he realized the moment might already be over in her mind and he hadn't even tried to shoot his shot yet.

He stopped, leaned back on his heel to fall in line with her again, and looked at her profile.

A beat. Maybe two. Enough to grow uncomfortable.

"Here?" he said because he needed to say something, to fill the silence, to give her an opening to apologize, make some excuse, and exit stage left if that's what she wanted.

"Y-yes," she replied airily. She had cocked her head as if in deep thought when she stopped and now found it difficult to change tack and meet his gaze. It was only for a moment, but it was there. Her recovery was worth all the self-doubt he experienced in her moment of pause. She smiled that beautiful smile at him as she took the first hesitant step toward the loveseat in front of her. She had to inch around a coffee table that was littered with coasters and books that people had changed their minds about to get to the free seat and she seemed nervous to do so, but when a man wearing the professorial garb of a professor waiting for his first lecture of the day to begin eyed the same space, she quickly moved into action to claim it.

She sat down a little harder than she meant to, jostling the other occupant as he read the newspaper.

He looked up.

CHAPTER 2

It was just a glance but it was enough to throw her off. What she saw in that moment, that fleeting second when the man on the loveseat's eyes flashed toward hers—not quite making it all the way but close enough... dear god, it was close enough—what she saw in them was forever.

Nicole faltered, might have fallen onto the seat—she didn't know... she had lost the feeling her legs.

And then she realized that the man with the pink hair, the first one to make her lose her grip that day, was looking at her.

She sniffed as if her nose had just suffered one of those phantom tickles, the ones that felt like the nose hairs had decided to reposition themselves all of a sudden—but it hadn't. She just needed to do something—make a sound, move her body... something!—to get her mind back in the game, and she hoped maybe the sharp intake of air would do it. At the very least she wanted to try to distract the pink-haired man she sat down with, turn his attention away from her for just a moment so she could screw her face on right.

Nicole was sure she looked every bit as stunned as she felt, so obviously affected by the man holding the newspaper. She needed some way to regain control of the moment and that, that weak little sniffing noise, was the only thing that had come to mind.

She almost did it again.

"So... interesting choice," she said instead, speaking the phrase as if in continuation of a conversation they had already been engaged in.

"Mmm," he hummed noncommittally, barely aware that he was responding at all. In fact, he hadn't realized he was sitting or that she was talking, or nearly anything that had had happened in the past few seconds. At least he hoped it had only been a few seconds. He didn't know. Would looking at his watch appear rude? Would she think that he wasn't interested in her anymore, that she had somehow bored him so much that he couldn't be bothered with the pleasantries of chit-chat? Did people even say chit-chat anymore? Or pleasantries? *What century am I from, anyway?*

He shook his head a little, just enough to clear it. He had to keep it together or else he would lose it all. But all of what... just what the hell was he talking about?

He looked at her.

She felt it too. He could tell by the way her body was drawn to him, leaning in without realizing it, as she fought not to look at him full on, unabashedly, the way her soul craved to.

And then he felt better. Because he wasn't in it alone; he wasn't seeing this in some dream or hallucination he might be having while waiting in line for the coffee he'd never drink. She saw it too, and that made it real.

He let out the breath he hadn't realized he was holding

and had the urge to rub his eyes to clear them, to make sure he was seeing the real world through them. She was looking at him expectantly, a little too eagerly, if he was being honest, like it was put on. And he couldn't blame her. Sitting next to someone like that has to make one feel disoriented and loopy, maybe even dizzy. Sitting across from him surely did.

The man that Nicole had sat next to on the loveseat was reading the newspaper, holding it low on his lap over his crossed legs. His face was still as he read–he didn't mouth the words, didn't move his eyes across the paper exaggeratedly, allowing a full, unobstructed view of his features for anyone who might choose to look. His golden skin peeked through the long, wavy bangs of his windswept hair that reached the nape of his neck. His cheekbones were high, full and round like apples at the tops, and his lips were incredibly full.

He was staring, he knew that. He told himself to stop doing it, but he couldn't. It was as if he was waiting for something—a moment, a second that held everything important within it.

How long had he been staring at this man, so unsuspecting behind his newspaper? Suddenly he was thankful that the man hadn't noticed him—he didn't think he could take another moment of awkwardness brought on by his own behavior today.

He swallowed.

The man kept reading, oblivious to him.

He looked at her.

She was waiting for an answer patiently, beautifully.

His heart surged. She was so damned stunning. The way her eyebrows knitted ever so slightly when she was curious about something. The way her lips twitched as she tried to keep her nervousness at bay. The way it seemed like she was trying not to bite her bottom lip just to have something to do in the silence.

Silence.

How long had he kept her waiting?

"What is?" he said after clearing his throat just to be sure that sound would actually come out as he formed the words. "Interesting, I mean?"

"Pin-"

The man reading the newspaper stretched as she spoke, cocking his chin sharply from one corner to the next as he cracked his neck. And then he did the thing that did them both in, ruined whatever façade they had been trying to uphold, whether consciously or unconsciously, and reduced them to infatuated teenagers.

He ran his hand through his longish hair, pulling the bangs away to expose his forehead.

As the man's hair cascaded down in messy layers on either side of his natural part, she could feel her stomach drop. She jolted in her seat, just a little, but enough to get his attention, and he turned his rich brown upturned eyes on her fully this time. He had been reaching for his cup of coffee but stopped midway, his arm suspended in air. She had time to notice the curve of his bicep as the flowy white shirt he wore clung to it, outlining the muscles, taut as they held his arm in place. She also had time to notice that his lips, plump and beautiful—kissable was the first word her mind flashed at her about said lips in neon, like a motel vacancy sign—had curved into the most endearingly quizzical grin.

She would be buying everyone in the hair salon gift cards when she got home.

CHAPTER 3

He was looking at her.

She was looking at him.

He was looking at him.

He felt outside himself.

When he woke up that morning he felt... different, like something about that day would be unlike any other day. Normally he didn't put a lot of stock into that kind of thing; premonitions, presque vu, *déjà vu—those were for the superstitious, for old ladies who crossed themselves whenever the wind rustled their hair and threw salt over their shoulder to ward off bad luck... and the French, apparently. Still, when he crawled back onto the hotel bed after jumping up and out of it at the sound of the alarm, the bed with its too soft mattress and feather pillows that wrapped around his relaxing body, holding it like a glove, after his mind told him that the shitty presentation for the shitty meeting he was in town for could wait and then proceeded to lull him into the most restful sleep he'd had in recent memory, he knew something was different. When he splashed his face with cold water in a bathroom that distantly reminded him of the sterile penthouse suite where the entomophobic landlord met his end in Creepshow; even when he smiled in the mirror at himself and audibly congratulated his reflection for pulling entomophobic out of his ass like that, he knew something was up.*

He didn't know if he should be happy or frightened by that momentary clairvoyance... that, dare he admit it, premonition. But there it was.

Prickly.

His skin felt prickly under their gazes. Tingly in a way that was not unpleasant in the slightest.

Euphoric?

Really?

Where were all these SAT-level words coming from? He felt like he had stepped out of lit class on a campus far more prestigious than his own had been only to find out that he was actually the professor.

He smirked to himself. Where was all this next-level shit coming from? Was this why he woke up feeling different, off in some way...so he could spout heady shit in the meeting and then drop the mike on the executives, their mouths hanging open in surprise? But what kind of surprise would that be? The good kind, 'You have a great roadmap planned out for this line of business, Mark. Excellent work.' Or the bad kind, 'What the fuck is this bullshit here, Mark? It's like you don't know anything about the product at all or the market we are trying to penetrate. What are you doing all day, jerking off?'.

They wouldn't say that, off course, probably wouldn't think it either. Mark knew that. He also knew his shit and had done well at the company for the almost 10 years he had been working there. But his working from home bothered them, and that always made him nervous. He knew they hadn't liked it when he asked to transition to a remote model after moving into the new house, which was over 70 miles away from the closest office—just barely, but who's counting? They agreed to the remote working situation, but it was a sort of reluctant approval. He figured they'd get used to it, that it would get better over time. But 'better' only meant they didn't say anything about it, at least not directly. Who knew what they thought he was doing when it took him longer than 30 minutes to reply to an email or when they called at 12:30 p.m. and he didn't pick up because he was, gasp, eating his lunch? Did they think he was outside soaking up the sun, that he had driven to the beach and was out playing in the water? When they called at 2:00 a.m. did they think it was ok because hell, he was only sleeping? Did a delayed response to a message always mean he had been playing guitar, painting a picture, taking a gourmet cooking class, watching porn, doing anything other than working on a report on another screen with his head down and his mind focused when it came in?

Jesus, why am I going off on such a tangent? Am I having a stroke?

He breathed deeply through his nose and let it out slowly. No, not having a stroke. Just feeling like every other person who has to work a job they don't like as much as they used to feels. He didn't even need to struggle to find the right word to describe it, not that day: precarious.

That's how he found himself sitting there, where he normally would not have been that morning, or any morning. He needed to be there if only because it was different from his norm. On any other day he would have driven right by that little bookstore with coffee shop attached, claimed a hotel cube at the company's office space, and gone over the presentation once, twice, as many times as he could before the meeting started, never even considering stopping for a drink. That had been his routine since he added travel to his toolkit, volunteering to be the presentation guy for his team, the one who made eye-catching slides and spoke to the data in front of executives, internal and external alike. Because he liked working from home and he wanted to keep doing it. So he carved a niche for himself, made the company think they needed the service he was providing and dominated it so that he and only he had the historical knowledge. So even if that meant he had to fly all over the world for meetings and be away from home more often than he wanted to, it was—

The meeting... crap!

Like a light switch had been turned on, Mark's eyes darted away from the newspaper in his hands to the clock over the door. He had noticed it before sitting down, a huge face with roman numerals and ornate minute and second hands. An eccentric selection for this place, he thought, reveling again at how his mind seemed to be working that day. Normally he wouldn't have even noticed a thing like that, let alone taken the time to consider whether or not it fit the décor. Even if he had noticed it, he would have chosen, instead, to check the time using his cell phone like everyone else did. Looking at a clock on the wall reminded him of checking a wristwatch. Then he thought of his Fossil watch with the interchangeable wristbands. Camouflage. He loved the camouflage one.

He started to rethink that stroke idea.

The line for coffee had grown since he had been in it, nearly reaching the door. He noticed it after looking at the clock and feeling silly that it took him a moment to be sure he was reading the roman numerals right. On this day of enlightenment he found that his memory didn't extend to trivial things such as what 11 looked like written in roman numerals or if a farmer walking into his country cottage, as the coffee place seemed to be going for, would know how to write those minutes in said archaic form. He laughed at himself. He had never been more thankful that inner monologue was precisely that.

It wasn't too late, but he needed to get going soon if he wanted to have time for a shower before getting dressed, because again, unlike usual, that day he had rolled out of his comfy hotel bed and gone out wearing casual clothes instead of the suit he would don for the meeting. He had packed the casual shirt, more like something he might wear on vacation, on the off chance that he went out to dinner with the people he had likely bored to tears during the meeting. But he rarely did that. Still, he packed it anyway, just for the heck of it.

The meeting was at 1:30, right after lunch when their bellies would be full and they would feel a little drowsy. There was nothing like speaking to an audience fighting to stay awake, their attention split between trying to listen and trying not to let their heavy eyelids close or their heads to bob embarrassingly on their necks. They would give a valiant effort but, in the end, would do a half-hearted job at both. That usually meant cursory questions and veritable radio silence all the way through so they could end early and slink away in guilt-ridden acquiescence, which was just fine to him.

Just smile and wave, fellas.

Unless, of course, some overzealous exec trying to make a name for himself was intent on ruzzing the mouthpiece, throwing a wrench in the roadmap, asking questions that were more like challenges.

He never knew what he was walking into.

His eyes cascaded over the people in the line, seeing but not seeing them, trying to decide whether he would finish the article he was reading before getting up or doing it after the meeting.

But then...

He saw surprise on the faces of two of the most beautiful people he had ever seen in his life. There had been some kind of mishap, that much was clear. Either she had stumbled or he had stumbled; when Mark saw them, they were embroiled in an off-balance kind of cha-cha as they righted themselves. But that isn't what he noticed first, in fact, it barely registered at all. What he noticed was how beautiful her smile was, her teeth perfectly imperfect as they peeked out from behind shapely lips. He noticed the slope of her nose, proportioned and sleek, and the arch of her brow, meticulously done. And her eyes. He noticed how, as her smile grew bigger, her cheeks rose, closing her eyes ever so slowly. He wondered if she smiled her hardest, maybe when she was laughing at something full-bodily or thinking of something that brought her joy, in those moments, would her eyes disappear altogether? Then Mark noticed his smile, muted a bit by stubble that looked more deliberate than from neglect, manicured in a way meant to distract. Mark noticed the hollow of a cleft in his chin, more a suggestion than anything tangible, and wondered what it might look like without the facial hair covering it. He noticed the shape of his neck, muscular and strong, the hint of a tan. He noticed all those things about them as he watched them recover and was sure his facial expression matched theirs.

Surprise.

Excitement.

Interest.

He didn't know what do with that.

He should get up.

He should get up, go back to the hotel, and get ready for the meeting but Mark couldn't make himself move, not when the scene in front of him was playing out the way it was... not when he was having a hard time turning away. He shook the newspaper, calling upon that age-old practice of making as much noise as one can to clear his mind. Maybe the sound would jar him, break him out of whatever mood he was in, stop him from doing what he was doing. Because he was staring and he knew it, and even though he had told himself to stop, it just wasn't happening.

She got her coffee from the barista... had she been calling for a 'Nicole'?

Nicole.

The way the name swirled around in his head, settling in a place that seemed made for it, gave him pause.

She got her coffee. Then the two who bumped into each other nodded agreement and started moving.

They were approaching the seating area.

Mark became keenly aware of the open seat next to him on the loveseat.

Should he move over a little, make room for one of them to sit? Condense, shrink his footprint—he might or might not have been sprawled over most of the available space—to accommodate?

Yes.

Yes, he should.

He wanted to.

But... why?

He shook the newspaper again.

Shit.

The loveseat.

Who the hell came up with the name 'loveseat' for a smaller than average sofa? What kind of name is that? It's a setup, that's what it is. Imagine asking someone to join you on the 'loveseat'. You sound like you're suggesting something, maybe even asking for something. You might as well say, 'come with me to my bed.' Didn't Morris Day say something like that in Purple Rain? Something about a brass waterbed...'

They're sitting.

They have already sat down, actually, he realized as an afterthought.

He could feel her body next to his on the loveseat, which seemed smaller than it had before. Was it normal to feel someone's warmth radiating off them like that? Or was it his own heat he was feeling? He could believe it was—he felt like he was on fire.

She said something, and her voice sounded melodic, like chimes on a front porch that is too far away to see, but the delicate notes travel on the wind that blows them. The man with her responded, more of a hum really, and up close, up close dear god, he looked like a model. His face was chiseled, freaking carved. He had a widow's peak that Mark couldn't take his eyes off of. It gave texture to the flip of his hair, and Mark knew he was looking longer than he should have, longer than a casual glance called for. He wondered if they saw him staring—- irredeemably staring in a way that was probably borderline indecent—eavesdropping, being the creeper he warned his children about.

He wondered if, after the man brushed his hair—*pink...? Is his hair actually pink?*—in the opposite direction of the widow's peak, it would just flop back into place.

Oh my god.

Mark blinked finally, feeling like he hadn't done so in hours, and tried to take stock of himself. What the hell was going on? He had woken up feeling off-kilter, had done things that were out of his routine all morning, and now this? He stretched his neck, cracking it as he did, relying on an old habit from when he was a kid to ground him. Maybe he was sick. That's it. Maybe he was coming down with something, something that was altering his perception and making him, what, see the world through somebody else's lens? Because he had never, not once in his entire life, looked at a man the way he was looking at the one across from him. Never once had he had the urge to lean into a woman the way he wanted to now, like she was a magnet and he was metal, like when that soldier in one of those Indiana Jones movies threw gunpowder in the air so that the magnetism of the crystal skull would pull it forward, creating a path Indy and his captors could follow.

Where the hell are all these random references coming from?

He had to get control of himself. Mark ran his hand through his hair subconsciously, pulling out all the stops on his ticks to try and bring himself back to a reality that he understood. He knew the best way to do that was to leave, remove himself from the situation and get on with the day ahead of him, as uninteresting as it might be. He could chalk this experience up as bad coffee in a strange town, as long as he wasn't really having a stroke, and move on like it never happened. But he didn't think he could do that, didn't think he'd ever be able to do that. He felt certain that if something made him leave the room in that very moment, he would make his way back to them no matter what, even though they didn't know who he was... even though they didn't even realize he was there.

He reached for his coffee.

She jumped ever so slightly, twitching as one does when surprised.

Was she surprised?

Did I startle her?

Did she not notice me before and did my sudden, Neanderthal-like lunge toward my coffee make her frighteningly aware of my presence... of how close she was to me?

Did she want to move, to do that polite scooting over thing that people did when their personal space was encroached?

Did she—

CHAPTER 4

They looked at each other.

All three of them looked at each other.

None of them knew what to say or what to do. But none of them stopped looking.

They *wanted* to look. Each of them was certain that there had never been anything they had ever wanted to do more.

Mark realized his arm was still extended towards his drink. He had time to think about whether or not he still wanted it, understanding immediately that if he tried to drink it, he would make a mess of himself. He couldn't do that. Not now.

Mark pulled his arm in, consciously going slower than his self-conscious side wanted him to, trying to retain some semblance of cool.

Ha, cool. Like anything about him was cool in that moment.

A lopsided smile spread across his lips.

Nicole couldn't take her eyes off of them, shifting her eyes every few seconds to one or the other because she missed them. She had been trying to ignore the man sitting next to her, trying to focus on the one in front of her because he was more than enough to take in at one time. But she couldn't help but see how the tone of his skin contrasted against his white shirt or the delicate wave of his hair. She couldn't help but see his long eyelashes as they dusted the tops of his cheeks when he blinked. When he turned to her, his eyes also dancing between her and the man she met in the line, she felt as if she could sink into their warmth, letting it enfold her forever.

What in the world was happening?

"I'm Eric," the man across from her said, bravely speaking first and addressing them both as if it were understood.

And it was.

Hesitation graveled Eric's voice before he pushed through with the lazy tenor she grew fond of instantly. "I... I just wanted to say that because I hadn't... I hadn't yet..."

"Mark... I'm Mark," the dark-haired man who had captivated her with a simple hair flip said, his voice eager, whether to participate, to be heard, or to lift the burden from the shoulders of the other in their group.

Eric and Mark.

Mark and Eric.

The names rolled around in her head easily, filling the crevices they found and calling them home. She had watched a seminar once, some self-help tip about ways to remember people's names. Nicole knew she wouldn't have to repeat those names ten times, associate them with some celebrity, or use them in a sentence to remember. Eric and Mark. They tasted perfect on her tongue, like honey, like candy. Mark and Eric. She felt like she had known their names her whole life.

Eric and Mark were looking at each other with so many emotions on their faces, it was hard to pick one out. Nicole could feel Mark fidgeting, the slight adjustments he made shifted the cushion they shared ever so slightly. She could see Eric fiddling with his fingers, clasping his hands to rub his thumbs together, then letting go and placing one hand over the other. He was nervous. So was Mark. So was she.

Had she started biting her bottom lip yet?

"I'm N-," she started, realizing she hadn't introduced herself yet.

"Nicole," Eric and Mark said in unison. And then, beautifully, all three of them laughed. It was a sound that felt more real than anything they had ever experienced in their separate lives. It was a response to the funniest joke, a reaction to tickling fingers, the most important thing that any of them had ever said or done. As they recovered, as their chuckles wound down and the woman sitting across from them, who had looked up from her book unenthused by their raucousness, had turned her attention away from them, they knew that they had been destined to hear that very sound at that very moment from the time they were born.

The conversation was immediate, though not necessarily easy, but not because of any lack of interest or connection. It was good in that way that you anticipate how satisfying a candy bar will be or how interesting a movie will turn out based on the trailer. In those moments you want to find out if you're right but harbor a little hesitation, a bit of trepidation in case it goes south. Because you want the candy bar to be the best candy bar you have ever brought to your lips, the payment for your unexpected find down the candy aisle of the convenience store. You want the movie to be good after sitting through the trailer filled with booms and bangs, oohs and ahhs, subtle glances and demure chuckles. So you dive in headlong, hoping for the best, but that niggling worry sits at the back of your neck all the while, tickling the short hairs ever so slightly.

But they pushed through. They opened up. They listened. They each had divulged more in 10 minutes to people who were nothing less than perfect strangers than they had to acquaintances who had known them for several years already. They bantered. And boy, did they laugh. Full-bodied, all-encompassing, belly-grabbing laughter that made their eyes water and their cheeks hurt. Because it felt right to do it. As Eric would admit later, when there was more time behind them than in front, it felt *natural.*

But still there was the question of the pink hair.

"Not that I don't like it," Mark found himself saying when color rose in Eric's cheeks at the question. "Actually, it—"

Eric was shaking his head before he could finish, his blue eyes looking into Mark's brown ones playfully, stopping the other's heart right then and there.

"It works, somehow," Nicole said, picking up where Mark had left off, hoping the quaver in her voice didn't give away how very much she liked it, as unconventional and as utterly different from anything in her life it was.

Eric cast his eyes onto Nicole and found her looking at him as if he and his ridiculous hair were the most wondrous things in the world. He sniffed a laugh and looked up at the ceiling. He couldn't believe it. Of all the times that he could have chosen to do this, *today* was the day his hair was the color of cotton candy.

"Well, you're very kind, but it's not my usual."

He was blushing. He couldn't help it.

She wanted to ask him what other colors he had tried, what he liked the look of most. She had never been with anyone who was free-spirited enough to change their hair color so drastically, if at all. Had he tried red or purple, or maybe turquoise or cobalt blue? She had seen those colors on men online, models whose hair was dyed to match their outfits or singing groups with heads that looked like a handful of unwrapped Dum Dum lollipops. But he had the face for it, she thought as she let her eyes take in ever contour, every inch of it. She could imagine him with tangerine hair spilling into his face as he angled his face toward hers, and—

"It's for a role," he said, continuing before he got lost staring at her. "I'm an actor. Onstage. A stage actor... in plays?"

Calm down, man. What the hell?

Eric took a deep breath to reset.

"I'm here to audition for a part in *Body*. I thought the hair might give me an edge because the character is supposed to be part of the scene, very much entrenched in pop culture, and all that." Eric ruffled his own hair—an action that, unbeknownst to him, made both Mark and Nicole's hearts skip a beat—before continuing. "Now I think I might have gone a little overboard."

He smiled.

So did they.

"Baby pink," Eric sighed. "Jesus."

Eric's smile was so endearing that Nicole thought she might scrap the pleasantries and kiss him right then and there. No last names, no family history—not even an hour of time invested. She didn't understand herself, felt like she was on the outside watching as she oohed and ahhed and batted her eyes like a schoolgirl. But it didn't matter—she literally didn't care. She wanted to know more, to know everything. She wanted him. The revelation made her breathing hitch, almost made her gasp out loud.

"*Body*?" she heard herself asking, all but begging him to keep talking. "I don't think I've heard of it." She almost laughed out loud at herself. She hadn't been to a play in years. *Body* could have been 10 years into its run, and she still wouldn't have known about it.

"It's new," Eric said and wrenched his eyes away from hers. He felt like he had been hit in the face with cold water. The path they had gone down had sobered him up a bit and as resentful as he was for the clarity, he could see the pin puncturing the balloon for what it was. How would he say it? What did it mean to speak it aloud?

How would they take it?

"The play... it will open at the festival."

He waited a beat.

No recognition dawned on their faces, neither of them had recoiled in their seats... yet.

It was now or never.

"The Toronto... Queer Theatre Festival."

When Eric came out, he did so quietly, telling his family first and then a handful of friends. It wasn't that he was keeping a secret, not really, but he was in high school and on the swim team and he had enough to think about with qualifiers and standardized tests. He didn't feel the need to add defending himself to that list. When he moved away for college he opened up a little, started going out more, found some gay-friendly clubs, went to gay sports meet-ups before they were called that. He made some friends both closeted and out and embraced who he was. For him, coming out didn't mean showing out. He wasn't flamboyant or effeminate—he just liked men, plain and simple. His straight friends told him he didn't seem gay. He told them he was sorry to disappoint.

In the end, he was who he was, take it or leave it. Giving a damn how that impacted someone was not a problem he cared to take on.

But now, as he sat in front of two people whom he cared about more than he had anyone else ever, he found that he *did* care what they thought about what he just said because it might change things... whatever *thing* this was. He *did* care what they thought about him.

And who *was* he, anyway? As he looked into the shy eyes of the woman across the table from him, Eric couldn't help but wonder.

When he walked into the coffee shop to get an espresso, he was gay. Very gay. As in, never been with a woman and never wanted to, gay. It wasn't that he hated women or anything like that. He didn't want to *be* a woman either—that oddly possessive perspective always made him laugh under his breath. He could even recognize a woman's beauty and call it out for what it was in a manner that was at the same time non-threatening and non-threatened. But this was different. As he sat there trying not to play with his cup to keep his hand busy, he definitely felt very unsure about the whole gay thing after all.

"You're here for an audition? Have you already done it?"

Eric looked at Mark and found genuine excitement in his eyes. He wanted to keep looking at those eyes, wanted to fall into them—let them see what they wanted to see. Eric began to wonder if they understood what he was trying to tell them. Admittedly, he had only skirted the issue. Just because he was auditioning for a role in a play that was going to open in a gay festival and was written by a gay playwright did not mean that all of the actors were gay. He sighed inwardly, hating the way that he had stereotyped himself. He had to be clearer, even though things were the very definition of unclear at the moment. If he was gay why did her eyes, her smile, the way she inhaled and exhaled, for goodness sake, send a chill down his spine? Why did the thought of hugging her, nuzzling her neck to smell the faint scent of her perfume make him shift in his seat? Was he bisexual now? Pansexual? Was his interest so fluid that it could change at the drop of a hat?

He felt like he was suffering through teenage hormones all over again.

Nicole studied Eric, anticipating what he would say next. She hoped he would say it again, repeat the bit about the gay festival just one more time for her to be sure she heard him right. He said he was auditioning for a play. A gay play, she presumed, or at least a play with a premise that was suitable for a gay festival. What did that mean? It didn't have to mean anything at all, she knew, and she wanted to hold onto that for dear life, but she had a feeling she would be deluding herself if she did.

Ok.

So, what did *that* mean?

Was he gay and she was in the way, cockblocking? She regarded Eric. He *was* looking at Mark in the most starstruck of ways... But no—they'd also had a moment, back in line...

Hadn't they?

So...

Was he bisexual?

Was he bi-curious and thought maybe she would let him, what, try it out? No, no it was more than that—Nicole could see that in his eyes. What she also saw confused her more: his *own* confusion.

"Are you nervous?" she asked suddenly, throwing out the most loaded question of the day without meaning to.

Eric smiled genuinely because yes, yes, yes he was nervous. He was nervous that he had just fucked up something that could have been so amazing—the most amazing thing in his life. He was nervous that he had no idea how to find out if he had ruined everything, not without making things so, so awkward. He was nervous that when he left the bookstore he might never see them again. The fact that he was sure he had forgotten his lines didn't even cross his mind.

But he didn't say any of that. Instead, he said, "I am, but I'm used to it. I just have to push through and try not to look silly."

"You'll do fine."

"You'll be great."

Nicole and Mark tripped over each other as they offered encouragement. Then, as though they had done it for years, they said, "Don't worry," in unison.

Nicole and Mark looked at each other with soft eyes and then smiled shyly as they looked away.

Eric was sprung.

"I'd love to tell you how it went... later... if you... I mean, if you wanted to get together and maybe, I don't know, talk again."

Eric's inner voice was cheering.

Nicole's smile took over her whole face, lighting up the

room while it did. She nodded, vigorously at first, then slower, more controlled as she tried to reign herself back in.

Hurriedly, Mark said, "Yeah! Yes...I... yes, I want to see you again."

He almost let it go, letting the truth hang in the air between them, but before he realized he was speaking, his words stuttered on.

"You know, to hear what happened... at the audition... today."

"Maybe we could eat? I'm too nervous to eat now, but I will be starving later."

That part was true to form if nothing else had been. Eric never ate before auditions.

"I'll be ready to eat my weight in whatever we choose after a few more hours manning my booth," Nicole added, calmer now that she knew it wasn't over, that they wanted to get together—they *all* did.

"I know I'll be ready to eat and relax after my presentation," Mark chimed in.

"You sure you want to spend time hearing about my audition after such long days of your own? I might bore you to tears."

It was supposed to be funny, just something to say to wind down the conversation, but Eric felt his heartbeat speed up in the silence that came after. What if they decided that yeah, it *would* be too much after a long day at work and they didn't feel like hanging out again after all? He would never forgive himself if he had just screwed it all up... again.

Nicole didn't want to tell him that there wasn't any other place she would rather be that night than back in their presence, that she would break plans and might definitely have to decline offers—if she was reading Ananda right—

and it would be fine because she wanted to see them again, wanted to spend more time with them, wanted this, all of this.

"I would like nothing more," is what she ended up saying, and Mark nodded his agreement. And even though it had only been a few seconds, Eric had felt the possibility of loss in them. He struggled to keep the all-encompassing relief he felt off his face.

They talked logistics, deciding to text each other at the end of the day and talk about food options then. They left the coffee shop where Nicole had let her coffee grow cold only to be discarded without even a taste and went their separate ways with the promise of seeing each other in a few hours on their lips. As she walked back to the trade show she couldn't help but go over it all again, revisiting Mark's masculine profile and Eric's toned physique evident even through the jacket he wore. Even when thoughts of how wrong this was, how even entertaining feelings like the ones she was having was a form of deceit, Nicole couldn't stop. There was something about Mark and Eric that wouldn't let her go. Speaking of Eric... she opened his contact entry and changed his name to Pinky, the smirk on her lips threatening to spread into a full-on smile even as the band on her wedding ring tightened its grip.

CHAPTER 5

1:18 p.m.
Run-walking to the conference room.
Tripping over a cord.
Realizing that was the cord he needed.
Fumbling the same cord as he tried to plug it in.
Laptop booting up.
Presentation pulled up, title slide in technicolor on the SMART Board.
1:24 p.m.
Need water.
Must have water.
Or coffee.
Or something.
Something to help him focus.

Heading to the break room, head in the clouds. Thank goodness he'd visited that office before, or he would have been walking around aimlessly. Gotta speak about roadmaps and projections and service models, yet all Mark could think about was beautiful skin, smiling eyes, and pink hair.

Pink hair.

Did he really want to run his hands through that pink hair, feel how soft it was, watch it move, bend to his intentions?

Did he really want to rub his thumb along that cheek, feel the stubble there, allow his hand to lay flat against it, relishing the texture against his palm?

Was that really what he wanted now? After living his entire life as a straight man, were his thoughts really filled with a man he had met at a coffee shop he wasn't even supposed to be in?

Yes... and no.

His thoughts were only half filled with the visage of a man, an actor: *Eric*. The other half was filled completely by Nicole.

Nicole.

So stunning that he almost couldn't look at her dead on, having to avert his eyes after only mere seconds for fear of losing control. She was, quite definitely, the most beautiful woman he had ever laid eyes on. And there was so much more to her than that. It excited Mark to think about all the things he would learn about her when they saw each other next. Considering what he already knew—that she loved to travel yet had no penchant for learning languages whatsoever; that she had been a film critic in college who was supposed to focus on horror films but secretly was a sucker for rom-coms; that she was working up the nerve to write her first book—Mark was sure he would never get enough of her.

Or him.

Oh, shit.

1:27 p.m.

No time for coffee.

Only water, and from the kitchen faucet at that.

Water threatened to spill over the sides of the cup as he speed-walked down the hall from the break room, nearly missing a suit who clearly didn't get the message that the 90s were over and wearing slacks to work could be considered overdoing it. Unless you were a sales guy trying to make an impression. Or a travelling presenter from some small town north of Irvine that was so small it wasn't even on some maps.

Unless you were him.

Mark dodged the man, giving him an acknowledging nod as he covered ground toward the conference room door.

He stopped in front of it, straightened his tie, let the water settle in his cup.

As it turns out, the suit was on his way to Mark's presentation. Oh, joy. So it was going to be one of those types of meetings, was it?

A hasty sip of the tepid water still swirling in the cup.

Tinny.

Why did that happen, again? Too much copper or lead or iron, maybe? Eric would know. From what Mark had learned about him so far, it was like he was a wealth of knowledge when it came to the decidedly random. Probably made a fantastic Trivial Pursuit partner.

Mark took another sip. Definitely metallic. Zinc, maybe? He'd have to ask Eric what he thought la—

Footsteps approaching.

The suit cometh.

Mark plastered his practiced smile onto his face, the one

that looked welcoming and maybe even appealing, unless you realized it never truly reached his eyes.

Hold door open, 'good afternoons' and 'welcomes' all around as they enter.

1:29 p.m.

Made it by the skin of his teeth.

Cue stage lights.

CHAPTER 6

Nicole had been right. She did have to sidestep Ananda.

And as she tried on the remaining two casual outfits in her suitcase, she figured that was all right. Nicole knew that, at some point, she would have had to turn Ananda's sights away from her somehow, especially if his intentions became more pronounced, more deliberate. It was flattering, for sure, but that was all it was ever going to be—a compliment blown into the wind. So, when he asked her to dinner that night under the guise of recapping the trade show thus far and strategizing for the next one—an argument that would have held water if their divisions were even remotely aligned, but marketing and IT had very little overlap—it was easy to decline. Ananda made her smile, and his sideways glances, nervous chattering, and unspoken forlorn appeals in the break room or in the hallways as they passed by each other would continue to make her feel beautiful and interesting, sought after, even when she didn't want them to, but there would never be anything more because she was in no position to do anything other than smile back.

She did not allow herself to consider the contradiction of her thoughts.

Sweat stood out on her brow, and she silently cursed herself for getting so worked up—now she would have to curl her hair again. And what about her makeup? She didn't wear makeup ordinarily, just lip gloss. The bright red she wore earlier that day did its job, but tonight she wanted something softer, something more natural.

Tonight.

Nicole pulled her dress over her head carefully, trying not to mess up her hair even more than it already was, hoping that any touch up to her makeup would be minimal. She let the dress cascade over her on its own, the lightweight rayon feeling barely there. As she debated buttoning the few open buttons at the V-neck, trying to decide how much visual interest was too much, Nicole appraised her reflection in the hotel's full-length mirror. Turquoise midi with small copper flower accents and a copper double hem separated by a strip of lace that allowed for the slightest peek at her legs beneath.

Pretty.

She smiled despite herself.

She loved that dress. It always made her feel confident, sure, tall even, though she was far from that. At 5'5", no one would ever make that mistake. But this dress, the way it fell just below the knee, the way it hugged her waist yet flowed loosely, effortlessly everywhere else, the subtle crop of the sleeves—the dress just made her feel like it was made for her.

Nicole was glad she brought it. The fact that she almost hadn't made her cringe.

Why?

She had been asking herself that very question a lot in the past few hours—as she walked the few blocks back to the convention center after the encounter, lost in thought; when Ananda asked her if she had found anything good while she was at the bookstore and she felt the hot flush of embarrassment coloring her cheeks under his stare; every single time she checked her phone during the trade show, after the trade show, as she watched tv to try to settle her mind.

Why?

The same question kept coming back to her, forcing her to confront it... to answer: if she was not in a position to do anything other than smile back at Ananda, why did she have butterflies in her stomach now?

Why did she rush back to her hotel after the trade show?

Why did she panic when she found her phone dead in her purse, slamming the plug in so violently it could have shattered the casing?

Why had she tried on her clothes at least three times before finally deciding that her favorite dress was actually perfect for dinner, perfect even though the weather was just a little chillier than expected... perfect for them to see her in?

Why had she stopped at a store to pick up eyeliner and rouge knowing she would only use it once, would likely throw it out before returning home?

Why was she curling her hair again so that it fell just right?

Why, why, why?

Why was she going to dinner with two men she had just

met in a coffee shop, the name of which she couldn't remember?

Why, indeed?

Nicole looked at herself in the mirror, taking a deep breath and letting it out as her eyes silently ticked off a checklist:

- Natural makeup on—not too much, but just a touch? Check.
- Hair curled, styled to casually fall just to the side of one eye, giving the illusion that she's peeking out at the world? Check.
- Teeth brushed, breath fresh? Check.
- Deodorant on? Check.
- Body mist on? Check.

She chuckled at that one—she almost walked out of the store with some sparkly, glimmering thing that would have made her look like she was heading to the club instead of out to dinner. Her with glimmer all over her chest and Eric with his pink hair. What a pair they would have made. She laughed and laughed until she realized that her mind had preoccupied itself with wondering what things they might be able to talk Mark into.

Why?

She wanted to answer it, really she did. She kept trying to make her mind bend around the truth, take ownership of it and spit it back to her, to be honest instead of creating the lies that kept bubbling to the surface, but something inside her resisted. When she asked herself why she was being so meticulous about her look, she attributed it to always wanting to look nice when she went out. When she asked herself why she wanted to go out at all, she reminded herself how much she enjoyed eating in restaurants; being served and not having to cook or deal with the aftermath of pots, pans, and dishes, eating her meal when it was actually hot instead of lukewarm after everyone's food had been cut, drinks poured, and arguments about whose portion was bigger were over. When she asked herself why she would spend an evening in the company of two strangers, she rationalized that she didn't know the people she had come to town with any better than her soon-to-be dinner partners.

Sure.

The phone chimed. A text came in.

Nicole noticed the way her heart jumped in her chest as she reached for the phone but tried to ignore it. She picked up the phone, swiping the screen and feigning a casualness that wouldn't have fooled anybody if they had been there to witness it.

The phone chimed again before she had opened the chat.

She smiled.

It started small, all lips and closed mouth, but then quickly spread, revealing her teeth and the dimples that only showed themselves when her whole face was engaged.

Another response came in before her very eyes, and she nodded in agreement, pulling her bottom lip into her mouth as she did.

She typed her reply and put the phone down, going over herself in the mirror again, just to be sure, because it was time to go, and she wanted to be ready, wanted to make sure she looked the way she thought she did when they saw her —fresh and groomed and really, really good. She brushed her teeth again, smoothed down her tapered sides one more time, considered laying her edges again, but decided they were perfect the way they were. She reapplied her deodorant and spritzed the air next to her before walking into it, letting the droplets fall on her. The body mist she had ended up buying was perfect. It was a light and airy scent, one that made her think of sunflowers and sunshine. She hoped she could find it in stores when she got home, hoped it wasn't a local brand made by somebody who wasn't enterprising enough to put it online.

She hoped they liked it as much as she did.

Why?

CHAPTER 7

His hair was still pink.

Damn the box that said it would rinse out in two or three washings.

Damn the advice he found on the internet claiming that plain old white vinegar and water would do the trick.

Because it didn't... at least not all the way. Now, instead of looking like cotton candy, his hair looked more like champagne blond or what he had started to call Maybe Pink. Eric washed it again, really sudsing it up this time, but it was still Maybe Pink. He thought about trying the vinegar again before getting scared and pouring the rest of the small bottle he had picked up on his way back to his hotel room into the toilet. What if he stripped more color off and his hair started to look silvery pink like hair extensions that turned under bleach? No, Maybe Pink would have to be ok. It was closer to his natural dirty blond than the cotton candy had been, so there was that.

He was early. Of the three of them, he had been to Toronto most often, so he knew where some of the better restaurants were. Avoiding The Village because he wasn't sure how he would handle being interrupted by someone that knew who he had been before that morning, Eric chose a newish place on Adelaide Street. The restaurant wasn't far from Union Station, just in case one of them wanted to make a quick exit. The place was quiet, but not secluded, fancy but not romantic. The food was moderately priced so that going Dutch would feel natural, be less noticeable as a decision. Steak and chicken on the menu with a smattering of seafood: right down the middle, avoiding ethnic choices that might make Eric seem like he was pandering.

So many things to think about. So many things to get wrong.

He thought long and hard about the restaurant they went to, most of it while trying not to blind himself with the vinegar. He gave considerable thought toward what he was going to wear too, whether or not he should get a shave and clean up at the barber shop in the lobby of his hotel, whether he should bring something with him or show up empty handed... whether this was a date or not.

He tripped over that one, about whether or not he wanted it to be.

If it were a date he would bring Nicole a flower—just a single stem. Maybe an iris or a daisy—something that stood out but didn't overwhelm. He would bring Mark some kind of small, fancy chocolate box, go Amelia Rope style: simple, yet elegant.

If it was a date.

Eric knew how he was supposed to behave if it was a date—his mother had raised him right.

But this wasn't a date.

Right?

It was the three of them getting together to talk about what happened in their days after leaving the coffee shop. Just three fast friends who met randomly and connected over cold coffee amidst the din that permeated that little place.

Right?

Not a date.

How could it be a date?

Eric turned this thought over again, revisiting it for the fiftieth time since leaving them, at least. If this were a real and true date, he would only be interested in one of them, right? Only one, not both of them because Eric... he was gay, right?

And even if he took his sexuality off the table, how could he want both of them...?

Eric struggled with that question more than the repercussions of suddenly not being as gay as he thought he was. The question wouldn't go away; it stayed right there, in the front of his mind, persistent and unavoidable like a blinking neon sign: how could it be a date if there were *three* of them?

Eric was thinking, kept thinking and overthinking, rationalizing, adding, subtracting, coming up with a number that didn't make sense to him every time. His rumination distracted him, so much so that he found himself in front of the restaurant where he had planned to meet his newfound friends—because they were *friends,* and that was all, he had decided—without ever having texted them about where to go.

Shit.

He looked at his watch.

6:30 p.m.—later than he told them he might be.

Did they think he was standing them up, ghosting them

after making them sit by the phone waiting for him to get out of the audition? Did they think he had better-dealed them and was hanging out with his friends somewhere, their plans forgotten?

Were they sitting by the phone, waiting for him? No one had texted him yet either. Had they found something else to do with the people they came to town with? Maybe they made plans with each other, deciding they didn't need him in the end? There was definitely chemistry between them—any fool could see that. Did they even care if Eric texted them at all?

Eric looked through the glass door and noticed that there were several tables already taken. As he stepped aside to let someone enter, he realized that the place was quickly filling up. Eric took a deep breath there on the sidewalk and thought maybe he should hold on for a second, think things through. It was late, later than expected, but they hadn't texted him yet. Facts. He bristled a bit at the insecurity trying to take up residence. His subconscious, the part that never had a problem saying the right words to put him in his place, was gearing up, ready to pepper him with all the reasons why they weren't waiting for him—why they didn't care if he texted. It was the same voice that always told him he was pitchy in auditions or that he delivered his lines as flat as a guy off the street would. Eric knew that acrimonious bastard well and hated that he was trying to barge into his thoughts now.

No.

He nearly laughed out loud as inner Eric slammed the door in the other's face and brought the truth to bear. They hadn't reached out because they probably thought he was still auditioning and didn't want to disturb him. The idea of

Eric's cell phone dinging and him somehow hearing it while on stage... the thought that he might have heard it, might actually have thought it was them, made his stomach drop. He wouldn't have been able to focus if that had happened. He would have been thinking of shy smiles and winking eyes and dimples instead of stage placement and lines.

Good call on their parts.

If they had found other things to do, the adult way to handle it would be to let him know. There was nothing about the two people he was more anxious to see than he was willing to admit that made him think that either of them would play a silly game like standing him up just because they could. And he certainly wouldn't do that to them. And anyway, this was just a casual meeting, a nothing, a hangout among fellow travelers who just so happened to meet and find common ground. Talking about standing people up was for someone who was about to go on a date. And this was not a date...

Right?

A couple went inside.

Then a group of four.

Eric realized he'd better get a table before he lost his chance. As he claimed one of the last tables in the restaurant, he texted the address to Nicole and Mark. He sat down, let a nervous sigh pass over his lips, and waited for his "not date" to begin.

CHAPTER 8

Z's pool never really closed, not if you didn't want it to.

Mark couldn't help but think about that as he felt himself giving in to sleep on the daybed tucked away inside one of the private cabanas that bordered the hot tub. There was a word for that weird state he was in, half awake but half not, conscious of existing but not entirely sure in what dimension. The faint smell of chlorine kept him grounded even as the combination of the other smells in that space coalesced to remind him, to confuse him, to drive him wild.

The fresh smell of sunflowers.

The clean smell of shampoo.

The spicy smell of his own cologne.

Some kind of tangy smell that he couldn't put his finger on.

The provocative smell of sex.

Mark inhaled reflexively, sighing into the concoction as he slipped deeper into sleep.

Warm.

He was warm from the press of bodies on his own, and

he felt good, so good that he never wanted to get up, never wanted to be let free. So good that he feared the cool air that would accost him if they moved, if either of them moved at all, would freeze him to death.

How very dramatic.

Over the top.

So metaphorically corny that it went past the border of ridiculous to seat itself squarely in the middle.

But how incredibly apropos.

Mark felt a smile creep across his face as he snuggled deeper into the warmth that surrounded him, nuzzling hair and rubbing skin because he was sure of one thing, even through the haze of bliss and sheer exhaustion that was winning the battle to close his eyes: Mark knew that nothing had ever come close to the feeling of home that engulfed him there, as he lay in the oasis that was The Zerzura Hotel with two beings who were most certainly mirages.

Nothing.

Ever.

CHAPTER 9

Eric would tell them later, while they were filling their stomachs with omelets made with gourmet cheese, tuxedo chocolate chip muffins, polenta pancakes, and a host of other items that took standard breakfast fare and kicked it up a notch, that he didn't think they were going to come. When he said it, when he told them how the beep that signaled a text had come in, though delicate, like a wind chime, made him jump out of his skin. He thought they had changed their minds, were bailing out on him while he sat waiting in the restaurant. The honesty in his eyes brought Mark's hand to Eric's knee and Nicole's to his cheek, the heat pooling from their touches causing him to be still for a moment and just feel. His mind reeled in the seconds between their touches and his next words, at once amazed that he could have thought such a thing and thankful that he hadn't acted on his fear. Because that's what it had been —fear. He had been afraid that he'd misjudged the situation and made a fool of himself; afraid that he had made two of the most amazing people he had ever had the pleasure of spending time with uncomfortable and wary; afraid that he had been so desperate for what he had been feeling to be reciprocated that he'd created the whole narrative in his head. Similar thoughts tried to get in Eric's way later too, tried to color his judgement, stop him in his tracks even when it was obvious that what he had thought was going on —what he had *hoped* for with every fiber of his being—was *really* happening and that they were as into it as he was. But when he felt Nicole's lips on his... felt Mark's fingertips on the backs of his thighs...

Eric exhaled a shuddering breath before he could continue.

"The place got busy really fast," Eric said as he cut into the first crab and avocado eggs benedict he had ever had. He eyed the bite, the perfect combination of English muffin, egg, hollandaise, avocado, and crab. He smiled at Mark, who had ordered it for him, and put the loaded fork into his mouth. He couldn't stop his eyes from closing as the essence of the dish came together with disarming potency, as if the combination of such inherently mild flavors made them all the more intense. He hummed his appreciation and opened his eyes to find Mark's eyes smiling back at him, his mouth filled with a bite of his own snagged from Eric's plate. Nicole's bite of it was met with the same enthusiasm as Mark and Eric's and they smiled at each other, contented in more ways than one.

"I watched the place fill up while I sat there alone, sticking out like a sore thumb," Eric's smile belied the self-consciousness from the night before.

He chuckled under his breath and said as offhandedly as he could before trying a grilled heirloom tomato, "I must have looked like I'd been stood up."

Mark nodded his understanding because that's what Eric looked like when Mark saw him. Dejected. Alone. Smaller somehow, in that large space filled with people laughing and smiling around him. But now, as the benefit of hindsight kicked in, Mark could apply a better description to the man he saw when he walked into the restaurant, the one trying not to search the line at the door or stare incessantly at the host stand waiting for one of them to show up: Eric had looked disappointed.

"I guess somebody had to be first though, right?" Eric said, trying to recover, not wanting to dampen the mood, especially when his initial impression had been wrong, wrong, so very wrong.

"Yeah, but you were early," Mark said around a mouthful of baked currant donut.

"Really early," Nicole echoed as she took a sip of coffee.

"It would have helped if I had texted you about where to meet before I found myself standing in front of the building."

Mark's eyebrows furrowed incredulously as Nicole fought to keep the sip of coffee she was relishing—Arabic coffee, the server had called it, presented in a demitasse cup... demitasse... word of the day—from spraying out of her mouth as she laughed.

Mark snorted through his words, barely able to ask why Eric hadn't told them that last night and Eric laughed right along with him. The truth was once he saw Mark walking toward his table, sidestepping a server who wasn't looking where he was going and nearly backing into him, once he saw the way his black field jacket sat open to reveal a copper crew-neck t-shirt that clung to the crest of his pectoral muscles, all the self-doubt melted away.

The host, the scientist Ryan as he would look on modern Earth, had set Eric up at a table instead of a booth and that was ok. He hadn't asked for it, hadn't thought ahead enough to consider the seating arrangements, but it was better that way. They could all see each other at the same time without having to turn their heads or block someone's view. He didn't know how important that would be until Nicole joined them.

Mark's gait was casual, exuding a confidence that reached out and touched Eric where he sat. Mark was working on a smile that was almost sly. It built gradually as he walked, starting in his eyes and then spreading lazily over his lips as he initiated and maintained contact with Eric.

He saw him.

And it made him smile like *that*.

Eric's stomach dropped from sheer excitement.

Mark had spotted him almost from the door and was making his way toward their table, only slowing to let the host know who he was with.

With me, Eric couldn't help but think possessively. *He's with me.*

Eric could feel his eyes widening as Mark walked toward him and try as he might, he couldn't stop them. It was already taking everything he had not to let his jaw fall open. So when inner Eric, the one who always pumped him up, reassured him, and level-set him lost his shit, Eric could do nothing but freeze in the wake of the freak out and hope his face didn't reflect every single thing he was thinking.

Whoa.

D-did he—did he look like that earlier? I mean, he was gorgeous then too, but oh my god, this is... this is a different level.

He looks like a model but without all the attitude... like it's by mistake or something. Like he doesn't even know how amazing he looks. Like he—

Oh shit, almost here. Get it together!

Shit... SHIT!

Ok.

Ok, shit.

Ok.

His eyes were darting away from Mark, then back, away, then back. He could feel it. Oh god, he could *feel* it. The thought of what it might look like, how ridiculously immature he must appear, almost made him sick.

Make it stop!

Inner Eric recovered a little, shook off the shock and tried to calm things down.

You got this. You can handle this. It's not like he's the first good-looking man you've ever gone out with.

But damn...

Ok.

It's just dinner anyway, there's no indication that there will be anything after that. You may not even want *anything else after talking to him. He could open his mouth and sound like an idiot. You only talked a little bit earlier and yeah, you might know the name of the farmer's market where his mother buys her produce, but that doesn't mean that he can carry on a real conversation. What if you have nothing in common beyond the things you talked about earlier?*

Eric wanted to nod in agreement at the logic, but what inner Eric was saying sounded nothing short of absurd. But still inner Eric pressed on.

What if he hates the theater? What if his measuring stick is a kid's magic show in the mall and if there're no flowers in a hat, it just ain't good?

Inner Eric was working himself into a frenzy.

What if he chews with his mouth open or kisses with his eyes open or...?

Mark flashed Eric an even brighter smile.

He was almost at their table.

Shit

What if...

I mean, what if he's...

Inner Eric was crashing and burning, offering nothing, absolutely nothing to consider, leaving Eric to fend for himself.

Shit!

"Hi."

Had his voice always sounded so silky smooth?

Eric didn't know if it was inner Eric, or the Eric who ran the show most days, asking that question.

"Hi," Eric replied, his voice clipped as he tried to conceal how breathless it had become. He stood without thinking and then, finding himself close enough to smell the star anise and vanilla notes in Mark's cologne, he froze.

Should they hug? Shake hands? Nod and sit down?

Shit. What do straight men do when they meet up for dinner? What do gay men do?

His mind warred with itself, toggling between being appalled that he somehow reduced greeting protocol down to sexual orientation and irritated that he didn't know the answer either way.

Inner Eric might have been hyperventilating.

Come on!

Think!!

Eric stepped through the last time he met a friend out for dinner. They had said their hellos. Then they hugged.

Should I...?

No!

Some guys shake hands, some hug, some pat each other on the back, and some do nothing at all.

Eric sighed inwardly, keenly aware that his hands were hanging limply at his sides.

Awkward.

He was awkward as hell right now.

Good job, genius. You wiped the ability to do nothing off the board when you stood up like that, like something had bitten you, didn't you? Like something had scared you.

Eric cleared his throat as his smile faltered the slightest of bits in the corners at the realization that something *had* scared him. And it had scared the shit out of him.

Mark's smile was wide as he clapped Eric on the back. Eric received it well enough, even though Mark was certain he had hit him harder that he should have. Eric had flinched a little with the first strike like he hadn't expected it. Mark almost apologized but then thought that would make the whole thing even more ridiculous. But he couldn't get his mind off the way Eric's shoulder had twitched a bit when Mark's hand struck it with a blow that would have knocked him down if he hadn't been blocked in by the table... at least, that's the way it seemed.

Overzealous.

Over the top.

What the hell was he doing?

As he took off his coat, Mark wondered about the loss of control he seemed to be exhibiting. When he opened the door to the restaurant he nearly flung it off its hinges; he nearly pushed a man waiting for his table near the host stand to the ground as he navigated the crowd, trying to reach Eric. And then this. But was there really a 'this'? Mark didn't know—he might just as easily be behaving normally, using the amount of strength each activity required, like any person would. That he didn't know troubled him, but who pays attention to things like that anyway? How would one know if they were using the proper amount of strength to do anything at –

One man, $100, and a one-track mind.

Mark sighed inwardly. Random shit like that didn't use to happen.

Song lyrics from some old Go-Go track from the 90s popping into his head while he was embroiled in an existential crisis about free will and requisite force... that shit happened to other people, not Mark. He was usually pretty level-headed, some might say too focused. It wasn't that he didn't know how to laugh or have fun or do something unpredictable... he just thought there was a time and place for everything. Approaching what was very surely a date with a man *and* a woman when he wasn't at liberty to date either one, marveling at how well Eric's black long-sleeved shirt brought out his ice blue eyes, realizing that he was staring at Eric, maybe even making him uncomfortable after very likely bruising his shoulder—this was not the time to be calling up the lyrics of a one-hit wonder from an obscure music genre.

But he was.

God help him, he was.

Mark draped his coat across the back of the chair and smiled at Eric again... he hadn't stopped smiling at Eric since he got there.

They sat down at the same time.

Eric's biceps flexed as he pulled the seat beneath him.

Mark noticed.

One man, $100, and a

one

track

mind.

Mark snickered as much about the song popping into his head again as the sabotage that his mind had engaged in against him.

"What?" Eric asked, curious.

Mark considered not telling him—it was so damned stupid... almost too stupid to say out loud. But then he saw Eric's face, inquisitive, but not purely so. Even though he tried to look like he was just asking what was on Mark's mind—a little 'penny for your thoughts' sincerity—the question went deeper than that. Much, much deeper.

There was no question in Mark's mind that this was absolutely a date. Not anymore, if there ever really had been. And the scary thing about it was that it wasn't scary at all.

"It's nothing, really. It's just so stupid..."

"What is? Tell me," Eric urged.

Mark dipped his chin and peeked at Eric through his hair.

Eric grinned and leaned forward, elbows on the table, trying to capture Mark's eyes.

They were being playful with each other, if not flirting just a little bit.

Ok, flirting for sure.

Mark didn't even know he knew how to do that anymore.

Mark lifted his gaze to look at Eric straight on. He saw Eric's eyebrow twitch ever so slightly.

Wow.

"Ok, I warned you. This is ridiculous."

"Try me," Eric said, more eagerly than he wanted to but unable to stop himself.

"Well," Mark started, smiling even more, "All day I've felt like I've had no control over my thoughts. Like this morning, I kept coming up with words that I have never used before to describe things—random things... whatever I was looking at or thinking about. During my meeting I was talking about new products and it's all jargon and acronyms and just silly-speak, you know? I was supposed to say that we think launching the new line of business in Q2 is the best plan, but I said there 'was a preponderance of evidence to suggest that Q2 is ideal'. Preponderance—I can't even spell preponderance, let alone use it properly in a sentence."

They laughed together and it was so damned easy. Mark went on because he really wanted to talk, really wanted to engage, especially if it would make Eric laugh like that again.

"So, just then I was thinking about a ton of things all at once because, well, you're here and I'm here, and just..."

Eric's eyes were on him. He was looking at Mark like he was the most fascinating man in the world.

Mark looked away, nervous all of a sudden.

"Yeah," Eric said as he touched the hand that Mark had rested on the table. Just a little contact, nothing lingering, nothing that meant anything. But it was enough to bring Mark's eyes back to his, that rich chocolate brown intensity making Eric feel like he might fall into them and not care if he ever got out.

"We're actually here," Eric finished, nudging Mark along.

"Yeah," Mark said, a smile playing on his lips. "So, I was preoccupied by all these random thoughts filling my head and then all of a sudden," he chuckles, unable to speak without laughing through it. "A song cuts through all of it. But not just any song. Some old Go-Go song from back in the 90s."

"Go-Go? Like DC Go-Go?"

"Yeah! I spent some time there, so I heard more than just the few commercial songs that made it on the radio in the rest of the country. Real underground shit, you know? Rare Essence, Junkyard Band, Northeast Groovers..."

"I feel like you've started speaking another language right now."

They laughed again. Mark thought he could listen to that sound every day for the rest of his life.

"I can't remember this guy's name, though. It's on the tip of my tongue, but I can't get it."

"How does the song go?"

"Oh, you want me to sing now? Embarrass myself in front of all these people?" Mark smiled genuinely at Eric because at that moment he knew he would do anything the man across from him asked without batting an eye, if it would make him happy.

"No, not in front of all these people," Eric said quietly. "Just in front of me."

Mark sighed, through the smile on his lips. He was having more fun in that moment than he had in years.

"One man, $100, and a one-track mind," Mark sang, emulating the version that played in his head, unsure if that one was true to the original or not.

“One man, $100, and a one... track... mind,” Mark continued, the apples in his cheeks high as his smile took over his whole face. Eric smiled back, thoroughly enamored. Mark was running away with his heart, and he didn’t even know it.

Mark sighed, the memory he was reaching for just out of his reach. “I can’t remember if the guy’s name was Sugar Bear or Super Cat or—”

“Thundercats,” Eric added with a nod that made them both descend into laughter once again.

“It’s worse,” they heard from beside them. Their conversation had distracted them so much, they didn’t see Nicole as she approached the table. But boy, did they see her now.

Eric’s first thought was that she looked like sunshine, all warmth and happiness. He could feel her as much as see her, the aura she brought into their space reminding him of a breeze by the sea, a calming wind under the shade of a tree—life-giving air. He breathed deeply of her and was happy that he did.

For Mark, Nicole became the focal point where everything else around her blurred or faded away. Her beauty was crisp and fresh, layered on top of the room rather than merged into it. She took his breath away.

Nicole’s eyes bounced from one of them to another, awed by what she was seeing. She knew they would look good, better than they had earlier that day when they hadn’t expected their lives to be changed in a quaint little coffee shop. She knew she would have to tap into some long-forgotten reservoir of cool buried inside her to get through the night. But this... this was more than she expected.

They were laughing, full teeth and squinted eyes. Uninhibited. Happy. She supposed that anyone seeing two people having a good time would smile at the sight, but she was feeling a contentment that she didn't understand the origin of. Why did the sight of Eric and Mark's eyes nearly closed in what could only be described as glee make her feel euphoric?

How could she care about them so much already?

She opened her mouth to speak but closed it again to swallow down her nerves. Once she was ready, once their rapt—enchanted?—eyes were trained on her, she said, "His name is... Stinky Dink."

She caught them off guard.

They had been so wrapped up in feeling what they were feeling now that she had entered the room that they didn't expect her answer to hit them quite the way it did. Mark heard his voice climb a few octaves as he laughed unabashedly. Eric's laughing had degraded to gasping and wheezing, Nicole's addition to the conversation pushing him over the edge of control. Tears blurred their vision as they struggled to stand and greet Nicole properly.

Eric and Mark stood on either side of Nicole and brought their lips to her cheeks at the same time.

It was too fast to pick out the way their lips felt, too chaste to read too far into anything, but Nicole's heart somersaulted in her chest just the same.

Because it was perfect.

Natural.

It was them.

CHAPTER 10

Holy shit.
Ho-ly shit.

It was happening—it was actually happening now instead of playing out like a scenario in his head. He was there with Nicole and Mark, and it was good. So good. Already it was better than he ever could have imagined.

Nicole looked so beautiful, so jaw-droppingly stunning that Eric almost couldn't believe she was real. And the thing about it was that it was effortless. She wasn't wearing a ton of makeup, hadn't done something elaborate with her hair in the hours they had been apart, hadn't worked the shadows to try to appear more mysterious. She didn't look like she had tried to do anything at all because she was naturally beautiful, gorgeous in a way that magazine models always miss. And it had him spellbound, bewitched, captivated—pick a word, that was what he was. He felt like he couldn't take in a proper breath to save his life.

And Mark. Dear god, did he look good next to Nicole. In the second between when Mark released the press of his lips to her cheek and pulled back to smile—and to gather himself, Eric noticed, commiserating on more levels than one—he had the chance to really see them together. Mark was not quite as tall as he was, but that still put him head and shoulders over Nicole. From where Eric was standing he could see how perfectly Nicole's head aligned with the crook of Mark's shoulder, actually had a second to envision it nestled there, eyes closed in relaxation, before snapping himself out of it. Their caramel and golden complexions seemed to glow in the mood lighting set by the trendy lantern that hung above the table; they seemed to swirl around each other in an intoxicating dance. Eric wondered how his fair skin would look surrounded by their warm tones, couldn't wait to hold their hands to find out. Couldn't wait to—

His mouth was open.

His breathing had picked up embarrassingly.

Get it together!

Inner Eric had resorted to whisper-shouting now, afraid he had to do something uncharacteristic to call Eric back from the ledge.

You're supposed to be an actor, so fucking act!

But how could he when they looked like that together? How could he when all he wanted to do was stare at them?

"Why would you even remember that?" Eric heard Mark asking Nicole as they kept up the conversation while his brain short-circuited. "Wasn't he a flash in the pan? Not to mention that it was what, 20 years ago?"

"Yeah, but the song was all over the radio and playing in

every car in DC for a while. Even my parents played it all the time. Go-Go is DC's thing. It's what we do. We'll put a Go-Go beat on anything; just listen to some Chuck Brown and you'll see what I mean."

Nicole's eyes were warm as she smiled at Mark.

Mark's eyes were filled with stars.

Eric felt weightless.

"The bigger question is how in the world Stinky Dink came up in the first place," Nicole continued, settling into the conversation. "That song isn't usually part of dinner conversation, unless that's just how you do it out in LA."

Mark smiled and shook his head.

"Or in New York."

Nicole leveled her gaze onto Eric, and he thought his heart might stop right then and there.

She took a sip of the water Eric had ordered for the table, never taking her eyes off of him.

At first it seemed like she was waiting for a response about how the song came up, and honestly, Eric couldn't remember anymore, not with her looking at him like that. But then her expression changed. A question formed on her face as she regarded Eric, her eyes roaming over him in a way that was not at all unpleasant.

She looked.

She smiled.

She stopped drinking and sucked her bottom lip into her mouth.

Oh my god.

"Your hair... it's not pink anymore. Well, not really," Nicole said when she spoke again, hoping the comment would buy her a few moments to stare at him without making it weird. Because damn. He looked amazing with this new color, this faded pink that teased a glimpse of his natural hair color. He looked real and unreal at the same time. He looked... like a dream.

Eric could feel the heat rushing into his cheeks.

Nicole's eyes were filled with wonder. She looked as if she might reach out to touch a few strands herself to see if they were real.

Honestly, Eric would have been all right with that.

Eric smiled shyly and ran a hand through his hair. Because he had looked away, averted his eyes to look at a spot on the table as he tried to keep the newfound shyness that was creeping up his neck in check, he missed the way Mark reacted, the way his chin lifted unexpectedly as he pulled in a sharp breath. He didn't see Nicole's eyes squint, close, nearly roll in their sockets in ecstasy in response to the movement. By the time he looked at them again they had recovered outwardly even if there was a tingle in the pits of both of their stomachs.

"Ha, yeah. I tried to get some of it out," Eric responded, calling upon his acting chops to get him through... or, at least, trying to. "After the audition it felt more than a little silly to keep it."

What he didn't say was that he wanted to show them who he really was, gauge whether or not they liked what they saw.

Did they?

Mark's finger was on his lips before he realized it, rubbing them as he studied Eric's mane.

"It's lighter for sure," he started.

"Much," Eric chimed in. "Not quite as obnoxious."

"I wouldn't have called the pink *obnoxious*, necessarily," Nicole hedged.

"I don't know... maybe," Mark said slyly and the laughter commenced again. Eric knew right then and there that whatever it was they were starting would never be boring.

"What's the matter? You don't like your men a little extra?"

Mark smiled but that wasn't the only thing he did in the few seconds it took before he responded. He dropped his hand from his lips and laid it on the table. He snickered and looked away. He picked his hand back up to rub his jaw then laid it back on the table again to be clasped by the other. He looked back at Eric with eyes that were intense and all the more captivating because of it. When he finally spoke, it was as if the whole room had been waiting to hear what he had to say.

Mark replied, his voice laced with surprise, incredulity, and what might have been awe. "I didn't know I liked men at all."

Eric's smile seemed to curl into itself, dampening a bit as it moved from confident to this asymmetrical hybrid full of chagrin and self-judgment.

He'd overstepped.

Eric had overstepped and now it was all different.

He looked away, unable to hold Mark's gaze. Because he messed up.

Now everyone was going to feel weird about this—whatever it was—and it would be all his fault. Whatever might have been was over now, gone, finished before it had even started.

Eric fought to raise his eyes, deciding that he should at least be man enough to see the rejection coming. While that sounded like a good idea in his head, he still found himself studying the grain of the wooden table, eyes downcast... hiding.

Mark saw the way Eric's face fell and felt sick. Physically ill. He'd upset him, maybe even hurt him. For a moment, he marveled at the fact that he could feel so deeply for someone he had just met. But no, he admonished himself, that was skirting the issue, wasn't it? Flying above it, getting close but not landing. The fact was he actually *felt* something for this man. This *man*. He didn't know what it meant, didn't understand how it had come about nor how it could sneak up on him, surprise him with its presence the way it did, but it was most definitely true. Mark was interested in him. Him *and* the beautiful woman they were with. He had fought with himself after he got back to his room, after the presentation was over and he had nothing to do but wait for Eric's text. He could have chosen not to go out with them that night, could have told them that he should never have given them his number and that he wanted them to lose it as he would theirs, but that's not what he wanted. Mark wanted to explore the feelings he had, understand them, see what would happen, even when he knew he shouldn't.

But now he had compromised that.

Did Eric think he was posturing, wearing a heteronormative t-shirt and burning rainbow flags? Even before this new development of his, Mark was never about that. And now...

Nicole watched as Mark tilted his head in the same direction that Eric's was hung, his eyes imploring the man to look up. It took a second but Eric did, meeting Mark's eyes and maintaining contact with a degree of difficulty that did not go unnoticed. In a voice that was as smooth as honey but, more importantly, confident and clear, Mark said,

"Until now."

Nicole exhaled the breath she hadn't realized she was holding as the concern that had painted Eric's face was wiped away.

CHAPTER 11

Things in common:

- They loved to travel and had been to many of the same places.
- They had all lived on the east coast for some part of their lives.
- They loved to try new foods.
- They loved listening to live music, though their tastes in genres varied... and the jury was still out on dancing, too.
- They loved picking through museums and could spend whole days inside one without realizing what time it was.
- None of them had any idea what set of events had brought them into each other's orbits but they were so happy they occurred.

"What's your favorite city in the world?" Nicole asked as she forked a ring of calamari into her mouth. The conversation had been easy, had preoccupied them so much that, after nearly an hour, they had just gotten around to ordering food, and even then they had only put in for appetizers. It seemed that none of them wanted to stop talking long enough to look at the menu. None of them wanted to stop at all.

Mark mulled the question over as he chewed, and Nicole found herself trying not to look at the way his mouth moved. She turned her attention toward Eric, and that was no better. His smile was infectious, but when he was still, when he didn't know anyone was looking at him, he was breathtaking.

She fiddled with the napkin in her lap, hoping they didn't notice the fact that she had begun to fidget.

After a sip of soda and a moment to pick through the tentacles that he swore he could not bear to eat, Mark decided.

"London... It's the place for me."

Nicole felt her smile falter just a little. It had been on the tip of her own tongue; she had come so close to saying it, she was surprised it hadn't slipped out of her mouth already. Mark was being witty, batting quips in a way that seemed natural for him. It had been funny for sure, but it brought Nicole's head out of the clouds. In his answer, Mark had quoted a song from the movie *Paddington,* and it stopped her cold. She knew it well. She should, after all. Her kids had made her watch it over and over again.

Nicole felt a chill creep along the back of her neck. Children. Mark had children. That's not a reference that people without kids would readily make. It wasn't like a superhero movie, something that tapped into nostalgia for some and action for others. It was a movie about the antics of a talking bear who liked marmalade... not exactly prime adult viewing content.

Was he still married? Had he ever been married? They had been talking steadily, sharing things about themselves, gradually diving deeper as the night went on. But Nicole realized then that they had been weaving around potholes, avoiding the important things—the ones that could bring them back to their senses and stop the train before it got too far away from the station.

But now...

The questions bounced inside Nicole's head a few times, swirling around her image of him as she watched him talk about enjoying the British Museum so much that he visited it every time he travelled to London. Then, before she could even think about passing judgement, the questions turned inward, coiling around her psyche like a snake.

What about your own children, hmmm?

What about your husband?

They're home right now doing whatever it is they do when you go out of town—maybe staying up late to watch a movie, maybe running around the house until they're exhausted. They miss you. They want you to tuck them in, but they know you can't because you are supposed to be working. Working, Nicole. They definitely don't think you're out there in another country on a date.

"I—" Nicole uttered, completely by mistake. She regretted it the moment it happened, totally unsure of what she had wanted to say in the first place. The conversation had moved on without her, and she wasn't sure where they had ended up. Of course she was lost—she had been too busy wondering what the hell she was doing there to keep up.

Nicole looked at Eric and then at Mark with wide eyes that laid everything out like an open book... even the things she hadn't meant to show.

They noticed.

Eric touched her hand, and she let him because she really, really wanted him to even though her mind told her she shouldn't. When he spoke it was as if he had been reading her thoughts, as if he were answering an unspoken question.

"I was saying that I also love London, but that my favorite city is probably Paris."

He was rubbing her hand, coaxing her back.

"But I had a hard time choosing between there and New York."

Mark touched her forearm, gently caressing it with his fingers, and she almost melted. How did they know what she needed? They had just met—even if they felt like they had known each other for years, it hadn't even been a solid 24 hours yet. How could they know that she needed to feel grounded, to feel like she was still ok even though so much about this was not ok at all? How did they know that she was having second thoughts and that those second thoughts might eat her alive because, despite them, she wanted this, she wanted them, she wanted whatever was happening?

How did they know she needed to get out of her head so she didn't ruin everything?

"And I was saying that with all the places we have been to in common—London, Paris, Rome, Cairo, the islands..." Mark looked at her meaningfully then, and when he felt she understood, he looked at Eric the same way.

"I just wonder if we've ever met before. You know, maybe in the airport or on a beach."

"Oh, I doubt that," Eric said, pulling back to take a sip of his now lukewarm beer. "I think I would remember seeing either one of you in bathing suits." He wiggled his eyebrows mischievously and bit down on the straw.

Mark and Nicole worked hard not to look away even though they could feel color rising in their cheeks.

Mark continued through his suddenly shy smile, "Eric saw the King Tut exhibit in Cairo as an adult, but you and I saw it in New York back in the 70s. Maybe we were there the same day. I went to see it more than once, so it's entirely possible. We could have been standing right next to each other and never realized it."

Nicole nodded slowly, memories of that day at the Met coming back to her in snippets. She remembered being amazed by everything she saw—bread that had been left in King Tut's tomb, his underwear, the beautifully strong countenance on his death mask. She remembered looking at his young face, features captured in gold, and feeling such complete and total awe. She cried when the exhibition left New York, having dragged her parents back to see it at least three times since the field trip that brought her to the museum on the day of the opening; the exhibit moved her that much. The idea that she might have been in the same room with Mark, someone who would come into her life later and instantly become so very important, was mind-boggling.

"Right?" Mark continued, unaware of the scenarios

floating around in Nicole's head—the prospect of a past meeting and the way that made her feel.

"Then we all saw the unwrapped mummy at the British Museum—in fact, she's the reason I travelled to Egypt—after seeing her I knew I had to see the mummy room at the Egyptian Museum—but... but what if... what if we were there, in London, at the same time? What if we passed each other on the street or stole the other's cab?"

"Hackney," Nicole corrected, all the apprehension from before gone. She loved the feeling she was experiencing. Being with them, doing whatever it was they were doing, it just felt so right.

Eric couldn't resist. "Or if we're talking about New York, it would be a yellow cab."

"Yeah, but just what if?" Mark said, trying to bring them back to the conversation because suddenly he didn't know if he had ever been more serious about anything in his whole life.

"We could have met at the British Museum. Or at that park just a few blocks away. I always used to take a walk in that park after my museum visits, I don't know, to just process it all, I guess. I always found myself near the water fountain. I would just lose track of time."

Eric looked at Mark incredulously, disbelieving the words he was about to speak even as they came out of his mouth.

"The one in the center of the park?" Eric asked, but he already knew the answer. "I got tea from the café there and drank it on one of the benches. Watched people walking their dogs, kids playing in the water. I stayed until the outdoor lights of that big hotel behind it came on."

"The Kimpton Fitzroy," Mark said wistfully. "I tried to get a room there after falling in love with those same lights, but I couldn't—some dignitary was visiting, and they had cordoned off the whole area pretty much, even Russell Square."

"It's amazing. It's all pillars and statues, wrought iron and crests," Eric remembered, turning to Nicole to describe what he had called up from memory. "But even with all of that, it isn't gothic. It feels... I don't know... fresh. It's also unpretentious and distinguished at the same time, with all the brick and stone, and long balconies off of the great rooms—at least they look like great rooms from outside. And when the lights turned on, illuminating some spots and creating shadows in others, it was just... like, amazing doesn't cut it."

He laughed at his loss for words.

"I don't know—it's kinda hard to explain."

"It sounds amazing," Nicole said, and she meant it.

"It really is," Mark chimed in, wrapped up in the wonder of where his thoughts were taking him. "So, Eric and I have seen that, but you haven't. Only two of us, again." Boston and Spain had dropped off the list early on.

Mark took a deep breath before continuing.

"It... this... it feels deliberate, somehow, doesn't it? We've been talking about all these places we've visited or even lived in common and there has either been a discrepancy on the dates or just two of us had the chance to encounter each other, but never all three. What if..."

He paused, letting the idea settle in his mind before sharing it with them.

"What if this *is* the first time all three of us have been in the same place at the same time? Like all the other times just weren't the right times or the place wasn't the right place for whatever reason. What if, of all the amazing places we could have met, it was always supposed to happen in a coffee shop in Canada?"

"Fate..." Nicole said, neither asking a question nor making a statement. The word hung in the air before them.

Eric's lips parted as he considered what Mark was saying. And it seemed plausible, if that was the word that could be used in this off the wall situation. He had no intention of getting a cup of coffee that morning. He normally didn't drink it before auditions—the cream he liked to add to it always made his throat feel coated and thick. And while that was true for other people, he knew this was probably all in his head, because his throat never felt that way any other time. But none of that mattered: routine was routine, and superstition was, well, it was the theater, after all, and he was a theater guy through and through. But still he found himself in line at the coffee shop anyway, drink in hand and happy about it, in the perfect spot for Nicole to be distracted and bump into him, at the perfect time for them to find a table to sit and talk some more... the table where the other piece of their pie was waiting.

It was amazing when you thought about it.

Nicole had said that she hadn't planned to go to the coffee shop at all—that she had walked over to the bookstore at the suggestion of a colleague to get some fresh air. Mark had said that he had a presentation that morning and would normally have been in the office going over it again but found himself at a table at the coffee shop, newspaper in hand.

Coincidence?

Was it a coincidence that when they had stepped outside of themselves, stopped planning, rushing, thinking about what needed to be done next, and just let themselves relax that that is where their fates finally converged?

Mark looked at their faces and didn't know what to do. They had heard him out in silence, pretty much, and that alone scared him to death. Did they think he was crazy? Did they wonder if his next great topic of discussion would involve conspiracy theories or maybe extraterrestrial life forms walking the earth in human skin? He sighed inwardly, listening to his own thoughts and finding them odd upon closer scrutiny. They *had* to think he was off his rocker. Maybe he was.

"—wanted to see the T-Rex before they closed the exhibit for something like five years, but I ended up spending most of my time at the early man exhibit."

Nicole's eyes lit up as she smiled. Mark hadn't heard them talking about places they might have in common because he was too busy tearing the soundness of his psyche apart.

"I still have the picture of me as Neanderthal Nicole. But I didn't get it that week—I haven't been to the Museum of Natural History in years."

"That's ok," Eric said, his smile teasing his lips in a way that made them all feel happy to be alive in that moment. "We'll always have Paris."

Paris, Mark echoed in his mind, wondering. He'd had to find out about that later.

"I don't know if I'm explaining this well or if you think I'm a nutjob now or what but... I mean, I," Mark looked away, unsure of how to continue but knowing he needed to.

Nicole's hand found Mark's, and she rubbed it gently, urging him on.

He tried again.

"I mean, I shouldn't be here. You shouldn't be here either," he said, looking at Nicole. Then, casting his gaze over to Eric, he continued, "And neither should you. But still, we *are* here. And I don't know about you, but there is no place in the world that I would rather be right now."

Mark's self-deprecating chuckle caused Nicole to squeeze his hand and Eric's lips to part. Mark, who had dipped his head and averted his eyes in an effort to regain some semblance of control over himself, didn't see Eric's reaction, but he felt Nicole's hand, the gentle pressure she applied at his words, and he knew he could trust them with what he was feeling now and forever.

Buoyed by the confidence that his words hadn't been in vain, Mark finished, "As much as the reality of those words challenge everything I've ever known about who I am, they are the truest things I've ever said."

They were silent because that is what they needed to be.

It needed to sink in, the gravity of it all. It needed to settle.

And once it had, once she was sure that Mark had spoken her truth as much as his own, once she could see agreement in Eric's eyes as well, she did the thing that felt the most right to her there in the middle of a crowded restaurant filled with forgettable faces and indistinct voices, save two.

CHAPTER 12

Mark's cheeks were hot and probably beet red, but he didn't care. He was amazed, surprised, elated, and so very grateful.

She *kissed* us.

Nicole had brought both of their hands to her mouth and kissed them right there in the middle of the restaurant.

She kissed them one after the other, then pressed them side by side to kiss them together. She did it like it was at once a ham-handed attempt at something new and the most natural thing in the world.

Then she said simply, "Maybe you were in the crowd at Buckingham Palace. There were so many people waiting to see the changing of the guard."

And just like that, they were back on track.

"Ugh, the most underwhelming experience of my trip," Eric said and sighed into his drink.

"Right?" Mark chimed in, falling into their easy rhythm. "And the bagpipes—they were so faint where I was that they sounded like they were coming from two streets over."

"But the bacon bap I had at the coffee shop on the way probably makes my top 10 food list," Nicole said, eyes closing as she remembered.

She had let go of their hands somewhere between the kiss and then, missing their warmth immediately but not sure if reaching for them again would be too much. Mark had made a lot of sense; it kind of blew her mind to think about all the times they might have crossed paths, might have been close enough to touch. Would they have felt the pull, the almost physical connection they felt now if they had noticed each other but there were only two of them, or would something be missing, something they would both feel, both long for but not be able to name? Yes, Nicole determined as she opened her eyes and regarded the two men sitting with her. If either of them was missing she would feel the loss with her whole being.

"And they say the Brits can't cook," Eric chimed.

"Mmm, bangers and mash," Mark added, enjoying food memories of his own.

"Yes!" Eric exclaimed. "I must have tried it in three different places while I was in town, but if you can believe it, the best bangers and mash I found was—"

"At the airport," they all said in unison.

They looked at each other, all half smiles and barely concealed laughter. Another thing in common.

"Heathrow?" Nicole asked, knowing the answer was yes.

"Yep, terminal 4," Eric replied, feeling excited but trying to keep calm.

"Big place, long line, order and they bring it to your table?" Mark added, and they all nodded.

Coincidence.

"Guy at the table next to mine got sloshed, almost

missed his flight," Eric remembered. "He scrambled, made a big fuss, knocked someone's water over on another table,"

"Not hard to do in that place. They really cram them in," is what Nicole said but she was trying to remember if there had been a hubbub when she was there. Did anyone exclaim as water spilled into their lap? Had anyone taken off at a sprint to get to their gate?

Mark was thinking too, but he had a lot of meals at that restaurant to sort through. He must have been to Heathrow six times in the past few years, and he always ended up at that restaurant. There had been plenty of people who hurried away from their tables, trying to make their flight and likely failing. Heathrow is huge.

But still, regardless of when, they had eaten at the same restaurant.

He smiled, more at himself than at the two of them. When he started entertaining the notion that they might have been in the same place at the same time, the idea struck him as ridiculous, far-fetched. The world was too big for that. Except it was like fate had teased them in precisely that way... close, but not close enough... two but not three. He remembered the time when he recognized a man in the airport that he had seen looking up at the billboards that lined Times Square days before. Mark blew it off—tourists always seem to find each other, especially at the usual spots. It was weird, but it had happened to Mark enough that he didn't think much of it anymore. It was simple math; with only so many places to go, the laws of probability ruled. But *had* he seen Eric nursing a cold one as he waited for his flight? *Had* he seen Nicole thumbing through a magazine? What if they had been orbiting each other for a long time—like liquid swirling around in a funnel—sharing space, time, even air without knowing how important they would be to each other later? What if it was all by design, them flitting around each other, glimpsing what was to come but having to wait until it was their time?

What if they were always meant to be sitting right there, right then, no matter how they had set their lives up, no matter what other plans they had in mind... what if it had been so perfectly planned that all they had to do was show up?

The thought made him warm, happy in a way that he had never experienced before.

"Hey," Eric coaxed, his soft like velvet, "Where'd you go?"

Eric's hand was on Mark's shoulder, and Mark found that he liked that very much.

"Looking for you."

CHAPTER 13

Garlic prawns, porterhouse steak, and roasted chicken placed in front of the people who ordered them but quickly moved to the middle of the table, a fork's distance from each of them: this meal would be family style.

They talked while they ate, gestured with loaded forks, and laughed with full mouths. The more they learned about each other, the more they liked. To anyone looking they appeared to be three old friends out for dinner; three people who enjoyed each other's company very much. And that was true. It was as if they had always known one another, had always been Nicole, Eric, and Mark. The pauses were easy, the conversation even more so.

They just fit.

Potstickers made it to the table, as did buffalo wings, and bacon-wrapped scallops. Second round of appetizers after dinner... sue 'em.

"This menu is all over the place," Nicole commented as the mouth-watering third course hit the table.

"Yeah, that's why I chose this place. I wanted to make sure everybody had options."

"It's definitely eclectic," Mark said as he grabbed a drummie doused in sauce spicy enough to open his nostrils, "but I once saw a menu that had Rocky Mountain Oysters and fried alligator on the same page as sashimi, so I'm just glad I can identify what I'm eating right now."

Their expressions were classic.

"Good," Mark said through a mouthful of food. "At least I'm not the only one who didn't know what the hell I was looking at. The fried alligator was easy enough to figure out, but the Rocky Mountain Oysters and sashimi threw me for a loop."

They were both thinking it, but Nicole made the mistake of letting her surprise show. She cocked her head, questioning silently as she dipped her potsticker into the ginger soy sauce. She listened as Mark talked about the food he encountered with a curiosity that she hadn't realized was sitting so close to the surface before. She was suddenly conscious of everything—the fact that he had no discernable accent, or at least not one that would signal that he was from somewhere other than the United States; that his name was not traditional; that she had used chopsticks to eat her potstickers where Mark had not.

And then she went in on herself... hard. Was he supposed to be *ultra*-Asian, embodying every stereotype that she knew about, even ones she hadn't considered just because that was his ethnicity? What kind of name did she expect to hear—Mark Chen or maybe Haruto Takahashi... would that have been Asian enough for her?

She was embarrassed, ashamed of the assumptions she had made. She figured he was Asian so he knew Asian stuff, whatever that was. Would it have been fair to assume that because she was Black she knew Black stuff? What if they thought her name should be Tawana or Lakisha, or what if they expected something more ethnic, something African?

Holy shit.

She didn't even know she thought that way, that she categorized people like that, reduced them to caricatures. She wondered what other assumptions she had made about Mark and also about Eric. Did she assume that Eric came from a wealthy family who had allowed him to pursue his dream of acting "for fun," kind of like when people go backpacking through Europe taking a gap year to see the world? Yes, maybe she had. The thought made her sick.

One glance at Eric told her he had been putting himself through a similar castigation in his own head.

"You guys didn't hear a word I said for the past minute or so, did you? I mean, if ox testicles are your thing, I guess what I said was no big deal, but—"

"I—I'm sorry, Mark, I—" Nicole's words trailed off.

Her chopsticks hovered over the potsticker she had let drop into the sauce.

Mark saw.

Mark understood.

"How long have you been using those?" Mark asked, pointing at the chopsticks in her hand. She brought the hand closer to her, put them down.

"I don't know—I guess since high school?"

"Can you use them too?" he asked Eric, who nodded.

"I've been using them for as long as I can remember."

Mark nodded before speaking. "I can't." He forked a bacon-wrapped scallop into his mouth and let that information sit for a bit. Chewing, he continued,

"My parents could never figure it out well enough to teach me, and I just never picked it up when I got older."

Eric tried not to blink his confusion, tried not to move his face at all.

"I'm adopted. My parents got me when I was an infant. My *White* parents."

Nicole nodded slowly, hoping Mark would continue. She wanted to know more, wanted to know everything he was willing to tell them.

"They were originally from New Jersey, and that's where we lived for a few years until we moved out West. People do what they're used to doing because they're used to doing it, know what I mean? My mom and dad tried to make friends with Asian families and socialize me with other kids who were adopted into White American families like I was, but in the end, their friends were like them, and that's who we saw the most of. Sure, I had friends from other races growing up, but we were all doing the same things as everybody else—did the same activities, were in the same clubs, went to the same places to hang out. At that point, race wasn't the delineator—money was. We were middle-classed and so were the people we socialized with. I went to the public school and it was mostly White. My AP classes—because there is always *some* truth to stereotypes, right?"

Mark was happy to see both Nicole and Eric's faces soften at his offhanded comment. He pressed on,

"Those classes were filled with more White students than any other race, and so was the mock trial team. The tennis and AV clubs too. Those were the things I was interested in, so I did it with people who liked that kind of stuff. What race they were didn't really factor in. Besides, most of the Asian people near us were Filipino or Chinese. I wasn't even with the right people to learn anything about myself."

"What ki—" Eric stopped himself, certain that wasn't the way to ask what he wanted to know, but unable to call up the right words.

"Where am I from?" Mark supplied with kind eyes.

"Yeah... I'm so sorry, Mark. I—I feel so ignorant. I didn't know I was like this before."

Nicole nodded. She couldn't have said it better herself.

Mark breathed deeply through his nose and placed both his hands over theirs.

"Tell me," he said looking into both of their eyes imploringly, "And I need you to be honest here. When you met me was the first thing that jumped into your mind, 'hey, there's an Asian guy'?"

The cacophony of 'Nos' was immediate. Mark asked another question over the din,

"Did you automatically fetishize me? Though, I don't know if I have a problem with that..."

They laughed. All of them. Because not only was that the most honest response, they *needed* to.

"If this, whatever it is, if it's going to work, we have to be honest with each other. We can't worry about social constructs and stereotypes or any of that shit. Not inside our bubble. We have to keep that garbage out of it because it has no place in what we are building here."

Mark rubbed the skin on the top of Nicole's wrist as he spoke to her, "I didn't look at you and say, 'now that is a beautiful Black woman. Look at her black skin, so black and beautiful.'"

Nicole could feel the blush rising her cheeks. When

Mark said it that way, out loud for all to hear, the whole damned thing sounded even more ridiculous.

"I saw a woman with intriguing eyes and a smile that made it hard for me to catch my breath. I saw a beautiful woman that I was drawn to, one I couldn't bear the thought of never seeing again."

Mark's smile let Nicole know that everything was all right.

"And you," Mark said, turning his attention to Eric. "I didn't see a White man and his confidence and his blue-eyed Nordic Whiteness and say, yes, that Whiteness is definitely for me. I saw a man who was interesting in ways that I have never experienced before. I saw a man whose voice hypnotized me."

Mark looked at both of them meaningfully, all laughter drained from his voice.

"Race never came into play. I am attracted to you, and that's it. Is it the same for you? If not, let's get it out on the table now before we go any further."

Eric spoke first. He rubbed the underside of Mark's pinky as he did, eliciting a decidedly pleased look from the man.

"I am drawn to you both. Your race, how tall you are, what you do for a living or how much money you have—those things don't matter to me at all. I can't fight this thing... I don't want to."

"Race has always been something I was aware of—I had to be," Nicole added. "But with you two, it isn't a qualifying or deciding factor. It's just a characteristic."

Mark smiled, looking relieved. Later, when he'd had time to think about why he made the decisions he'd made, Mark would remember that moment as when he knew in his soul that everything was as it should be. He'd think about the fact that he couldn't remember a time when he had come out of tough conversations like the ones they'd had that night feeling the way he did right then—invigorated and hopeful rather than irritated and full of regret. Ever. Most of the time, when talks like these were finally over and sentences had become clipped to ward against tempers flaring again, Mark would find himself wondering if he even wanted to share space with the people he had fought with anymore—then or ever again... and that included his wife.

But not them. He was sure he would never feel that way about them.

At that moment Mark was just grateful. He had been worried that the conversation might not be as simple as he hoped it would be—was afraid that they might have hit an impasse that was bigger than the three of them, one that would prove insurmountable in the long run. He wasn't 20 years old and idealistic anymore: life had taught him just how difficult relationships could be. He mourned that possibility subconsciously, afraid that its reality would show itself—*had* to show itself—and that it was only a matter of when. But it didn't happen that way, and they had touched on things that could have made any one of them get up from the table and run for the hills, leaving all the potential drama for someone else to deal with. But no one did. Thank God, no one did.

They released each other's hands and started to eat again. Nicole snagged the potsticker she had dropped and, as she prepared to pop it into her mouth, she said,

"I'll teach you how to use chopsticks. Can't have my hot Asian boyfriend out there lacking."

Laughter, always laughter. Raucous, uncontained, beautiful.

CHAPTER 14

"I've never been with a woman before."

Eric panted the words onto Nicole's skin, acknowledging their truth but not their importance... not anymore.

She replied with an airy moan, a response to his hands on her hips or Mark's mouth on her collarbone or the combination of both. Her lips sought Eric out as she allowed herself to simply feel everything that was happening. Eric joined his lips with hers, his tongue dipping into her mouth automatically, as if coming home.

Her hand played with the hair at the nape of his neck, staying there once finding the welcoming patch as they kissed. He was used to that. Past lovers had told Eric that those short hairs, the ones closest to the base of his neck, felt as soft as Lamb's Ear. They liked to run their hands over it, linger there, kiss there. Nicole felt that same way, wanting to touch it, making plans to lick it when she had the chance to turn Eric around. Normally Eric had no reaction to it—it was fine, not unpleasant, but not something that turned him on or felt particularly good. But this time, when it was Nicole's fingers that caressed him there, Eric felt like he was feeling sensations anew. He leaned into it, giving her more access. And yeah, he liked the way it felt.

His own hand rubbing his neck, touching that patch of short hair in the process, was enough to draw him out of his memory and back to the present, which was like a dream in and of itself.

Eric had gone back up to the buffet to get a pastry plate for the table. It had been hard to detach himself from them and get into the line which was longer than he had first perceived. He felt like a teenager not wanting to leave them, not even for a second. He hadn't felt that kind of enamored, that butterflies in your stomach kind of excitement, in years... so many years he could hardly remember the last time. It was as if everything they knew about each other, everything they embodied together, was the sum total of his life thus far. Eric chuckled at himself for waxing poetic as he stood in line, but it was true—truer than he was willing to admit.

He had been in a rut. There was nothing *wrong*, per say, nothing that had been going off the rails in his life. But still it was all very run of the mill. As far as stage actors went, he had been doing pretty well. He had gotten most of the roles he went out for, had performed on stage in most of the major cities in the US—the Shubert in Boston, the Fox in Atlanta, the Ahmanson in LA—and had even had a few runs on Broadway. He had played the lead a handful of timesbut was more often supporting cast and that was just fine—that usually meant almost as much stage time and more flexibility in the way he played his character or how he interpreted the role depending upon what audience he was performing for. Eric had created enough of a name for himself that he didn't have to audition for every role anymore, which was more than fine. He had also socked away enough money that he didn't have to try for every single play that came to town—he knew where his next meal was coming from and then some.

Part of it was because he didn't actually live in New York City anymore, even though he called it NY—people had a tendency to call the metropolitan area NY because it was easier to pinpoint than smaller towns. He didn't spend an exorbitant amount of money on an apartment the size of a closet, didn't have a refrigerator that was only big enough to hold two- or three-days worth of food. He lived just over the river in Weehawken, New Jersey, a nice little commuter town full of families looking to escape the New York noise, an abundance of Targets, and all the other middle-class suburban trappings. It was nice, and it was cheap, and that was also just fine for him. Eric could have splurged on a more expensive place, maybe a condo by the water, but there was no need. He had a rowhouse in a quiet neighborhood and people around him who were friendly enough but minded their business beyond pleasantries. Again, that was just fine.

He wasn't in a relationship, and that was by choice. The men he had encountered recently just seemed so damned young, whether in age or mindset. And theater guys? That was just a whole other problem entirely. Dramatic, over the top, excessive, all of the above. He was tired of the party boys and the fuckboys alike. That was for when he was in his twenties. And, sure, some people might have accused him of being both at one time in his life, using the terms interchangeably to describe him, but that was a long time ago—back when he lived in the city and enjoyed partying all night, waking up hung over or maybe not going to sleep at all—that crazy life. Now, at 29, Eric felt like he was too old for all of that. Give him a jog to Hamilton Park on a mild, sunny day so he could feel the breeze off the Hudson while he looked at the Manhattan skyline. He called that winning... with or without someone pretty on his arm.

Eric stepped forward, filling the space vacated by the person in front of him as he drew ever closer to the mountain of pastries ahead. He was still in his head, amazed at how one day, one set of hours, could change so much. He hadn't been looking for anything when he entered that coffee shop—he wasn't even sure if he wanted coffee or tea, if he wanted to get his usual half dark or try something new when he walked in. He wasn't considering the things he wanted to change in his life, wasn't thinking about resetting his thoughts and starting fresh when he got back home. Life had been good, albeit predictable. Even being there, in another country at that moment in time, was part of his usual routine—he was no stranger to the Toronto Queer Theatre Festival. In fact, he had landed his first leading role in one of the plays in rotation way back when it was called Gay Play Day. He used to tell his friends in New York, the ones who were too snobbish to step off their high horses on Broadway to deign to audition for a role in *Canada*, of all places—how gauche—that he was gay and ready to play for a day. He thought he sounded witty. Repeating that phrase to his more mature, road-weathered self, he realized just how silly he sounded then.

Way back then.

Seemingly so long ago.

Eric was different now, had been for some time. Had turned over a new leaf. Really, he had just grown up, and he liked the adult version of himself very much. This Eric knew what he wanted out of life and was pretty good at getting it. He had hit paydirt in that he was working a job he loved—he could actually confirm the truth in the saying that you're never really working if you love what you do. The more mature Eric was ok by himself, didn't feel like he needed to be in a relationship with someone in order to feel whole. So he wasn't. He had time to be picky–there was no rush. There was no ticking biological clock to be aware of—if he and his partner decided they wanted children, time wasn't a consideration. So he didn't have to accept any of the casual offers for dates that he got after every show, could acknowledge that they were just code for casual sex and move on. He didn't have to waste his time in a relationship with someone who really wasn't appealing to him after the first few months because they had invested in each other and marriage was the expected next step. Being gay had allowed him flexibility in that regard. He had freedom, choice. Most importantly, he had time—all the time in the world.

But now, as his memory flooded his senses with the smell of Nicole's perfume, the way her nipples felt as he rolled them between his fingers, the way she tasted –

The man behind Eric cleared his throat in a deliberate yet polite way, bringing him back to the present, back to The Zerzura Hotel, back to the buffet line mere steps away from the two people who had come out of the woodwork to turn his life upside down the night before.

Two daydreams in, what, three minutes?

Eric laughed out loud as he took a step forward, ever closer to the pastries. He couldn't even try to admonish himself for it. If this was what happiness was, he wanted more of it. He didn't think he could ever get enough.

But would he have enough time? As he piled their plate

with pastries he couldn't name, he thought he could hear a ticking clock in the recesses of his mind.

When he got back to the table, Eric found Mark on his phone and Nicole looking up at the ceiling, lost in thought. It was beautiful—*they* were beautiful in how natural they were. The whole scene looked like a glimpse into the type of weekend morning he was supposed to be having—the one happening in some other dimension.

And it was good. So very good.

It was everything Eric had every wanted.

So as quickly as thoughts of running out of time had come, he silenced them. What else could he do? To entertain them would be to invite pain, and he couldn't do that... not now. Not ever, if he could avoid it. To do that would shine a light on how precarious it all was, how goddamned fleeting. It would ruin the moment, ruin *them*... maybe irrevocably.

"... And we've become an old married couple in the span of 24 hours?" Eric asked, laughing.

Nicole's eyes were pure joy when she turned them on him. Eric almost dropped the cheese Danish he had selected off the top of the mound under the weight of it.

"We're trying to remember what the guy said last night about the hotel. What the 'Z' stood for," Nicole said before grabbing a butter croissant for herself.

"Yeah, but I all I can remember is that I thought he was full of shit," Mark chimed in, his head still bent over the phone. "I had... other things on my mind."

Heavy breathing. Hot, fevered skin. Breathy, sinful moans.

Eric saw it all, the way Mark's head turned sharply, but just a little, enough to shake away the cobwebs discreetly, the way his eyes closed for a second longer than they would for a normal blink.

Eric's laugh was all air and silence. When Mark's eyes met his, Eric said, "Yeah, it happened to me too over there in line."

Mark's lopsided grin was the best thing Eric had seen all morning, and that was saying something.

"I don't think I'll ever get us out of my head," Mark added, and at that moment Eric was sure he and Nicole would be the death of him.

Nicole smiled at the two of them smiling at each other and it all felt so surreal but no less right for it. She selected a scone from the pastry pile and held it out for Mark to take a bite.

With a mouth full of deliciousness, Mark found what he was looking for. "Zerzura. It's a mythical oasis in Egypt."

No surprise, Eric thought. *This place is like paradise found.*

"I knew I'd heard of it before," Nicole chirped. "Zerzura. I think it was on one of those lists or something—those 'wonders of the world' lists. I think it's on the same one as Atlantis and Shangri-La."

Mark nodded as he skimmed the page. "Yep. People really thought it existed—some guy looking for his camel claimed to have found it back in 1835. Supposed to have palm trees and sleeping royalty and guards. Giant guards."

"So, *that's* why this place is so swanky. The whole sleeping royalty thing," Eric said around a particularly sweet bite.

Mark looked up from his phone, a smirk painted on his face. His eyes were dancing.

"No," Nicole said, her eyes issuing a warning, "Don't say it. Mark, don't. Eat this instead."

She held out the scone she had been feeding him, and he happily took another bite, but the smirk was still there.

Eric shook his head and dropped his eyes.

"I think it's useless, babe," he said over his plate. "I don't think he could stop now if he tried."

Mark, nearly shaking with silent laughter, tried to straighten his face enough to deliver the quip properly but just couldn't. He didn't let his mind linger on the fact that they knew, already just *knew*, he was going to say something trite, corny in the most tiresome of ways. He didn't let his mind linger on how free he felt in that moment. He just went for it.

The words burst through his mouth like a torrent.

"Only the best for my King and my Queen."

It was so silly, but it made Nicole blush and made Eric laugh quietly—the kind of laugh that people issued when they had been flattered by someone that mattered to them. And it made Mark feel good to elicit those responses from them. He couldn't wait to do it over and over again.

"Your head looked perfect against the royal pillows as well," Nicole said before sipping her coffee. "The filigree–patterned pillowcases looked like they were made to have your hair fanned out on top of them."

Mark looked at her, the smile faltering on his lips because he remembered... he remembered when he was on his back and she was on top of him, staring at him, moving her hips in torturously slow circles, driving him crazy.

She licked her lips.

Mark inhaled a shaky breath.

For Eric's part, he could only hum in agreement because he too remembered what Mark looked like on his back, hair wild and pupils blown. He remembered kissing Mark while he was underneath Nicole, could feel himself licking into his mouth and capturing his moans. The memory did things to him. He wouldn't have been surprised if he looked visibly aroused right there, in the middle of the restaurant.

Nicole shifted in her seat as the memory took hold of her in full force. Mark's hands on her skin, caressing, pressing, kneading, doing anything and everything to get more of it in his grasp, always more. Eric's tongue along her spine, travelling lower, lower, following every roll of her hips with his kisses and licks and playful nips until his mouth was there, right there tasting her and Mark at the same time. Her mouth was agape, she knew it was, but she couldn't help it. She only hoped she wasn't echoing the sounds she had made at the sensation right there at the table.

The three of them looked at each other.

They had come undone.

Again.

CHAPTER 15

"11:00 p.m.," Nicole had said the night before, almost mournfully.

"Already?" Mark seemed genuinely surprised. Time had flown by, passing in what seemed to be triple time. He remembered walking into the place, spotting Eric before being noticed. He remembered kissing Nicole's cheek when she came in. It all went by so fast, yet he felt like he had spent the evening with two old and dear friends. He wasn't ready for it to end.

The overhead lights in the restaurant had been turned on, the mood lighting affected by the dimmed lantern ruined in favor of a more blatant message: you don't have to go home, but you have to get the hell out of here. They weren't the last table left in the restaurant, but close to it; there were still a few people at the bar, but they were settling their tabs when Mark, Eric, and Nicole finally came up for air and took a look around. Their bill had been paid long ago, hands fumbling for wallets, credit cards coming out, fighting over who would pay for the whole thing. It wasn't that they wanted to go Dutch and be contemporary about this dating thing that seemed to be happening. They each wanted to treat the others, pay for their meals, be chivalrous, if that's what it could be called. In the end, Dutch it was, and that was ok because the conversation about who would pay now or next time allowed them sit and talk a little while longer.

But now what?

It was on each of their minds as they gathered their things and put on their coats, the finality of it all making them grow silent. They made their way out of the restaurant at a reluctant shuffle, each of their minds racing, trying to come up some way to make the moment last.

It was cold outside, cold enough to see their breath.

"So..." Mark started, but let it hang, embarrassed.

Excellent start. You're a real stud.

"So..." Eric echoed. He had intended to say more but couldn't. It wasn't his nerve so much as not knowing how to tell them that he didn't want the night to be over, that he wanted more time with them, more *of* them without sounding too forward or too desperate, or just too... much. So, he too let his voice falter and began to examine his shoes.

"So..." Nicole said, knowing she had to say something before it all fell apart. She had been afraid before that when they walked outside the magic would wear off, that when they saw each other under the bright streetlight that shone like a spotlight in front of the restaurant they would see each other's flaws and change their minds. The fear was so palpable that, on the way out, she had felt the urge to dig in her heels and protest leaving, throwing a tantrum like a baby. But now she could see that hadn't happened. Despite Mark and Eric's inept attempts that any one of them could have misconstrued as an awkward preamble to goodbye, Nicole could see that exactly the opposite was really going on. They didn't want to the night to end any more than she did.

"I'm... I'm cold," Nicole added quickly, before she lost her nerve. And then, like a light switch being turned off, she did lose it. Her nerve disappeared utterly and completely, causing her to tuck in her chin and fall mute.

Damnit!

This was all so new to her. She had never been the one to speak up, to be the aggressive one—not in relationships, at least. She did enough of that at work. She didn't consider herself passive—no one would have—but she hadn't had to make the first move with any of the men she had dated. Her husband ran two blocks to catch up to her on the street. She had passed by him, and he wanted to meet her, so he ducked into a florist, bought the first bouquet of flowers he saw, and bolted out the door to catch her. When she was a teenager, guys used to call the local radio station and dedicate songs to her. It had always been like that for Nicole—she didn't have to ask to receive. But now, when not saying anything might mean letting go of the chance at something incredible, something she hadn't known she was missing, hadn't known she even wanted, she was afraid to wait and see what would happen.

But the stakes were so high. She felt like a fish out of water.

Nicole wanted to say more, do more, show she wanted more, but couldn't figure out how.

Should she?

Could she?

Her heart was beating wildly in her chest as she shivered from a wayward breeze.

Eric and Mark jumped into action immediately, putting their arms around her, one at the shoulders, one at the waist, flanking her to create a 'C' shape. Eric reached toward Mark, instinctually moving to close the circle, wanting to keep him warm also, but stopped midway, second guessing himself. Would Mark be receptive to it? Eric didn't think his straight friends would be ok with him holding them to keep them warm. It was a deliberate 'let me take care of you' move, and Eric couldn't even try to pretend that he meant it any other way.

Eric brought his hand back to himself, deciding to spare Mark the awkwardness of too much too soon.

But then Mark reached for Eric.

It was awkward, and he ended up latching on to the front of Eric's shirt after a choppy, uncoordinated grab, but he didn't let go. Mark looked Eric in the eyes and didn't let go.

"Can we go somewhere? Maybe to get coffee or something? I just..." Nicole felt tears welling in her eyes, stinging them.

"Yeah, anywhere... anything," Mark said, his voice cracking. "I don't... I don't want..."

Mark looked at Nicole and then at Eric and found himself at a loss for words.

"Me neither," Eric said and pulled Nicole closer into him, rubbing the arm that Mark had wrapped around her waist at the same time.

Mark felt like he could have stayed just like that forever,

feeling their warmth around him and sharing his own in kind. They all did.

"Come on," Eric said, suddenly getting his bearings. He looked down one side of the street and then the other, squinted as he did, trying to make out the storefront signs that lit up the darkness. Had they been in The Village, they would have had their pick of at least six places that Eric could personally attest to either having decent coffee, good dessert, or a nice lounge—like atmosphere with great drinks. But Eric intended to steer clear of those places, would stay away from The Village all together if he could help it. The last thing he needed was for someone to see them out. Because it wouldn't just be that someone would see them together—Eric would like nothing more than to show them off, to let the world know that those two amazing people were interested in him. No, that wouldn't be the problem at all. Eric wouldn't just be seen—he would be recognized. Recognized as someone from the scene. Maybe as an actor they saw on stage or maybe by someone from the cast of past shows. And yes, there were straight people who attended the plays in the festival and yes, there were straight performers in the plays also... but he wasn't one of them. He really didn't want any more attention to be drawn to that than was necessary.

Eric wasn't ashamed of who he was, and he hadn't hidden it from Mark and Nicole. They had all been honest about the lives they had led before meeting that morning. But there was something different about knowing a thing and seeing a thing, something about seeing the man you might be interested in interacting with his crowd, pretenses thrown to the wind, that kind of burns away the rose—colored glasses. It's not that he wasn't being himself with Mark and Nicole, because he was. He was being himself in ways that he hadn't with anyone in a very long time. But there was the side of him that enjoyed drama, flamboyance, and a tad of the catty, even if he wasn't actively participating in it himself. He liked donning that mask every once in a while. The Village restaurants were undoubtedly filled with dramatic, flamboyant, catty gay theater folks blowing off steam after the first round of auditions. He would know many of them; the side of Eric they knew would be embroiled in the scene, toasting, talking loudly, being rambunctious or being receptive of it in kind... they would *expect* it of him. Maybe one day Eric would show Nicole and Mark that side of himself. Maybe he would introduce them to his friends and watch how they fawned over them, listen as they hemmed and hawed about how beautiful his loves were. He knew his friends would lose it over Mark and how gorgeous he was and Nicole's style and grace would be positively idolized. They would be envious for sure, and who wouldn't be? Anyone who had either one of them on their arm would experience the same thing. And Eric had them both? Eric, who used to be the life of the party but had, in large part, turned a cold shoulder to the scene? Eric, who didn't have a boyfriend because he didn't think any of the pickings were good enough for him? Eric, who seemed so untouchable now that people wondered if he was getting any at all anymore? And he wouldn't have to say anything for them to know right away why things were different now, why he was smiling with his whole face again. Just five minutes with Nicole and Mark, and it would all come clear. And they would be per—

Eric shook his head, clearing it. If he didn't rein his

thoughts in, he'd imagine them married and living on a farm in the span of six months.

Or in London.

Off in the distance, Eric could see what he was looking for, the ornate letter glowing in the night sky like a guiding light.

Z.

"I think I know a place."

CHAPTER 16

The Zerzura Hotel was posh, gilded, and lush. The high ceilings and sculpted archways in the lobby made them feel as if they had stepped into another country just by coming in off the street. Each wall held a fractal pattern in its core; stark black and white abstracts so intricate one found themselves searching for hidden meanings within them. The abstracts floated in subtle dimension above antique gold walls; it took more than a passing glance to realize that the canvases were suspended from the ceiling rather than framed and mounted. Palm fronds stood in impossibly tall, ornate vases. The room was guarded by winged goddesses with gem-studded *usekhs* adorning their necks done in red, blues, and greens that made you believe they might be the rubies and turquoise and emeralds that would have accentuated an Egyptian queen's own jewelry. All of these things came together to transform the room into an ancient paradise that promised more beyond the palace gates. The ambiance, the opulence, the fantastical nature of it all was heady, intoxicating. It fed their fantasies perfectly.

"I remember hearing that the restaurant here has amazing desserts," Eric said as he held the door for both Nicole and Mark. Mark had reached out a hand to do the same but pulled it back when Eric beat him to it. It made them both chuckle, then the most wonderful thing happened: Mark blushed.

He was shy about it, looking off, not meeting Eric's eyes in a way that let Eric know he wasn't used to doing so and that... that made Eric feel fantastic. He hadn't meant to cause it, hadn't done anything in particular to bring it on, but wow, it felt good to know he could have that kind of effect on Mark.

It felt really, really good.

Nicole wanted to say that it didn't matter whether or not the place had good food, that she literally didn't care if it served day old bread and burnt coffee from some discount reseller. The only thing she wanted was for the place to stay open so that they could be together, even if they never said another word.

They were shown to a table by a wiry server with tanned skin and a thin moustache holding a white cloth over his right forearm. He was comical, really, like a character right out of a 1940s movie set somewhere exotic. She supposed this was the right room for it too; the dining room had lush ferns along the arcaded walls, creating the atmosphere of being outside, and every table held its own bouquet of red poppy and cornflower, the red and blue contrasting startlingly against the white tablecloth. Nicole tried to remind herself to tell them about the server and how he made her think of *Casablanca* without really knowing why, but by the time they ordered drinks they would soon abandon without so much as a sip, she had forgotten all about the man with his slicked down hair and slight build.

They took off their coats and sat down again, same spots as they had in the restaurant, but that was the only thing that felt similar. Something had changed. There was a shift, something different in the air, and everyone felt it.

No matter how nervous it might have made them, how wary or disoriented, each of them was still there.

"I feel a little like the lion did in that scene in *The Wiz,*" Nicole started. "You know, when those women threw the dust in the air and he and Dorothy got high?"

Mark's mouth worked around a question he struggled to form, but Eric knew what Nicole was talking about right away.

"Yeah, the Poppy Girls scene."

Mark looked at Eric incredulously.

Eric shrugged. "I'm a theater guy. *The Wiz* is requisite education depending upon where you work. But what I want to know," Eric said, turning his attention back to Nicole, "is why you chose the lion over Dorothy?"

Good question, Nicole thought and one she was definitely going to answer. Even though the words scared her, she was going to say them... no more holding back.

"Because when the dust affected Dorothy she tried to shake it off, clear her head. Not the lion. He let the dust have its way with him, enjoyed the way it felt going down. He didn't want to fight it. Neither do I."

Nicole's words hit Mark and Eric right in the pits of their stomachs causing one to squirm and the other to take an audible breath. Nicole smiled, just a little thing, just enough to raise the corners of her mouth before she bit it back down.

Suddenly Eric felt responsible for what had to be perceived as pressure. He'd brought them to a hotel. A freaking hotel! Of all the places they could have gone.

Jesus!

If he had just taken a little more time to think about where they could go, maybe even asked them what they wanted to do, but no, he had to take the lead and look where that had gotten them.

A hotel.

A hotel... it made it seem like he only wanted one thing from them. It was like he was making it easier for them to fall into bed by coming to this specific restaurant when there were countless others to choose from. It wasn't like Toronto shut down completely at night—hell, it was only midnight. Eric could have found another place because he didn't only want to take the party to the next level. He didn't want them to think he only wanted to have sex even though he wanted to, he definitely wanted to, and he would, if that's what they wanted to do too—he would do it in a heartbeat. But now he had made it seem like that was the only thing on his mind. Now Nicole felt pressured into being there with them... with him. Now Mark felt like he had to do things he wasn't ready to do, didn't want to do, and he—

"I," Eric blurted out, going from aroused to scared to death in an instant. "I didn't mean... I don't want you to think I—"

"You don't *want* to?"

It was Mark who spoke next, his eyes darker than they had been before.

And oh, Eric very much wanted to.

"What can I get you this evening?" the server asked, her smile warm and welcoming.

Nicole recovered first. "Just a cup of coffee, please, with cream."

"S—same," Eric said, clearing his throat.

"Me too," Mark said and glanced at the server with a quick smile.

"Three coffees with cream, of course. I'll be right back."

They didn't see her leave, only knew that she must have because the space around their table was quiet again. There weren't many people in the restaurant; they pretty much had the place to themselves. That was both good and bad. It was good that they didn't have to worry about whether other people could tell what they were up to, because Mark had become confident that anyone glancing their way would know they were more than just friends hanging out at this point, but it was bad because without the din of conversation, their voices could be overheard... and with all the innuendo and the outright mood between them now, there would be no question what was going on between the three of them.

"So?" Mark asked, behaving more forwardly than he ever had in his life. He'd had time. Time to think about what he was doing, why he was still walking with them when the night could have been over and he could have taken the train back to his hotel. They had walked in relative silence, each of them off in their own heads, considering, measuring, deciding. He thought about everything in the space of the three blocks between the restaurant and the hotel—how if anyone ever found out, the reputation he had always worked so hard to keep straight and narrow would be ruined, how if his kids found out, they would never understand, how his wife would never forgive him. He thought about what all of that meant. He wondered how he could want two people—two! Wondered about his sexuality and when it had changed or if this had always been there, lying dormant, waiting for a chance to show its face. He thought about the hard conversations that would happen if everything came to light, and the guilt he would feel forever whether it did or didn't. He thought hard, yet he kept walking.

So, he asked... because he needed to.

Nicole couldn't believe how brazen she was being. Her heart was still beating wildly in her chest at her own wanton words. But she had decided on the way to the hotel that she was ready for this. She hadn't been looking for anything, hadn't felt anything more than complacent after she'd been married to the same person for nearly 20 years, but there she was. It wasn't just that the two men before her offered something fresh and new—it truly felt like this—all of it—was meant to be, that this whole thing was preordained: kismet. Come what may, she didn't think she had it in her to fight it. As terrible as that sounded, as terrible as it made her feel as a mother and a wife, she knew it was true. Thinking about the possible consequences of such a thing was enough to make her sick, but she had to see it through. If never before, Nicole knew then that she was following the path that had been laid out for her. Come what may.

Three. Eric kept thinking of the word, seeing it flash and weave and scroll in his head.

Three.

Beyond the sex, beyond this night, there would be three of them. Three people unsure of what they were feeling, three people trying to deal with the aftermath of what they might start there, on that chilly night in Toronto..

Three.

He liked to think that he would be ok with whatever happened. He was the one who was single in the world, no children, no partner, no guilt... right? But he knew that wasn't true. It would have been true if it was just sex. They were the married ones and, therefore, the ones who had to think about what they could lose if they did this thing. They were the ones who would get the lion's share of the blame when it was passed around. But this wasn't just about sex; he knew that much even as he imagined what their skin might feel like pressed against his.

This was something else entirely.

He was feeling things that he hadn't felt before, and it was enough to give him pause. Eric thought back to his most serious relationship—two years with a director. They'd had to hide their relationship so that people didn't accuse his partner of helping Eric's career. They grew close over the first few months of being together and learned more about each other with every passing day, it seemed. Eric could remember being happy with him almost until the end, remembered feeling comfortable with him and vice versa, not needing to fill the space with words or activities... just allowing themselves to be quiet in the same room.

Eric already felt that same kind of comfort with Nicole and Mark.

At first, he didn't believe it, didn't want to allow himself to become that smitten in one day. But it was true. They had already told each other more than Eric, for one, had ever shared with anyone else. They already got each other's jokes, read each other's faces, understood each other's pauses. And it all came so naturally, they just fell into it without noticing. So, when the two of them walked away from this night feeling guilty, he would share in it. Because this was so much more than just sex. It was...

He needed to be sure.

The server delivered the coffees with another of her beautiful smiles, but it went unnoticed.

"Mark, are—" Eric started when she left, but was cut off quickly.

"Do you?" Mark said as he covered Eric's hand with his own. He rubbed his thumb over the back of Eric's hand, tracing his way to the tip of the middle finger ever so slowly, watching his finger as it moved.

Eric watched too, enjoying how Mark's fingers looked against his own. He reached out to Nicole suddenly, needing to feel her touch like he was feeling Mark's, then her hand was there, in his. Eric's eyes closed with the sensation, with the perfection of it all.

From a place deep inside himself where his need and desire had been sleeping quietly for longer than he cared to think about. Eric spoke the only word that needed to be said.

"Yes."

CHAPTER 17

Fast.

Fast.

Everything was going so fast.

Too fast, Nicole thought as they met in the middle of the California King that seemed to be nudging them together, the downy mattress so supple that every move was smothered and repositioned, inching them that much closer to each other.

Not that they needed any help.

Nicole barely remembered Eric getting the room and them riding up to it separately after hatching their amateurish plan to evade prying eyes. But Nicole was sure Mark had been right—anyone seeing them going upstairs now would just be getting confirmation of what they already knew to be true. It was all over them—the looks that had turned lustful as the night went on, the connection they shared, the give and take that only existed between lovers... it was almost palpable. People might wonder about what was going on, but not about whether or not there was a connection between them, some kind of spark. That much was very clear.

But still...

Nicole was the second to arrive, just as the door was swinging closed, with Mark a close third. Eric let them in one by one as agreed upon, allowing himself to only ghost a touch over Nicole's cheek before she moved further into the room. It was gorgeous, the room that would witness this thing they didn't have a name for, well-appointed and contemporary, done in brushed gold and turquoise, midnight blue and the softest ivory. She only had a few moments to register that before she heard the door close for the final time and felt a hand at the small of her back.

So fast.

Too fast.

No one was rushing, but meeting at the coffee shop, pining all day, the dinner and coffee afterward, anticipation that filled her stomach with butterflies—it all felt like a whirlwind.

She felt unsteady, breathless.

And so, so ready.

Nicole turned, reached out to touch, and felt Eric's chest beneath her hand.

Her eyes acted of their own volition then, rolling and closing in pleasure.

Her breathing might have stopped. She might have been on her way to the floor in a faint as otherworldly as everything felt all of a sudden. Nicole didn't know. She could only feel Eric's chest, his strong heartbeat against her hand. She could only envision the skin hidden by the shirt, could only wonder whether it was bare or covered with light brown hair, hair that matched his normal shade but would be different from the champagne color on his head now. She could only wonder if his nipples were pink or brown, small or large. She couldn't help but fantasize about how toned his chest might be, how sculpted.

And then she couldn't move.

Eric reached for Nicole's hand and raised it higher so that he could kiss the inside of her wrist. She visibly relaxed as she felt his lips part, first to place an open kiss on the sensitive skin, then to lick a thin strip from her bracelet to the base of her hand. She melted a little, breathed into it. His tongue, his lips that trailed behind it... it felt like just what she needed. Eric smiled against her skin as he kissed her there again, relishing her reaction.

Because Eric was nervous about pleasing Nicole. He was nervous about hurting Mark. He was nervous about everything that was about to happen. But he wanted it. Eric wanted it all, and he'd be damned if he let fear get in the way.

She felt good.

He was making her feel good.

Eric sighed with relief.

Mark was taking his coat off when Eric began kissing Nicole's wrist and felt momentarily awed. They were gorgeous together. He knew it before but now, giving into this thing and allowing themselves to be vulnerable, the truth of how well they fit together really rang true. He wanted to join them, knew he would as soon as he could pick his jaw up from the floor, but for the moment he was content to watch, enjoying the gentle tilt of Nicole's neck as she savored the sensations she was feeling. He wanted to watch Eric's mouth move as he kissed her skin, catch a glimpse of his tongue as it caressed, teased. Mark wanted to watch Eric please Nicole because it pleased him, too.

But only for a little while.

Mark couldn't stay away for long, not when Eric smiling against Nicole's wrist looked so endearing. Not when Nicole had begun to bite the corner of her bottom lip. Mark crossed the room unnoticed, loving the fact that they were already in their own little world. He touched them both at the same time, cradling the backs of their heads, allowing himself to feel their hair in his hands, run his fingers through. As though planned, Nicole and Eric turned to Mark at the same time, their eyes telling him what would come next if he let it. And he would. Even though he had no idea what had come over him or where this desire was coming from, he would let it happen. All of it. They hadn't talked about what that meant, but Mark knew he wanted it. Just like he knew he wanted to be there, in that room, at that moment.

Mark kissed Nicole first, moving his hand to cup her cheek before dipping down to meet her lips. They were soft, so very soft. He kissed her gently, lingering to appreciate the feel of her mouth against his, enjoying the hitch in her breath as he took his time. When he parted his lips and reached his tongue toward hers, he found it with ease. Their tongues danced, touching and swirling, working smooth, slow circles around each other until neither of them could resist moaning into the other's mouth. They stayed that way, leaning into each other, Nicole's hand gripping his shoulder as she surrendered into the kiss, Mark's hand caressing her scalp with his fingertips. When they broke the kiss, they pulled apart to look at each other in wonder.

Mark turned to Eric, whose head he still cradled in his other hand, and stared at him. He was a gorgeous man, modelesque yet unpretentiously so. *Real.* Mark felt like he could have stared into Eric's blue eyes forever, especially the way he was looking at him then, with a mixture of restraint and longing dancing inside him. Mark knew Eric was thinking of him, what might be going on inside his head, how he might be feeling. Mark was grateful that Eric was so considerate of him, and he trusted that this night would be special because of it. But no matter how confused he might be about these new feelings he was having, Mark knew he would explore them. Tonight. With the two of them.

Mark bit his lip as he looked at Eric, his champagne hair pushed off his face as he took in the man before him. He could feel the attraction welling in his body the longer he let his eyes cascade over Eric's face, his shoulders, his chest hugged so beautifully by his shirt. As Eric took in a breath under the weight of Mark's stare, he knew he couldn't wait anymore.

Mark tilted his head, having to reach up just a little to catch Eric's lips in a kiss, and he found that he liked that. Eric leaned in to bridge the gap, wanting desperately to deepen the kiss but restraining himself to follow Mark's pace. Mark pressed their lips together once, twice, three times before deepening the kiss himself, opening his mouth on the fourth meeting. Eric's hand found its way into Mark's hair as he let the tip of his tongue touch Mark's lip.

Eric would have been lying if he said that he hadn't braced himself for Mark to pull away, to come back to his senses the moment he felt Mark's tongue. He even had an unwanted flash of Mark's face turning stony and angry as he lashed out at Eric, swinging his fists. But that didn't happen. Instead, Mark moaned from low in his throat as he let himself go. He met Eric's tongue with his own and kissed him greedily.

Nicole couldn't stop watching the way they looked when they kissed. She could feel her breathing increasing in time with theirs even though she wasn't actively involved at the moment. It was sexy in a way that nothing else had been for her before. She had seen her fair share of porn, had had more than one or two partners—it wasn't that she was inexperienced or a prude. This was different... more. This was *them*.

Neither Mark nor Eric had let go of Nicole when they started kissing, and neither of them wanted to now. They caressed her as they did each other, hoping she felt some of what they were feeling. The result was heady, bliss-filled, and sensual. Mark's hand moved down her neck to rub her shoulder blades, his fingers dancing inside the crease they formed. Eric's thumb rubbed the space where his lips had been at her wrist, creating a different, intensely pleasurable sensation even with such a light touch, before caressing her forearm. As Mark drove his tongue deeper into Eric's mouth, Eric's hold on Nicole's forearm tightened. When Eric nipped playfully at Mark's bottom lip, Mark curled his fingers on her back, pressing through the material into her skin. She found herself beginning to writhe as they shared their pleasure with her.

It was intoxicating.

When Mark and Eric pulled away, the three of them found themselves in an embrace. Lopsided smiles and appreciative chuckles emitted from one or all of them, it was hard to tell. They each felt a bit shy after that, vulnerable after that first sharing of intimacy. They also felt elated, their worries over whether or not everyone felt the same way dashed.

Each felt more aroused than they had ever been before.

The bed.

Slow down, slow down, the mantra sang in Nicole's head but she could do nothing of the sort. As she took her shoes off then turned to look at her soon-to-be lovers, she knew she wouldn't do anything to get in the way of where this thing was headed. Even though she didn't want the moment to end, she also couldn't wait for more.

Eric put his knee on the bed, having removed his shoes as well. Mark followed suit. Both of them looked at Nicole.

Nicole dipped her head, causing her hair to nearly cover one of her eyes. She looked up at them through the fringe coyly as she fingered the top button of her dress. She saw their reactions, saw their chests heave as they watched her watching them.

"I almost didn't pack this dress," she started, her voice low and sultry. "But something told me I should."

She unbuttoned the top button. The dress opened like petals of a flower in the nurturing sun, revealing the hint of cleavage.

Mark licked his lips.

"Something told me to pick this dress over all the others I have, because I needed to have it."

Another button gone.

Eric inched further onto the bed, his body moving before he was even aware of it.

"I wore this dress tonight...for you."

She ran her finger down the open buttons, barely grazing her freed skin. Could they see the flush that had bloomed there, the alertness of her nipples? She smiled despite herself, proud of herself for not shying away, happy that she laid it all out on the table.

She felt sexy as hell.

"It's b-beautiful," Eric struggled out, his mouth dry as he struggled to look her in the eyes. But it was difficult when he could see the round of her breasts peeking out at him, right where they met her ribcage. He imagined what it would be like to kiss that spot, to lick it. Would she like it? Would she squirm beneath his touch?

Nicole joined them on the bed, drew closer to them as she did, the magnetic pull between them making it impossible not to. She looked at them, their eyes speaking volumes. They wanted her. She knew that already, but seeing it in their eyes as they knelt before each other—before her—was exhilarating. Eric looked at her like she was the most amazing woman in the world, and Mark's expression wasn't much different. She wanted more of that, she knew all of a sudden; the feeling was impossible to ignore.

She wanted to tease.

"You're sure you like it?" Nicole asked, leaning into Mark as though to kiss. She got so close that his eyes closed instinctively as his head cocked to the side to receive her. But she didn't kiss him, even after parting her lips to do so. She pulled back instead to stare into Eric's blue eyes, now clouded with desire. As she continued to speak, Mark leaned in, his eyes opening wide at the realization that he was not getting kissed and that she wasn't even where he thought she was. It was such a rush. He could feel excitement coursing through his body.

"It isn't too, I don't know, matronly?" she asked Eric as she unbuttoned another button, revealing more of the black lace bra hiding beneath the turquoise material.

"Ma—no. Not at all. It's..."

Nicole moved toward Eric, and he raised himself up onto his knees. He hadn't realized he had slumped as he watched Nicole undress, his body nearly giving way, but he had. Now, emboldened by her behavior, he rose to his knees again, hovering tall above her, bigger in a way that made her feel safe.

"It's...?" Nicole asked, her voice nothing more than a whisper as she moved ever closer, until her lips almost touched his.

"It's... you're..."

"What?" Nicole asked softly, her lips teasing, almost touching.

Eric looked at her mouth, so close to his now he hardly needed to move to kiss her lips. Her mouth was open—he could feel her warm breath on his skin. He tilted his chin slightly, letting his own mouth open to match hers, his tongue wetting his lips. He could feel as much as hear her take a shuddering breath.

Eric exhaled a breath of his own and enjoyed the way she moved closer still, her body nearly pressed against his. The way she looked, the way she smelled, her perfect mouth, that gorgeous dress. She was simply...

"Perfect."

Eric kissed Nicole then, starting slow. She kissed him back, feeling herself arch into him as he grew more confident. Before long he had latched onto her bottom lip to suckle it, eliciting the sweetest sounding moan he had ever heard. Nicole's tongue met Eric's, and they chased the electric spark they felt, tumbling, rolling, pressing into each other. She could feel the moment when Eric's composure dissipated, could hear it in the clipped moans he almost begrudgingly gave. She wanted more of that, wanted to make him come completely undone.

She wanted more of him.

When they separated, Nicole found her hands gently lifting the bottom of Eric's shirt.

Eric pressed his forehead to Nicole's, his mind divulging a truth he was no longer sure mattered.

"I've never been with a woman before."

Nicole moaned her response, though whether it was because of his words or a reaction to Mark's mouth on her collarbone, no one could tell. She felt like she was on fire, could feel her nipples reaching, straining to be touched, kissed, sucked. Her hand found its way to Eric's neck even as her eyes closed while Mark made his way up, up, up, his lips blazing a trail from her shoulder to her mouth. Mark kissed her and his tongue was hot, as hot as Nicole's skin felt.

Eric hummed his appreciation of her touch on his neck, pressing into it for more. Nicole pulled him closer, as close as she could get him, and Eric came willingly, eagerly. Mark moved away from Nicole's mouth only to lick the shell of her ear. Eric took up residence there instead, licking into her mouth passionately, as if it was his solace.

Mark and Nicole's hands met at the nape of Eric's neck, and they interlaced their fingers on contact, wanting to touch each other, wanting to touch Eric, wanting to touch Eric together. A chuckle emitted from Eric, muffled by Nicole's mouth on his, as they played in his hair. He felt like he was having the best, most vivid dream of his life.

"I've never done *anything* like this before," Nicole said breaking the kiss to look into Eric's eyes.

"Me neither," Mark said breathily as he continued to kiss the back of Nicole's ear.

Eric touched the material of Nicole's dress where it hung open to reveal her bra. He traced her collarbone with her fingertips, his bottom lip clenched between his teeth. He slipped his fingers beneath the strap of Nicole's bra and pushed it toward her shoulder ever so slowly, enjoying the glide, until it fell over the side. He did the same on the other one, marveling at how smooth her skin was. Nicole undid the remaining two buttons, letting the dress hang open, clearing the way for Eric to go at his own pace.

Mark had other plans.

He moved behind Eric, wanting to kiss him the same way he had Nicole. He wanted to find the places that made him squirm, wanted to know he could make Eric feel good, too. Mark ran his hands down Eric's back, stopping at the belt loop of his pants, moving slowly and adding pressure as he approached his lower back. He felt Eric arch the tiniest bit and felt pleased with himself. Mark teased his fingers beneath Eric's t-shirt to feel his skin and couldn't contain a moan of his own when he found it. His back was smooth, the muscles defined. Mark couldn't wait—he had to see.

The air on Eric's skin was a surprise. He had felt Mark's hands on him, thought he might touch him higher on his back, hoped he would run his hands over onto his pecs, then over his stomach as his confidence grew, but he wasn't prepared for Mark to remove his shirt before doing any of that.

Mark lifted Eric's shirt over his head, the shirt helped along by Nicole who kissed the surprise away from Eric's mouth as soon as he realized what happened. Her eyes searched his imploringly, making sure this next step was ok, and Eric loved her for it. He initiated the next kiss, tracing the outline of her upper lip slowly before pressing their lips together. It was delicate. It was sweet. It was affirmation.

Mark closed his eyes as Eric's shirt came off, suddenly nervous. He hadn't asked if this was ok. He hadn't thought about what he was doing until he had almost finished fishing Eric's arms out. Eric hadn't resisted, had actually helped him get the shirt off, in fact—they both had. But still.

And he was scared to see Eric's skin because he didn't know what his reaction would be.

What if all of this was some sort of mistake? What if he wasn't feeling attraction, but was having some kind of reaction to something? Something airborne maybe, or something he ate? What if he was getting sick? Not with a cold or anything so pedestrian—maybe he was getting something major. He remembered seeing some show where they talked about signs of major illnesses—smelling something sweet when nothing like that was around was a symptom. So was promiscuity. It sounded ridiculous, and he was embarrassed by the thought even though no one else knew he was having it, but the trepidation was still there. He had never been attracted to a man before, so why now? Why all of a sudden? It didn't make sense that he wanted to see Eric's body, feel all of the curves and the textures. It didn't make sense that he wanted to taste him, satisfy him in whatever way Eric wanted. Did Mark even understand what that meant? Was he prepared to–

Mark felt Eric's hands on his. He had reached behind himself to touch Mark, careful not to turn around or change what Mark was seeing. Eric wanted Mark to do whatever he wanted to do to him, and he was willing to wait. He just wanted Mark to know that it was ok.

Mark leaned forward to lay his forehead onto Eric's

back, kissing him chastely there before he took a deep breath.

You can stop now.

You don't have to do anything else.

What are you doing here anyway, Mark?

Mark's mind threw rapid fire questions out, and one side of him stood back to assess their merit. He didn't *have* to go on. While he had done some things that would be hard to explain in the light of day, he hadn't gone all the way with anything. He hadn't even taken his clothes off yet, and before he had acted so brazenly and taken Eric's shirt off of him, no one had. No one had touched places that didn't see the sun; it was akin to petting in the basement while the adults were upstairs, nervous and tentative at best. The whole thing had only lasted a few minutes, but that was bullshit. If this was just about sex, all of that was true. But this wasn't just about sex, and he knew it. This was something so much more.

He needed this. Mark needed to touch Nicole, he needed to touch Eric, he needed to be touched by them. His body was reacting to them in ways that he had never felt before. So was his mind. Even outside of that room and the physical contact—the heat that felt like it was engulfing him—Mark needed Nicole and Eric. Now. Maybe forever.

Eric brought Mark's hands to his own waist, pressing his fingers to the exposed skin. He looked at Mark over his shoulder, resting his chin there just long enough to catch a glimpse.

Mark exhaled resolutely. What was he doing? Even as the answer felt ludicrous considering everything he knew about himself, Mark was certain it was fact.

What was he doing?

Loving them.

CHAPTER 18

There was so much Nicole didn't know—so much she hadn't done, or seen, or heard about.

So much she didn't know about herself.

She didn't know that not every orgasm she had needed to be the screaming, gasping, sensory overload kind—that she was capable of smaller ones that quickened her heartbeat and took her breath away but didn't exhaust or bowl her over.

She didn't know that a man could get as wet as she could, messing his stomach up with so much precum that it could fill his navel to overflowing.

She didn't know she liked to watch so much, that she could have one of those quiet orgasms from it and be ready for more.

But she knew that now.

As she lay beneath Mark, feeling his mouth on her breast and her back arching because of it, she was excited to learn even more.

Nicole's breasts were gorgeous. Mark didn't think he

would ever get enough of looking at them, touching them, kissing them. Her nipples craved attention, remaining firm in his mouth as he sucked them, licked them, nibbled just a bit. He loved to pull off of them and see his saliva shining there, her nipples pert from the attention. He loved how her breasts moved as her chest heaved. He loved them, pure and simple.

They were naked now, clothing coming off easily enough after Eric's shirt had been discarded, each of them desperate to see more, to touch more. They had explored each other's bodies, tickling, teasing, touching in ways that excited, only to move on to something else, the reaction stored in each of their memory banks for later. There was so much they wanted to do, so much they wanted to feel. They were concerned they wouldn't be able to hold out anymore, afraid they would end up chasing their releases and then it would be over. No one wanted it to be over. They had to make it last.

Eric rubbed circles into the backs of Mark's thighs. Positioned between both Mark's and Nicole's legs, Eric had a view that he never expected to have—the most sensual view he had ever had in his life. Nicole's body was beautiful. He couldn't take his eyes off it. The curve of her breasts, the delicate 'S' formed as her ribs reached toward her hips, the soft skin of her stomach, all of it was captivating. He wanted to touch. The instant he saw her bare shoulders revealed he knew he had to feel her skin beneath his hand, had to kiss it. And he did. She had let him do whatever he wanted to do, and so he did. He had lapped at her neck hungrily, excited by the prospect of more. He touched her breasts, first under cover of the bra, and then bare, the supple flesh sitting firmly in his hand. With his eyes he asked for permission to do more, and she kissed him in affirmation. When he took one of her nipples into his mouth, she moaned appreciatively.

So different from what he was used to.

So wonderfully different.

From behind them, watching them enjoy each other, Eric remembered how he had trailed his hands down her body, letting them follow her curves, touching everywhere he could. Eric had taken off her dress before he realized it, and Mark had removed her underwear ahead of him, knowing somehow encountering them would have given Eric pause. And so there she was, undressed and waiting, the heat of excitement coming off of her in tantalizing waves.

Eric had rested his hands on Nicole's hips, his ring and pinky fingers pressing into her buttocks as he looked at her. Nicole had tried not to squirm under the intensity, knowing that Eric needed this. It was new, being surveyed so closely—she couldn't remember the last time anyone had actually looked at her like that. Could he see how excited she was? She could feel herself pulsing in time with her quickened heart. And she was wet, so very wet, and they hadn't really begun. What did that look like to him?

As she tried to envision the picture her body was painting for Eric, she watched his face and the changes it went through as he stared. This was his first time, and the awe of the moment reflected in his expression. So was determination and desire, as well as a modicum of fear. She wanted to tell him that he didn't have anything to worry about, that this experience had already been so amazing that nothing else needed to happen to satisfy her. But she didn't say anything at all. If she had, she would have ruined the mood, might have shied him off doing anything else. And he wanted to—she could see how much he wanted to. So there she lay. It made her feel vulnerable for sure, but there was a more intense feeling at play as she lay prone beneath Eric's gaze, opening her legs a little wider so that he could see even more.

She felt desired.

Eric licked his lips as he remembered the way she tasted. He had to fight the urge to touch her then, to cover his fingers in her juices and bring them to his mouth again. But he had something else in mind, something else he wanted to do at that moment, so as enticing as the prospect of engaging with Nicole might have been, he had to set that side. For later.

It was Mark's turn.

Eric was back to staring, but this time at Mark. His golden skin was flushed with arousal, and that was slowly driving Eric crazy. Mark seemed to like the way Eric was touching him, and that was good. Eric had been watching his reactions to make sure he was still ok, and so far, Mark had been receptive to everything that had happened, including when Eric ran his hand over his hardening member. It has been clothed, covered by the boxer briefs Mark wore, and the touch was fleeting, barely there at all, but any touch, however brief, would have been too much for a man who was decidedly straight and entirely uninterested in exploring otherwise. Mark had thought that was who he was before that day, but if the way he pushed his hips forward, chasing Eric's hand in search of more was any indication, all of that had changed.

Eric had let his hands slide up Mark's legs as he considered how attractive the man before him was, how toned his legs were yet how supple the skin. He had expanded the circles he was making, using his whole hand now to rub and feel. His hands inched toward Mark's behind, and he slowed them, hesitating ever so slightly. Mark didn't stir, didn't ask him to stop... so he didn't.

Eric touched Mark's backside, kneading the flesh, enjoying the way it moved under his hands. He caressed Mark's hips and smiled when he saw goosebumps rise on his skin. He repeated the path from behind to hips and back at a slow pace, spreading his cheeks more and more with every pass. Mark seemed to enjoy the stretch, moaning as he felt himself become more and more exposed.

Eric could see it—the tight pucker clenched as Eric moved the flesh around it. Emboldened, Eric blew lightly on it, not too close to frighten Mark off, but deliberately enough to make him notice.

The curve of Mark's lower back deepened as he arched, exposing even more of himself to Eric. Eric bit back his own deep moans.

Ok.

Ok.

It's now or never.

Eric separated Mark's cheeks again, allowed himself to watch Mark quiver in anticipation and to feel his own penis twitch in response before he kissed him where he had never been kissed before.

Mark inhaled sharply at the new sensation, his arms growing weak in response. He laid his head on Nicole's stomach, his mouth open as he panted involuntarily. She cradled his head, and he nuzzled into her hand appreciatively as he looked back at Eric.

Eric raised his head to look at Mark, at the same time

circling the flat of his thumb around Mark's entrance, stimulating him differently than before.

"Is this ok?" Eric asked Mark quietly.

It was hard to think with Eric touching him the way he was, but he knew without a shadow of a doubt that this, all of it, was more than ok.

"Yes," he said, his voice sounding ruined already. His eyes begged Eric to continue. Eric learned quickly that he couldn't deny Mark or Nicole anything.

CHAPTER 19

Too late.

As Nicole sat looking at the still blue water of The Z's pool, she couldn't help but think those words.

Too late.

Her husband had texted her at some point during dinner. He wasn't texting about much, but at the same time his text was everything. It was after the kids would have gone to bed, even if he had let them stay up late to watch the scary movies they frightened themselves with when she wasn't around. He might be awake now dealing with the aftermath of it too; whichever ghost or ghoul that had terrorized the kids from the screen had likely met them in their dreams, and he might be up at that very moment, showing them that there was nothing in their closet. What time was it, anyway?

The clock above the candle wall read 2:56 a.m.

Just about the witching hour. And all the witches had already gone out to play.

Too late.

Too late to respond to his message acknowledging that she hadn't called and checking in on how trade show duty was going.

Too late to wish she hadn't glanced at her phone when she went to the bathroom.

Too late to worry about what she had done.

Too late to wonder why it didn't bother her as much as she thought it should.

Because it didn't.

Ok, yes, there were some things that really bothered her about her behavior, and if she dwelled on the potential aftermath she might start crying and never stop, but they weren't the things she thought she should be upset about. She had just had sex with two men... *two* whom she still hadn't known for 24 hours yet, and had done things with them that she never thought she would do—never knew she wanted to do. She had broken the trust of the man she had vowed to love for the rest of her life. She had cheated, and while she knew this should upset her greatly, it wasn't the thing that made her get up from the bed where she, Mark, and Eric had lain thoroughly spent nor what made her try the door to the pool and spa to miraculously find it unlocked, the indoor cabanas and pool still lit. What made her leave, made her separate herself from their warmth in search of a place to clear her head, was the fact that it was over, and she had no idea what came next.

Too late.

She couldn't take it back and wouldn't if the option were on the table. She was sure there was something to unpack there, but that was for another time. Nicole had never experienced the feeling she had just felt with Mark and Eric, never before had she felt so perfectly adored, so accepted, so needed. Even before they had explored each other's bodies, the conversation, the sharing and acceptance—she had never felt more understood. And she loved it. She loved every moment of it, would do it all again, would do it all forever. Did this make her a cheater? No, she didn't think so, not in the traditional sense. She didn't think she would sleep with someone else if given the chance; this had never been about physical pleasure. Did this mean she wasn't in love with her husband? She didn't think that was true either. In fact, and this part made her sad, she didn't think it had anything to do with him at all. She wasn't unhappy—she wasn't running from anything in her life. But when she met Mark and Eric it was as if she had found *life* for the first time, had finally opened her eyes to it. Her happiness, the part of her that had only been going through the motions, had put itself to sleep and let the rest of her deal with the life she was leading—that part of her had finally woken up.

It was too late to put that Nicole back in her box or make her go back to sleep.

But now what?

What were they supposed to do now?

Did she expect them all to uproot their lives and live together in a rose-colored bubble? There were so many reasons why that couldn't happen—wouldn't happen. She and Mark had their families to think about—their children. What would they think of their parents? First they would have to accept that one of their parents had cheated on the other one. They'd have to sort through the misplaced blame and confusion to settle on the one horrible truth. Then they'd have to accept that they would have not only one new person in their lives, but two. How would she and Mark ever be able to explain that? There would be so many questions, and those questions would spark new ones. Would her kids ever feel comfortable, ever be able to accept their relationship? Would they ever forgive her? And what about Eric? He was a single man before today—how would he cotton to taking on a ready-made family—two significant others and four kids' worth? Nicole shook her head and sighed. She didn't even know if Eric and Mark even wanted anything more after tonight.

Too late.

Too late to wonder if she had done the right thing.

Too late to wonder about whether or not she had done enough.

Too late to worry about what might happen next. Because that *was* next. And she would have to find out no matter what.

CHAPTER 20

She didn't come back.

Mark and Eric were thinking about what to do because she had been gone for longer than they thought she would be. They were thinking about it but not saying anything because to say it out loud would make real the possibility that...

She hadn't taken her phone, they discovered, or they would have texted her—this turned out to be a good thing because they would have blown her cover; the beeping of the incoming text would have caused an echo in the cavernous space and that echo would surely have caught someone's attention. But not knowing where she had gone off to after experiencing what they had made them feel helpless and empty.

Eric looked at Mark whose worry showed on his face. They were still naked, wrapped up in the sheet that they had drawn over themselves as they fell asleep, unable to move a muscle. They hadn't intended to doze off, but the warmth of their bodies in bed and the utter exhaustion of their muscles won out. Nicole woke up first and curled into the first person she could reach, wanting to go back to the dream she had been having, the one where two beautiful men kissed her until she was dizzy.

Mark had cradled her into his chest, wrapping his arm around Nicole and nuzzling her hair with his chin. He had fallen asleep using Eric's arm as a pillow, and he snuggled his back into his warmth once more. After a while, how long Mark didn't know, Nicole got up to use the bathroom. He groggily remembered seeing her get dressed and hearing her say she would be back. And then she was gone.

That was thirty minutes ago.

Mark looked over at the sofa in the sitting room fifteen minutes ago, noting that her coat and purse were still there lying on the coffee table, the useless cell phone half in and half out of the bag. She had taken a room key but nothing else. He found himself looking over there again just to be sure.

"I wonder if she remembers the room number?" Eric said, thinking out loud. "She doesn't know what name I put it under, so she can't ask the front desk."

She probably doesn't remember my last name, he thought but didn't say it.

This had occurred to both of them ten minutes before when they first started to worry about her individually—silently—but it had gone unsaid. Neither of them wanted to be overbearing, especially at that moment when everything was so raw. Instead, they'd looked at each other with eyes that tried to quell the concerns that sat between them. They shrugged off their worries; they shifted unconsciously on the bed; they waited. But now the prospect of her being lost seemed more and more likely. What else could have happened to her at 3 a.m.?

Unless she left, Mark thought. *Unless she decided she didn't want to face them again and just left.*

Mark pushed the thought out of his mind and started to get up.

"I wonder if that restaurant is still open," Mark started as he sat up. "She might be in there—"

Mark stopped talking abruptly, squeezing his eyes shut and affecting a look that was just short of a full—on grimace.

Eric sat up quickly, placing a hand on Mark's back.

"Are you ok, babe?"

It... it just slipped out. Eric wasn't even aware that he had started applying terms of endearment to them already. But when Mark turned to look at him, he could see that he didn't mind one bit.

"I'm ok, it just... damn, I'm just—I'm really sore."

Eric had been rubbing Mark's lower back without realizing it and continued to do so once he caught on. He kissed Mark's temple.

"I bet you are. I'm sorry. I tried to be gentle—"

"No," Mark said, cutting Eric off mid-sentence. "Don't apologize. You didn't hurt me, I mean, not on purpose. I've just.. never had anything... you know..."

Eric smiled, completely enamored by this wonderfully shy man who had stolen his heart.

"Yeah," Eric said in between kisses, "I know."

Mark smiled too, loving the attention.

"I'll go check downstairs and let you know," Eric offered, getting up from the bed to pad over to his clothes which were strewn unceremoniously around the room. The memory of how they had ended up there made him smile.

Mark stared at Eric's form as he moved away from the bed, unable to stop himself from remembering what it had felt like to be inside of him. The way Eric sounded when he moaned filled his ears all of a sudden, the way he whispered Mark's name so breathy and rich...

Eric bent over to pick up his pants, and Mark thought he might have blacked out for a moment.

Eric heard a huff and turned his head to see Mark's intent gaze. He smiled despite himself and held Mark's gaze as he pulled his pants up.

Mark shook his head, pulling himself out of his reverie, snickering to himself. Because his mind had moved on, calling up images and sensations that made his toes curl, like the one where he remembered Eric's fingers moving inside him, stretching him, touching places he never knew could bring him such pleasure before. Mark remembered wanting more even through the stinging newness, pleasure and pain weaving into one. He remembered whispered promises of future pleasure when he was ready, words pressed into his flesh as he whined, panted, begged. It was a daydream that he would happily revisit, and often, but later.

"No, I'll come with you. I probably should walk it off anyway, right?"

Mark got up gingerly but pushed through the new sensation, resisting the urge to grab at his backside and whimper. He took a step forward, and it felt, well, weird.

"You should really take it slow, babe," Eric said, his brow furrowing even as he smiled sympathetically. "She's probably just downstairs, drinking a cup of coffee."

"Full circle, huh?" Mark said, his voice a little strained as he anticipated the pain that lived in his next step and was pleasantly surprised to find that it wasn't quite as bad as the first. "It's coffee that got us into this mess," he finished, a chuckle punctuating his words.

Eric watched as Mark lifted his legs carefully as he put on his pants, his balance clearly off. He chuckled too, unable to stop himself.

"And what a mess it is."

CHAPTER 21

She wasn't in the lobby.

The café was closed.

She wasn't in the restroom off the main foyer. They knew that because Eric lost his battle with patience after waiting outside the door for a mere two minutes.

She wasn't in the rooftop seating area looking over the sleeping city.

She wasn't anywhere to be found.

"She wouldn't have left, right?" Eric's voice was small and timid as they stepped back into the quiet elevator.

"No," Mark said, trying to sound confident but unsure if he made it there or not. "She wouldn't have left—"

"—her stuff, I guess that's true," Eric said, unconvinced by his own words.

"I wasn't going to say that," Mark said as he touched Eric's arm. "I was going to say she wouldn't have left *us*."

They shared a meaningful glance as the doors shut, both of them hoping the words were true.

Eric looked at the button panel and was about to press

the one for their floor when his eye was drawn to the other selections. They had tried the lobby and the roof without success. But they had not tried the pool, the only other common area in the hotel.

He pressed the button labeled 'POOL/SPA' and smiled at Mark.

"She loves being by the water..."

Mark saw the lit button and picked up Eric's line of thinking. "And she feels like being near it, or better yet, *in* it helps her think."

Eric nodded at Mark as they felt the elevator glide smoothly toward the floor.

"But shouldn't it be closed? It's the middle of the night," Eric asked, starting to poke holes in his logic.

"I know, but where else can she be?"

The question hung in the air, full of implications that neither of them wanted to entertain.

As the elevator door opened, Eric said,

"If she's not here, we'll go back to the room. Maybe we just missed her and she beat us back there."

"And if she's not there?" Mark said but wished he hadn't. If she wasn't there that probably meant that she had left them, that she regretted what happened and wanted to put distance between herself and her mistake. Maybe she had been in the lobby after all and saw them looking for her. Maybe she had hidden herself where she could see them but they couldn't see her in the hopes that they would wander away, giving her the chance to dart upstairs and get her things. Maybe she would delete their numbers and try to forget the whole thing had ever happened, forget they had ever met.

If she wasn't there, ... oh god, what if she really wasn't there?

The door to the pool and spa required a keycard to enter, but it was curiously ajar. Eric and Mark looked at each other, trying not to let the optimism they suddenly felt show too much, but failing miserably. Eric grabbed the handle, and Mark placed a hand on the door itself, and together they pushed.

CHAPTER 22

The pool was still, the water placid and tranquil. The candles on the candle wall were extinguished, and the hot tub was turned off. There was a distinct feeling of trespass in the air, and Eric wasn't sure whether they would find Nicole or hotel security around the corner.

"Maybe over there," Mark whispered, the sound magnified in the humid, cavernous room. "By the cabanas."

And indeed, they thought they saw someone or *something* inside one of them—the curtain was drawn, and the light was dim. Whatever was in there was incredibly still, but they thought they could make out the detail of an arm, the shape of a head in the silhouette.

As they crept closer, Nicole heard their nervous whisper—chatter about whether it was her or not. A smile crept across her face as she opened the cabana curtain to wave them over, exhilaration wiping away the thoughts that had clouded her mind just moments before.

Exhilaration at just seeing them.

God, what had she gotten herself into?

"You found me," Nicole whispered as they crawled onto the daybed in the cabana to sit on either side of her.

Suddenly Mark wasn't sure if they *should* have found her. She had left the room for a reason, and as real as their concern about where she was had felt, it seemed more controlling, more like smothering now. Seeing her there on the daybed that was almost the size of the bed they shared upstairs in their room, Mark started to think they had intruded on her privacy. He looked at Eric and found a similar thought coloring his expression.

"We—we were worried about you. You've been gone for almost an hour, not that you can't do what you want to do. It's just... well, we didn't think you'd be gone that long," Mark said, trying not to stutter, trying not to sound guilty.

"You left your phone in the room," Eric said quietly, keenly aware that they were the only voices echoing off the walls of a place that was supposed to be closed for the night.

"But maybe we should have waited until you came back," Eric continued. "We just... we were afraid that..."

"No," Nicole said, placing her hands on their legs. "Please don't apologize." She looked at them for a moment feeling an emotion she couldn't place welling inside her. It was why she didn't feel the kind of guilt she thought she should feel. It was why she was sitting in the cabana by the pool in the first place.

Her eyes, filled with unexpected tears, looked them both in the eye, and spoke to their very souls. "I missed you, too."

CHAPTER 23

Z's pool never really closed, not if you didn't want it to.

That's how his memory would emblazon that moment in his mind if he had anything to do with it.

Mark couldn't help but think about that as he felt himself giving in to sleep on the daybed tucked away inside one of the private cabanas that bordered the hot tub. There was a word for that weird state he was in, half awake but half not, conscious of existing but not entirely sure in what dimension. The faint smell of chlorine kept him grounded even as the combination of the other smells in that space coalesced to remind him, to confuse him, to drive him wild.

The fresh smell of sunflowers.

The clean smell of shampoo.

The spicy smell of his own cologne.

Some kind of tangy smell that he couldn't put his finger on.

The provocative smell of sex.

Mark inhaled reflexively, sighing into the concoction as he slipped deeper into sleep.

Warm.

He was warm from the press of bodies on his own, and he felt good, so good that he never wanted to get up, never wanted to be let free. So good that he feared the cool air that would accost him if they moved, if either of them moved at all, would freeze him to death.

How very dramatic.

Over the top.

So metaphorically corny that it went past the border of ridiculous to seat itself squarely in the middle.

But how incredibly apropos.

Mark felt a smile creep across his face as he snuggled deeper into the warmth that surrounded him, nuzzling hair and rubbing skin because he was sure of one thing, even through the haze of bliss and sheer exhaustion that was winning the battle to close his eyes: Mark knew that nothing had ever come close to the feeling of home that engulfed him there, as he lay in the oasis that was The Zerzura Hotel with two beings who were most certainly mirages.

Nothing.

Ever.

They asked for more coffee even though they didn't really want it. They got another plate of food, gourmet mini quiches filled with spinach and goat cheese and wild mushrooms and roasted bell peppers, that they only picked at. They didn't really need anything else—their bellies were sufficiently full, and after the night of activity they'd had, that took some doing. All they needed right then was more time.

"I can't believe," Eric started, his face playful, but he bit back his words when the server came back with more of that fancy coffee. After she served them and left the table, Eric leaned in conspiratorially to finish what he was saying.

"I can't believe they didn't catch us in the cabana!"

Nicole giggled, and Mark nodded, smirking.

"Me neither," Nicole whispered, color coming to her cheeks.

"It was too perfect. The door being open like that..." Eric mused because it *had* been perfect. However it came to pass that they had been allowed that space and time, it had been something he would never forget.

"Somebody had to be asleep at the wheel," Mark supplied, remembering every touch, ever breath, every sound. "Or the cameras were off for some reason or... something."

After Mark and Eric had found Nicole in the cabana, after they had apologized clumsily for tracking her down in the first place, they had settled back into that easy rhythm they seemed to have, leaning into each other, enjoying the silence, enjoying the togetherness. Then Eric slid out from beside them to stand.

"Wait a sec," he said as he moved, turning off the light in their cabana. He made his way to each of the units, turning off the light switches methodically. Nicole and Mark watched as cubes of lights disappeared from the pool's calm surface until the room was bathed in darkness, the only light emanating from the pool floor. It was beautiful, really, the cool light seeming to glow, creating shades of celeste and aqua blue that shifted before their very eyes. Eric came back into the cabana and curled in behind Nicole.

"Just in case," he said as he settled.

Nicole smiled and rested her hand on Eric's forearm,

which had snaked around her, reclaiming its place. She caught a glimpse of their legs at the bottom of the daybed, how all of them entwined with each other, creating an intricate weave that seemed to go on forever.

Beautiful.

They were simply beautiful together.

Mark had been rubbing Nicole's arm gently, almost absently. He had also been looking at the same thing Nicole had, looking at the picture they created. He was awestruck.

"Baby," Mark finally breathed, needing something to keep him grounded.

Eric felt his own emotions roiling inside him. He wanted to tell them what he was feeling, wanted to say it and was so, so close to doing just that. The only reason he hadn't yet was because of fear. What would they say? What would they think? How could he really feel that way about them so soon?

But he did. He knew in his heart he did, and now there was a different kind of fear to contend with, one he couldn't think about right then, didn't want to think about at all, but it wouldn't go away. Regardless of what happened, it might never truly be gone.

What if when they woke up from the dream they were having and saw each other, really understood each other for the people they were and the lives they lived, what if... what if they looked at him and didn't like what they saw?

"I thought you left," Mark said, his voice determined but hushed. "I wasn't going to tell you that," he said, his hand moving from her arm to her thigh as it worked lazily. "I didn't want you to know that. I... I didn't want you to think badly of me."

Nicole's face changed slowly, morphing from relaxed

comfort to alarm, and it was all so mind—blowing. Eric could see, in that very moment, that they were all experiencing the same thing, feeling the same emotions, trying to stand still as vulnerability stripped them bare. When Nicole told Mark that she wouldn't leave them, didn't know how she ever would, Eric knew that this was as real for both of them as it was for him, and that scared him more than anything else had.

Nicole pushed Mark's hair out of his face, that soft brown hair that had fallen down to cover his forehead and hide his eyes when embarrassment forced him to turn away, and he leaned into the touch. She kissed him, her mouth exploring his without hesitation because there was no need for that, not anymore. Nicole straddled Mark as he reclined to lay flat on his back, neither one of them breaking the kiss, neither one of them wanting to bear even that momentary loss of contact. Nicole guided Mark's hands up, past his ears to a place above his head and held them there. She applied pressure, feeling his wrists sink into the mattress, her way of letting Mark know he should leave them there, to let her have her way. Then she trailed her hands down his arms, down his chest, to rest on the bed next to his sides. She released his mouth then, her lips swollen with want, and began to slide her body down between his legs. She left open—mouthed kisses on his neck and licked lazy circles around his nipples on her way down, relishing the beautiful sounds he could make. Her fingers grazed his ribs as she moved lower still, nipping at his navel, chasing each love bite with her tongue. Mark's was breathing heavy as he undulated beneath her hands. Nicole grabbed at his hips, teasing her fingers beneath the waistband of his pants to caress the skin there. She kissed over the zipper, raising her eyes to connect with his for just a moment before undoing the pants and pulling them down.

Nicole was slow with Mark, more focused on satisfying his mind, body, and soul than on giving him a quick release. She touched. She kissed. She tasted. She watched his reactions, found the twist of the wrist, the circle of the tongue that made him react the most.

She savored.

And when he was finished, she felt as enraptured as he did.

Nicole kissed Mark's thigh and curled up next to him, eyes lidded with arousal and a fatigue that was only barely being kept at bay. Eric sat at the foot of the daybed watching them, entranced. Nicole reached for Eric's hand with the intention of pulling him closer, her mind gearing up to please her second lover as she had the first, but Mark caught her hand and kissed it instead.

"Let me," he said, his eyes trained on Eric.

Eric bit down on his bottom lip, something about the look on Mark's face making his stomach drop, causing the hairs on the back of his neck to stand up and take notice.

Mark closed the space between himself and Eric quickly and kissed him with a gentleness he didn't know he possessed. Eric felt himself melting, instantly weak. Mark knelt before Eric and undressed him, and marveling at his body again, running his hands along the sculpted lines and curves, stopping only to give attention to the places that Eric liked most. Everywhere except...

Mark knew he wanted to do it, it wasn't a matter of him *not* wanting to... not at all. It was just that he had never done it before. He didn't want to hurt him, didn't want to do something stupid like not clearing his teeth and running the tip of Eric's member along his molars. Mark wanted it to be good for Eric, and he was afraid he couldn't make it that way. What if he didn't suck hard enough and it just felt like being in a hot, slimy hole? What if he sucked too hard and damn near sucked the life out of him? Include the balls or don't? Touch his ass or...

Mark sighed in his head. There was nothing worse than a bad blow job.

Mark ran a finger over Eric's penis. It was still clothed by his underwear, but it was prominently erect.

And Mark realized with full clarity that he really wanted to see it again.

He pulled back the elastic on his underwear and released Eric's penis from confinement. It was long and thin, flushed. Instinctively, Mark's hand stroked it up and down slowly as he looked, marveling, comparing. Eric's pubic hair was lighter than his own. The veins on his penis were more pronounced than Mark's were too. Eric seemed to really enjoy it when Mark encircled the head, beads of precum showing themselves every time he lingered there. This was different than what he liked himself; Mark preferred a firmer, more insistent stroke mid shaft. As Eric grew more and more aroused, he was inclined to roll his hips ever so slightly—Mark could see Eric's abs tensing as he tried to stop himself from doing that very thing, probably not wanting to do anything to ruin the moment... afraid he might scare Mark off with something so overt. Mark realized, as Eric fought to stay still, that he wanted Eric to do it. He wanted to feel Eric moving, feel the friction it would create. He wanted Eric to let go.

"Please," Mark whispered, stroking down then up again

to encircle the head, watching Eric's head drop backwards in appreciation. "Show me."

Eric panted through a half smile, feeling like he might go crazy if Mark kept talking to him like that, looking up at him like that, touching him like that. He was trying to stay still, to give Mark time to figure things out, not rush him. But good god, Mark's touch was driving him wild.

More precum wet the head of Eric's penis, and Mark didn't allow himself to overthink it. He dipped his head and licked it off, taking stock of the consistency, savoring it.

"You don't have to—" Eric started, his breathing starting to get away from him. Because Mark had no idea how amazing he looked on his knees with his mouth open, his fucking tongue out, glistening with Eric's juices. He had no idea how much Eric wanted him to put his mouth on him, wanted him to *want* to do it... wanted Mark to want *him*. But he couldn't force him. Eric couldn't ask Mark to do something he didn't want to do or allow him to do something because he thought he should. As much as Eric wanted this, it was more important that Mark wanted it too.

"It's ok," Eric panted. "You don't—"

"Shhh," Mark admonished, running his hand along the v-line that led to the thick tuft of Eric's light brown pubic hair. "You have no idea how much I want to."

Eric thought he might explode right then and there.

Mark looked at the head of Eric's penis, steeling himself for the work ahead. He stroked him once, twice, three times, pulling a moan from Eric that he had not anticipated—a moan that sparked his own desire again—before pressing his lips to the head.

It was hot, throbbing.

Mark felt his own hardening length twitch.

He licked the underside of Eric's member.

Eric's mouth dropped open as his eyes fluttered closed.

With a deep breath, Mark lowered his mouth onto Eric's penis, feeling his lips wrap around it, his tongue rise to cradle it.

And it was sweet, so very sweet... just like candy.

Later, when Eric thought about how they hadn't been caught even though he had been anything but quiet, he would remember how his orgasm erupted before he knew what was happening. Mark had been so interested in what Eric liked, so eager to please. When he found the right rhythm, he was relentless about making Eric feel good. The knot had formed in Eric's stomach before he realized how far gone he was, pleasure coiling tight like a spring. His toes curled, his body acted of its own volition, hips rolling, chest heaving. He ran his fingers through Mark's hair, not pulling or tugging... just touching. Eric hoped that his touch would serve as encouragement because he couldn't put together a cohesive sentence to save his life. Not then, with Mark's mouth working him the way it was.

And then he came.

He came hard and without warning, barely having time to tell Mark to pull off before exploding. Eric's moans were deep and guttural. And loud. Much louder than he ever expected to be, louder still as they echoed off the walls. But he couldn't stop himself.

Nicole, who had felt her own release come minutes before, the two of them loving each other proving more than she could withstand, kissed Eric, swallowing the last of his moans as he rode out his orgasm in Mark's hand. She peppered them both with kisses as they laid down on the daybed moments away from a deep, hard sleep. They knew they should go back to their room and indeed regretted not doing so later when they were awakened from their slumber by voices that sounded close enough to be right outside the cabana curtain, but in that moment, lying in each other's arms in the afterglow of their lovemaking was the only place in the world they wanted to be.

CHAPTER 24

"That you remembered about the water… that you even thought to look in the pool in the first place…" Nicole couldn't believe how simple things had been with them, how they seemed to gel so easily.

"It was meant to be… fate, or something like that—I don't know what to call it," Eric tried, his brow furrowing as he searched for the right word to describe what he was feeling. He felt like his steps had been ordered, like he wouldn't have been able to change course if he tried.

"Serendipity, destiny. I'm like a thesaurus over here." Mark laughed at himself but then grew pensive, twisting his fork over and over on the tablecloth as he thought. After a moment and with true sincerity, he finally said,

"This… this is kismet."

Nicole looked at Mark with wide eyes hearing the very word she had thought of earlier to describe this thing, this inexorable connection they had, fall from his lips.

Kismet.

CHAPTER 25

The staff at The Zerzura Hotel restaurant needed to prepare for the next shift.

Eric had gotten a callback for the play.

Mark's flight was leaving in less than four hours.

Nicole was late to the trade show.

It was all coming to an end.

But they couldn't say goodbye.

They kissed when they got to their room, knowing it would be the last time they would be able to do so the way they wanted to, the way their bodies craved to.

Standing just inside the doorway, they felt the need to be together, to slot their lips against the others to fashion their mouths around the columns of necks. And it was passionate, breathy, urgent, but they couldn't allow themselves to do more. Time had run out.

Eric had talked the concierge into letting him go up and gather his things without incurring any additional cost, arguing that he had only been in the restaurant finishing up a meeting and lost track of time. Mark and Nicole had gone upstairs separately, beating him to the door, unsure if it was safe to stand near each other or if they should circle back and approach the room again separately. If someone saw them, would they find it odd to see two people waiting outside of a room? Maybe, but only if they were still standing there when they ventured into the hall again.

Nicole and Mark looked at each other only once, nerves getting the best of them. Mark felt antsy just standing there on the cusp of one of the most difficult moments of his life. He was about to leave and come back in a few minutes, anxiety pushing him to do something—*anything*— when the elevator door opened, and Eric shot out of it almost at a run. They couldn't contain the smiles that spread across their faces nor the way their hearts pulled.

"They said they'd only give me a few minutes," Eric said as he closed his mouth over Nicole's, shutting the door behind himself before taking both her and Mark into his arms. "God, I want more time."

Mark drew close, rubbing their backs as their circle closed. Nicole broke the kiss with Eric only to latch onto Mark's neck as he and Eric kissed, careful not to bite, careful not to mar.

"We could pay for another night. Stay for an hour or two," Mark said, trying to push away the rhapsodic whine threatening to spill from his mouth over the attention Nicole was giving the hollow of his throat.

"I want to," Nicole said as her tongued played, licking up Mark's Adam's apple, all the way to his chin. "But I can't. The trade show... they called..."

Everyone had gotten a call. The producer had called Eric himself after he hadn't replied to the initial text saying he hoped Eric hadn't left for NY already because he really wanted him to read again. Ananda had called Nicole wondering why she had missed the start of the first shift at the trade show, concern evident in his voice. And Mark... his children had called to ask him if he could pick up ice cream on his way home.

They couldn't stay.

They nuzzled each other, pressing their foreheads together, sometimes lips meeting in the middle to share a three-way kiss, sometimes eyes closing against reality. They didn't know how long they stood there holding each other, silently willing time to rewind so that they could have more kisses, more laughing, just more. The sound of the housekeeping cart in the hallway ruined the fantasy, making clear what was real.

"Can we..." Eric let his words trail off. He knew there was nothing to be done, nothing that he could suggest that would squeeze out a little more time, nothing he could do to put off the inevitable. They couldn't share an Uber, ride the train together, walk each other to their hotel room doors. They couldn't even share the elevator to the lobby. It was over. And what was worse was that they had to say their goodbyes right then and there.

"I don't want to this to be over," Nicole said quietly.

"It's not o-" Eric started but was interrupted by the phone in the room. The front desk was calling.

"No," Mark said, feeling his resolve breaking.

"Please, just a little longer," Nicole said and pressed her body as close as she could to theirs.

They stood that way, holding on to each other for dear life until the end of the second call. But then, fearing that someone might come and check the room to see if Eric was really gone, they started to pull themselves together.

There were no belongings to pick up, no drawers to check. They hadn't even slept in the room, at least not for long. Just like that, it was time to say goodbye.

Nicole would leave first, but not before tripping over her words and feeling, for the first time in their presence, like she didn't know what to say.

"I—I feel like anything I say right now will cheapen this, and I don't mean to," she settled on, reluctantly. "I want to tell you how I feel, but part of me thinks it's better left unsaid."

She was standing closest to the door but had leaned away from it... had leaned closer to them. Again.

Mark reached toward her, his fingertips catching the knuckle of her middle finger. She looked down at his hand on hers, felt the sad and sorry smile that was forming at the corners of her mouth. Then she saw her wedding ring.

"I don't want this... this thing we've shared... this tryst or whatever you want to call it... I don't want it to end," Mark said as Nicole's mind was inundated with images of her husband, of her family. "I don't want *us* to end."

"We don't have to," Eric replied, his voice thick with emotion. "We can text. We can call. I—I can come to DC or the west coast. Or we could meet in the middle somewhere. This... it doesn't have to be goodbye."

Nicole looked at Eric with eyes that seemed as if they had awoken from a deep sleep. She regarded Mark with the same stare and then shook her head, moving in slow motion, as if she were underwater.

"I don't ... I don't live in DC," Nicole said, her voice no louder than a whisper. But they heard her as though she had been yelling into a megaphone. She recoiled—it wasn't an abrupt movement, but it was a deliberate moving away from them, a purposeful retraction.

Because they didn't know each other; that fact hit her like a ton of bricks. Even though they had felt so connected, had shared each other's bodies and shared each other's secrets, they didn't really know anything at all about each other. What they knew were snippets, little pieces of each other's lives that were pertinent to whatever conversation they were having. The subject of hometowns came up because of some music reference; favorite colors came up because of a piece of art in the restaurant's unique collection. Dog lover or cat lover? Because of a commercial on the TV next to the bar. She would have shared the same information with anyone at a happy hour or a dinner after work. But what did they *really* know? Did they know that she secretly cheered when rain was in the forecast because she loved the way it sounded? Or that she never read a book more than once? Did they know that, to this day, she loved Liberace because she used to watch reruns of his show with her grandmother? Of course not. They didn't even know where she lived.

Mark's stomach dropped. He could see Nicole pulling away in every way. He could see it in her eyes.

"Nicole, we can still—"

"I'd better go," she said, diverting her eyes from them, gesturing toward the room phone. "They've already called twice. If you don't get down there, they'll come check the room soon."

Nicole's voice sounded hollow, distant. She was coming out of it, she could feel the trance-like state she had been in starting to fray at the edges as real life slapped her squarely across the face, and that made her incredibly sad.

Mark couldn't let it end that way. He moved toward her, ignoring the fear of being rebuffed that tickled the back of his neck even as he braced himself for a restraining hand on his chest. It didn't come. He snaked an arm around her waist and reached his other one out to fold Eric in as well.

Nicole felt tears spill over onto her cheeks as Mark and Eric put the heads on her shoulders. She put her arms around their necks and hugged them back just as deeply. Whatever this was or wasn't, she would miss them. She would miss this.

Voices in the hallway.

Doors opening and closing.

Time to go.

They let go of each other reluctantly, straightening their clothes and wiping their faces. Nicole put her hand on the doorknob and took a deep breath. So many things were on the tip of her tongue, words she wanted to say but didn't know if she should, words like 'I'll miss you' and 'Thank you' and 'I'll text you later.' Even 'I love you.' But none of those words felt right to say out loud even if each and every one of them was unbelievably, ridiculously, foolishly true.

Nicole sighed, kissed them both on the cheek, and said simply, "Goodbye."

CHAPTER 26

The sound of the door slamming jarred him to his very soul. He'd had to listen to it twice, first when Nicole left and then when Mark did, their parting no less difficult for being just two. As he walked through the lobby Eric fought hard to keep his face straight. He tried to think of the callback and what it could mean. Callbacks the very next day were unusual, and he was optimistic about why it happened. He prepped himself, going over the character's backstory again, trying to channel what he might be feeling and why so that he could bring the proper emotion to whatever lines he read. It was important—this part of the process required an increased level of focus—but it wasn't enough to keep him from casting a glance around first the lobby and then the street hoping to catch a glimpse of one or both of them, conspicuousness be damned. He wasn't that far off their heels—they had each left within minutes of the other, unable to stay in the room longer than necessary now that the air had changed. There were a lot of people on the street—the hotel was in the restaurant district, and it was bustling seven days a week. He looked for Mark's confident gait, Nicole's stylish hair, trying to pick them out in the crowd making their way toward the restaurant they had eaten in, or waiting for the light to change so they could cross the street to the train, but to no avail.

They were gone.

The sense of loss was immense.

Eric had tried to chastise himself back in the elevator when he was coming up to meet them for the last time, tried to remind himself that this was as it had to be... maybe as it *should* be. He tried but he failed to convince himself that it was over and done, a wonderful time, but over, nonetheless. He wouldn't accept it. His heart had been beating so loudly in his chest he was afraid everyone around him could hear. The process at the front desk had been torturously slow. He'd had to speak to the concierge just so, affecting a charm that he knew worked when he turned it on just right. He was an hour late for checking out and that meant he owed them another night. If they had chosen a mid-range hotel that might have been fine. But at five-star rates, Eric really didn't want to eat the cost if he didn't have to.

So, Eric gave the concierge the eye contact she wanted after first glance. He let an unsure smile creep across his face, let absentminded man-child vibes flow before switching to a look he liked to think of as smoldering restraint. It was supposed to say, 'I want you but, I can't,' but he didn't practice it enough to know if it hit the mark. He let his stare linger, dipped his eyes toward her lips and took a breath, allowing his shoulder to rise ever so slightly, like it was hard to keep all that magnetism in check after seeing what he saw. Cartoonish and contrived, very Fabio and Dwayne Johnson-esque. He got lucky; it worked most of the time.

But it took time to get it right—you can't make someone think you're desperate for them while speed talking. By the time he got in the elevator, he felt sick with need. He'd been away from Nicole and Mark at a time when all he wanted to do was be in their arms. He'd been burning minutes making eyes with a woman he couldn't even remember after leaving the counter instead of kissing the people that he...

That he...

Come on, it couldn't really be love, could it?

Eric had climbed back into the elevator with that on his mind. He was afraid the people in there with him could actually hear his thoughts because they were so loud. Love? In a day? He had never subscribed to love at first sight, never put much stock into the sheer romance that something like that would require. He used to laugh at his friends who would meet someone and move in with them in the span of a month. Idiots. Goodbye freedom and goodbye money, and maybe even good credit, in a lot of those cases. He had never been one to fall head over heels, even when it was love he was looking at. Eric had always managed to protect himself from falling too far, from losing himself. Maybe it was an actor thing; it's easier to wear a character's emotions as your own if there is nothing competing with it. He preferred to call it living in a deliberately blank state. Whatever it was, it had worked for him.

Until now.

Before finding himself alone on a crowded street, he had been in an elevator yet again willing it to move faster, for the people he shared it with to get off on the same floor so the incessant rising and stopping could be mercifully over... so he could get to the two people his heart now beat for. And then it was over. Mark and Nicole were gone; whatever they were doing was over, and Eric didn't know what he should do next.

This wasn't his first rodeo—he'd had one-night stands before. That's all this was, albeit an incredibly intense one. And with two people—hot and fast, like a dirty movie. But...

But threesomes exist.

People did it all the time. It was probably the subject of most adolescent males' wet dreams. It had definitely been one of his.

Funny.

He hadn't thought about that until then.

Ménage á trois is pretty common. Well, relatively speaking, he corrected, societal norms being what they were. So, why was he tripping over it so much in his mind? Why couldn't he just think of how awesome it was to see one of his fantasies come true? Wasn't he all about the lived experience—all the travel, living in different places, all the people he knew... didn't that make up who he was? Why would this be any different? He had wanted to have a threesome; now he'd had one. Case closed. Why did it have to be anything more than that?

Was it maturity? Did him getting older, having life under his belt make him feel differently about it all? The sex, the using of someone else's body for release. Was his morality the problem now?

He'd almost laughed out loud in the not entirely empty elevator as he remembered having some nameless pretty boy's face pressed against the wall, his own knee between the man's legs as he slid a condom on and prepared to wreck him. And that was only a few months ago. No, it wasn't a sense of morality that was twisting Eric's gut.

But...

He had wondered why he was tripping over the idea of a threesome so much at first, but the better question was harder to ask. The truth was, if he was being honest with himself, it was more valid than the first.

Why *wasn't* he tripping over it?

The way Nicole's laughter faded into something introspective when she was done, leaving a faint smile on her lips...

The way Mark raised his right eyebrow when he heard something that interested him...

Eric's mind was busy with thoughts of them smiling, talking, laughing, the sights and sounds chaotic as they bounced around in his head, yet filling him with the most tranquil peace he'd felt in some time, if ever.

No, he told himself, deciding that the time for denial was over. *I've never felt anything like this before.*

When the elevator stopped on his floor, he nearly bumped into the man standing in front of him on his way out.

They were at the end of the hall waiting.

Waiting for him.

He almost ran down the hall, only succeeded in stopping himself from doing so because that would definitely be something that a person coming out of their room would remember. And that was good. It allowed him to keep a modicum of self-respect. But in the end, none of that even mattered anymore. He would have crawled to them if they wanted him to. Because he loved them. He did. He knew it the night before, when they'd met for dinner and fallen into each other's hearts. He probably had known it his whole life.

And now they were gone.

It was gone.

Everything was all over.

The day looked normal; the sun was shining, and the air was crisp; that strange Canadian springtime was in full swing. People walked in groups along the sidewalk studded with storefronts, chatting happily as they made their way to this restaurant or that, enjoying their day with a leisure that you never really saw in New York. The day was beautiful, and Eric felt like he could cry. Normally the sting of tears behind his eyes would be bothersome to him. It wasn't something he felt often, and that wasn't him being macho, it was just the way he was built. But he would have welcomed them that day if he could've made them fall. Because if he cried he might yell, and if he yelled he might be able to force out the sadness that was collecting around his heart.

Maybe.

But no, the tears wouldn't fall for him, so he had no release—he had no catharsis. He had only stark, gray anguish under the light of the sun and an appointment to make.

CHAPTER 27

It could have been worse.

Nicole showed up at the trade show halfway through lunch, thankful that the kiosk hall was relatively empty. One of her colleagues was there—Mitch? Rick? She was starting to wonder why she could never seem to remember any of their names. She gave him a break and stood behind the table filled with mugs and pens and mousepads all with her company's logo emblazoned on them. She felt unsteady. She *was* unsteady.

She had spoken with Ananda on her way in, telling him that she had overslept because she felt sick. Must have eaten something the night before that had gone off. Slept longer and deeper than she ever had. And he believed it—he had no reason not to. He didn't know her well enough to wonder if she was lying. And why would she be? It would be a hell of a thing to go all the way to a trade show after being chosen to be part of a team to represent the company and blow it off, wouldn't it?

Yeah, a hell of a thing.

Ananda wanted to rub her back, wanted to make her feel better because she did, indeed, not look like herself. Her eyes were watery when he saw her at their booth talking with the latest influx of people into the showroom, and she looked a little wobbly on her feet. He wanted to, but he didn't. Just like he didn't know her well enough to tell if she was lying or not, he didn't know her well enough to take such a liberty. Ananda definitely didn't want to invite an HR complaint. Instead he said,

"Gosh, I wonder if it was the coffee from that place over by the bookstore. Didn't you say you got something from there? I can't remember what flavor you said but you mentioned that it smelled really good."

Nicole nodded weakly, fresh tears prickling the corners of her eyes. She didn't want to cry. Dear god, she didn't want to cry at work. She had never cried at work before, always thought it was so unprofessional when people did that, especially women. She thought it set women back years in terms of progress toward being seen as equals in the office, made them seem weak. Nicole hated that she thought that way, but she did, and here she was about to do it. Sick... sick... she was sick... She would hang on to that, milk it for all it was worth. Because she *was* kind of sick, wasn't she? She hurt so badly she would have thought she was having a heart attack if she didn't know why.

"Yeah, you were a little off kilter then, too," Ananda continued, concern lacing his words. "You even forgot to get the pens."

Nicole looked at him, a question in her eyes.

"The pens. The errand you went out for in the first place!"

He chuckled in that way that people do when they don't

know what to say or do and all Nicole could do was nod again. She had forgotten about the pens. She had forgotten what time it was. She had forgotten what the focus of the next release of their product was, the demo that the more seasoned guys on the team were presenting upstairs. She had forgotten nearly everything in the hours between meeting Eric and Mark at the coffee shop and seeing them again at the restaurant. She wished she could blame it on something else—curdled milk, old coffee beans, mold in the machine, but she knew better. Hell, she didn't even think she had taken a sip of that awesome smelling coffee that had lured her there in the first place. That wasn't what was wrong... not by a long shot.

"Maybe," Nicole said, her voice shaky and thin.

"Yeah," Ananda said, closing his commentary on the subject with that one final word.

"Are you good to cover the afternoon shift? You don't have to stand up and, you know what, let me see if I can find a better chair for—"

"I'll be ok," Nicole said, suddenly uncomfortable with his attention, no matter how well-meaning. "It'll pass. I just need to let it run its course."

Ananda's eyes implored, but he didn't ask the question they held, the 'Are you sure?' perching on the edge of his tongue but going no further.

"I already feel better than I did an hour ago," Nicole supplied, releasing Ananda from obligation. She could almost hear him sigh in relief.

She smiled a little bigger this time, hoping it was more convincing than the last one.

"Well, ok," Ananda said, hesitating. "I've gotta head

upstairs for the demo in five. Text me if you need anything, ok?"

Nicole nodded then Ananda was gone. There was no one left in the room except for her, fellow booth jockeys, and an old man who strolled from table to table, touching pamphlets and looking like he was just there to wait for someone, his son maybe, to finish all that mumbo jumbo he was doing upstairs.

And that was good.

Because Nicole needed the room, the trade show, the world to be quiet so she could listen to the harmony of Eric and Mark's voices playing in her mind.

CHAPTER 28

A man sat across from him reading a book, a political satire that he had read before.

The music coming from the teenaged boy's earbuds two seats over was loud enough that he could make out the words.

A woman was having a conversation with someone on her cell phone that was both loud and obnoxious.

Two little kids watched the planes take off with their noses pressed against the window.

Mark looked around the gate at the people he would share a plane with and didn't know how he had gotten there. He didn't remember much about those last few hours —the mad dash to his hotel, frenzied packing, rushing out of town in the rental to get to the airport—only that he had done it. He had been operating on autopilot, a numbed kind of understanding and execution. Mark had taken enough of these trips to do what needed be done with his eyes closed... pack the clothes stacked on the desk chair; check the drawers to make sure he hadn't put anything in there, which he never did; get his toiletries off the bathroom vanity. Get the suit hanging in the closet as well as the shoes. Pat his pants for his wallet, his passport, his phone, and his keys. Then go. Out of the city, over a bridge if need be, then into the suburban area. Follow the signs—there were always signs—follow them to the airport, turn in the car, take the airport tram or bus or rail back to the terminal, and then go through the elaborate process of waiting.

Wait to check in.

Wait to get through security.

Wait at the gate.

Wait to board the plane.

Wait to take off.

Wait.

Wait.

Wait.

Apparently, Mark had done all of that successfully because there he was at one of the final checkpoints on his grand list of waiting. The *waitlist.* He had to chuckle at that. He could be so corny sometimes that it was actually funny.

But that, too, was to be expected. Everything was always the same, and while that was something that annoyed him—the predictability of life boring him to the core—on this day, it was welcomed. On this day he didn't think he could have gotten himself off the cold city block in front of The Zerzura Hotel if he'd had to consciously do something about it, let alone made it to the airport in time for his flight.

To say that he was distracted was an understatement.

Mark's body was there interacting with people, going through the motions, but his mind was back in the hotel room with Nicole and Eric. He was back in their arms, listening to their stories, feeling their touch on his skin. He rubbed his arm near the shoulder and thought of the way Nicole had kissed him there before laying her head on it contentedly. He ran his hand through his hair, only it was Eric's hair he felt against his palm. Maybe Pink, he had called it and that made Mark laugh again, even as he sat at the gate without them.

Alone.

As his laughter died in his throat, he began to wonder if any of it had been real. It was unlike him—the past day had been wholly unlike him, so much so that some little part of himself was starting to wonder if this wasn't some elaborate dream and he was still asleep in his hotel room. Did he really go to a coffee shop before a meeting just because? He hadn't even been wearing his suit—he wasn't ready to present at all. He never would have done that before. Check one in the crazy column. Had he really met a woman who had stunned him so much on first glance that he had felt himself tremble? Mark, who had never looked at another woman after meeting his wife right after college? Again, not something he would do.

Check two.

Was it possible that he met a man who made him forget how to speak for a moment? Mark, the one who made part of his living as a public speaker… *he* couldn't find any words? Not likely.

Check three.

Mark looked around himself then, more than a little afraid that perhaps there was some truth to his concern and that he was having some kind of lucid dream. The actions seemed like they weren't his own, almost like they were being executed by some other person entirely. Except that he remembered the smell of Nicole's perfume and the shade of her lipstick that morning. He remembered how blue Eric's eyes were and the way he smiled so openly.

Mark remembered. He remembered it all.

One of the kids standing at the window turned to look at him then, almost as if she could hear his thoughts. She smiled at him shyly and gave a little wave over her shoulder before turning back to the window to watch the plane taxiing to the gate, her braids masking most of her face as they cascaded over her shoulders and down her back. It was their plane that was coming in, navigating the turn into the gate and lining up for the jet bridge slowly. Soon they would be getting on it and flying away.

Soon he would be flying away, leaving Nicole and Eric behind.

Mark felt sick, reality feeling so much worse than the odd trip his mind was taking.

Because it had been real, all of it... every touch, every smile, every emotion. And he wanted it back. He wanted to be there with them again, having dinner again, talking again. He wanted to know more about the book Nicole wanted to write. He wanted to know more about what Eric loved about acting. He wanted to know more, to do more... to have more.

Mark didn't want to go home.

Home was what was to be expected. Home was predictable. At home he was Mark Lewis, father, husband, breadwinner. At home he was responsible, friendly, and a good neighbor. He strove to be those things because he thought that was what he was supposed to do. That's what grownups did, right? They got married, they bought homes, had children, were good neighbors... in that order. That's what his parents had done. That's what they taught him to do. So, Mark complied. And it wasn't that he didn't want to do that or had been forced to conform—he didn't wear khakis and polos like a uniform or keep his hair trimmed to the collar because there was some unwritten rule requiring all males who lived in the suburbs to do so... it was that he didn't know of any other way to be. Mark didn't know that he *wanted* to be any other way. This was life, and he was just living it.

Only he wasn't, at least not the way he was supposed to be. He knew that now, if he had learned nothing else. Being with Nicole and Eric showed him that he had been ignoring a part of himself that was not cookie-cutter or predictable. He was... more. He *wanted* more.

Mark sighed he watched people funnel out of the jet bridge and into the gate, departing the plane that would soon take him back to California. He took out his phone to check the time. Thirty minutes.

He must have broken all of the speed limits on his way to the airport.

Mark reached into the outside of his bag to grab his book, this time a lightweight mystery that he could devour between both flights but found the space empty. Right. He'd finished the book on the flight up, nearly five hours in the air had been enough time to burn through the pulpy novel. His vacation books, he liked to call them. Enjoyable, casual, no effort required.

He cast a glance over his shoulder, looking for one of those bookstore/convenience store hybrids you only found in airports where you could by a paperback and a sandwich at the same time. Nope. Only sunglasses kiosks and over-priced touristy t-shirts.

Mark sighed again, opening his phone.

His thumb hovered over the email icon, but he decided against it. He wasn't in the right headspace to deal with work, which would just be more of the usual—accolades for the presentation, ideas for the next round... all just proof that he was a good, predictable little worker bee. He thought about texting his wife. He usually did so before boarding under the pretense of just saying hello, but it was really to give her a timestamp by which to figure out when he would get home. That was a nice way of putting it when he really felt constricted by the check-in and how, without verbalizing as much, she had come to expect it. He had a knack for putting things the "nice" way so as not to offend anyone or make any waves. Apparently, he even did it to himself, placating and pacifying natural reflexes. Gauging his arrival was code for tracking him, and it had been going on for as long as he could remember. Who had instated this ritual, he wondered? Why did he keep doing it? The question that was trolling outside his conscious thought, the one that was silhouetted by the veil that he seemed so willing to throw over anything even remotely controversial, was why did he get angry when he thought of it that way?

No, he wouldn't text his wife right then. The prospect of doing what he always did—what he was *expected* to do—infuriated him.

What, then? If he sat there, just sat there allowing himself to think, he might go mad.

The internet.

Mark thought that was a safe enough bet. Maybe he would read the news or something, catch up on what he had missed. Maybe he would watch a movie on the plane and go to sleep, give his mind the rest it needed to deal with whatever came next.

Mark opened up his web browser and was accosted by sketches of golden palaces, of palm trees, of tranquil water. It was the last thing he had searched, the last page he had visited.

Zerzura.

He and Nicole had been trying to remember what the 'Z' stood for, and Mark had looked it up. A fabled oasis. A place that would live in his dreams forever.

Mark rubbed his eyes, squeezing the bridge of his nose until it hurt. Real. It was all real, just like the discomfort he had caused himself then, just like the sting of tears at the corners of his eyes. It *was* real. And it was all gone.

The crackle of the staticky microphone surprised him, the monotone flight attendant calling the first group to begin boarding shocking him more. Last he checked he had 30 minutes left before he could try to sleep and escape the torture of his memories. He'd spent that time on the periphery of bliss, remembering the way they smiled at him, the way they looked at him, the way they touched him. Even as he tried to avoid it, to clutter his thoughts with other things—things from the life he recognized—his mind made its way back to them.

He wanted them.

As Mark stood to fall in line with the other Group 1 passengers, he worried that he always would.

CHAPTER 29

"Nicole," Eric breathed, sadness, misery, and love warring, tumbling over each other in an erratic dance. "What do we do now?"

His words seemed loud though they were not. It was the room, the emptiness of it, the coldness. It was a lovely space, cream walls accented with antique cherry furniture and buffed brass. It was everything it was supposed to be—calming, innocuous, serene. It was everything it shouldn't have been—hollow, silent, final.

Nicole looked at Eric, all her memories, everything she had become since that moment in time coloring her vision to frame him. And still she saw him the way she did back then, the way she always would: beautiful.

"What more *can* we do?"

The door rattled before opening, the tongue banging against the strike plate once, twice, three times before opening slowly, even that a hesitation, as if in warning. The grace was short, mere seconds, but that was long enough. They had grown accustomed to changing expressions, dropping touches, creating distance between them. Young lovers hiding their petting and panting from an intuitive parent had nothing on them.

But they didn't want to.

It hurt Nicole and Eric to step away from each other, almost to the point of physical pain. For the first time since the whole thing had started, this time felt like the last time.

Nicole stepped away from the casket, releasing Mark's hand and leaving Eric's warmth, every step feeling like betrayal. Her face was wet, and she could feel it. That couldn't be. Too many tears would raise questions. Too few would as well, and about more than she could ever explain.

Nicole moved away from her loves wanting nothing more than to go back, to fall into Eric's embrace and cry over Mark, to mourn the realization that their forever had been wrenched away from them before they had the chance to seize it.

Forever.

Never.

She wanted to look back, to see him one more time. She wanted to reach out her hand, let one of the only men she had ever truly loved grasp it in his own and come with her, leave with her, stay with her, and promise to never go away again. But she couldn't. She knew she couldn't, not only because someone was coming into the room, was already in, was walking up the aisle toward the casket that held the man who never failed to make her smile, make her laugh, make her wish for another hour or minute of time so they could spend it together, but because they would see. If she and Eric touched, they would see, and they would know all, know everything, about Mark, and about them. Nicole didn't want that, couldn't bear to be the reason that Mark's family found out now, after he had passed away. Even though she was part of the secret he couldn't share, it was not her secret to tell.

But it wasn't just that.

She couldn't reach out to Eric because they were lost. Lost together for sure, but lost just all the same.

Nicole blotted the fresh tears pooling in the corners her eyes. She patted her cheeks, finding them as wet as she suspected. She took a deep breath. But none of that helped. The tears kept coming, flowing consistently like a slow, persistent drizzle… like the lazy trickle of the bathroom faucet in the hotel where they spent two blissful days. Where had that been… The Keys? Jamaica? Sint Maarten? Somewhere warm with gorgeous sand and beautiful water. Somewhere secluded, off the beaten path, where they could go outside and hold hands and kiss in the sun. The place had been old, but there was a path near it that led to a private beach. Birds of Paradise grew wild near the bedroom window. The cabinet doors creaked. The mattress was lumpy. The faucet dripped.

It was heaven on earth.

The tears kept coming, and she knew they wouldn't stop… not now… not ever. But she could make it—for Mark, she would make it through this. As long as she kept moving, she could make it out of the room without screaming.

Nicole walked on the outside of the pews, leaving the center aisle free. She didn't make eye contact, but that didn't stop her from seeing. Mark's wife was flanked by their sons, each of them dressed in black suits, jackets that looked out of place on their young shoulders, tie knots crafted by unsure hands. Their father would have tightened and flattened and taught, standing beside them as they fumbled in the mirror, encouraging them when they got frustrated. But not this day. Not ever again. His wife was beautiful even in mourning. She was familiar even though grief had taken its toll. Nicole recognized the dark brown eyes, contoured cheeks, and delicate chin that peeked through the black veil she wore from the picture Mark kept in his wallet. She was stunning, but different now. Changed. Her chin quivered, trembling under the weight of keeping her emotions at bay. Her cheeks, unadorned by makeup on this day, looked sallow and oily. And her eyes, normally such a vibrant brown, the reddish hue reflecting the fire Mark always said she possessed, were tired and muted... weary.

Nicole didn't want to see. She was afraid that looking closely at her would be like looking in a mirror.

Mark's boys were almost grown now. Sixteen-year-old twins who were just growing into their feet and becoming men in their own right. Nicole remembered how pleased Mark had sounded the last time he spoke of them, how in awe he was of the adults they were becoming. Football for one, baseball for the other. All the travel games and practices and trips to the store to replace one thing or another, and Mark loved every minute of it. And she loved it for Mark. Because she loved Mark.

Nicole hadn't realized she had turned toward Mark's family, had begun to watch them as they moved down the aisle. She wouldn't have known it had happened at all were it not for one of the boys—*oh my gosh, is that William?*—looking back at her. She resisted the urge to smile at him kindly, to open her mouth and tell him how sorry she was for he and his brother, tell him how much his father loved him and that she would do anything she could to bring him back. Because who was she? How would she know about their father's love? Beyond platitudes, what could she offer those boys who had lost the most important man in their lives?

She was just a stranger.

And Mark was gone.

Nicole kept her face straight as though she wasn't really looking at the boy, but rather at something outside her reach. She cast her eyes down to the floor before looking away, turning the knob and pushing herself through the door without hesitating. She kept going in the same manner out of the funeral home and onto the pathway leading to the sidewalk, never slowing, never looking back... not even at Eric. She had to dodge mourners on their way inside, ready to share memories and condolences in the lobby as they were expected to do because after all, there are funerary rituals to be carried out. Nicole's stomach clenched at the thought that she would not have that release, would not be able to share stories and memories about Mark in an attempt to heal because she was on the outside looking in. She did not belong there.

Eric...

As Nicole rounded the corner; the sheen of sweat that had covered her face as she made her escape chilled in the air.

It was over.

She had gotten away with it, with seeing Mark one last time without being caught, had been among his people—the ones who were supposed to know him best—and not been spotted for who she was... they both had. Together. In some ways, that was the most thrilling part. What would Mark have said had they pulled it off together, all three of them? She couldn't help but hear his laughter, rich and full, in her ear. He might say something like,

'That was the heist of the century!'

And Eric would probably reply, 'How did I fall in love with such an old man? *Heist*? Who even says that anymore? Besides, no one stole anything, boomer.'

And then Mark would most definitely say something like, 'You did... the day you stole my heart.'

Nicole laughed then, considering a conversation that never happened, never had the chance to. And then she actually *heard* herself, laughing unabashedly while tears streamed down her face, and she was wearing a black dress with black heels and carrying a black purse, and she was right around the corner from the funeral home where one of her lovers lay dead and the other was surrounded by people who would hate him if they knew who he was.

The boy, the one she thought was William... had he seen her? Had he truly seen her, into her soul, and figured it out?

Did he know who she was and what she was doing there?

Did he know who Eric was and what he was doing there?

Did he see them and know who his father was?

What would he say if he approached them?

What would he think?

Eric.

Nicole turned back to the funeral home, breaking into a run as thoughts of Eric locked in a room with Mark's sons and his mother flooded her mind. Eric being cornered into explaining himself, explaining their father, explaining what their love had been.

How long did had it gone on?

The woman from before, was she involved too?

How dare you corrupt my father in that way?

How could he do this to his family?

Would they yell? Would they scream? Would they put their hands on Eric, try to beat the answers out of him?

Would they pin him in a corner, surround him, berate him, call him names he could withstand out in the world because they held no power, but would break him coming from Mark's family, Mark's blood, the people Mark held dear because it would feel too much like it was coming from Mark himself about himself, about them and what they were doing... about it all?

Were they hurting Eric right now, her poor, sweet Eric, as he stayed there and took it, stayed there fighting every urge he had to run because he wanted *her* to escape?

Nicole didn't know and that terrified her.

She had to save him.

She couldn't save Mark, but she would damn well save Eric.

CHAPTER 30

Babe, what's taking you so long?

It starts at 10:30!

10:20 AM

10:20 AM

Still waiting.

He's getting antsy. Wants to go out.

10:21 AM

No! I'm right outside. Stop him.

10:22 AM

I know you can think of something.

Maybe…

10:22 AM

10:22 AM

...?

10:23 AM

Ah! Don't get started without me!

10:25 AM

OMG...

But you told me to distract him...

10:26 AM

Ugh...

10:27 AM

U R killing me.

I'll save some for you, don't worry.

10:27 AM

10:28 AM

I'm on my way up now.

No lol! Wait for the guy!

10:28 AM

10:29 AM

He's here. Coming now.

Nicole still hadn't gotten over the time change, but how could she have? It's not like they had gotten any sleep since she landed. It was incredible how eager they had felt, how desperate to be in each other's presence. She had felt butterflies in her stomach the whole flight over, barely able to settle down long enough to read more than a few paragraphs of her book at a time. Her logical brain told her to go to sleep, that she would be happy she had rested before getting there because they would likely stay up all night out of sheer excitement, but that was never going to happen. And, as expected, they did stay up all night talking, and laughing, and kissing, and reacquainting themselves with each other's nuances... the curve of Nicole's back of particular interest to Eric, the sensitivity of Mark's neck Nicole's focus. And it was all as beautiful as they remembered, as wonderful as the first time. It had been a year since they had been in each other's arms. It simultaneously felt like just yesterday and as if lifetimes had been lived in between.

They had tried to be good.

They had tried to walk away from each other, to count their interaction as a momentary lapse of judgement and move on with the rest of their lives as planned before that strange detour in Canada. Eric, who had the least to lose of their three, did what they asked even though he could feel his heart breaking during their one and only phone call, the only time they had heard each other's voices since that morning at The Z. As he waited for one of the only people they would deliberately interact with during their trip, Eric's mind was inundated with the details of that conversation. It was unwanted, the memory of the day that almost tore him apart, but it was coming, flooding his mind with the sounds, saturating his senses with the feelings.

They had to stop.

'Stop what?' Eric had asked, feigning confusion trying to avoid what was coming. He protested, said they weren't doing anything, they weren't seeing each other, they weren't touching each other. 'They were just talking,' he said, the sound of his voice closer to obstinate than he liked. It was just a conversation, he said. If he had punctuated it with a stomp of his foot he didn't think anyone would have been surprised.

He got belligerent, asking if they should stop their friendship, because what was wrong with being friends with people? He qualified that by listing people he was friends with, other married people, some of whom were high profile, at least in his world. He said all those things knowing how ridiculous they sounded, but he couldn't stop himself because he didn't want it to end. He didn't want Mark to say what he was saying and make the sense that he was making. Eric didn't know what he would do if Mark kept talking, kept going... kept leaving.

Nicole had been oddly silent while Mark said the words that were slowly ripping Eric apart. Somehow that was just as unsettling, and Eric felt like he might go crazy if he didn't hear her say something—anything. She had been like that since they said goodbye in the hotel room, cool since she had clammed up, sobered up—whatever had happened. Nicole didn't always participate in their group texts, didn't always respond with any substance. Not that she needed to write pages of words to make him feel like she was present, but the one word answers she sometimes gave left him feeling hollow. What did that mean? Eric had been wondering, too afraid to ask Mark if he noticed anything, too afraid to ask Nicole why. Saying something—actually verbalizing it—would make it real, whatever 'it' was. What if 'it' meant that she had gotten bored with them? What if 'it' was that she had never really been as into it as she said she was? What if 'it' meant that she wanted to move on but didn't know how to say it? Eric wasn't ready for that—he wasn't ready for anything even remotely like that, but the possibility was there, slapping him in the face.

Nicole... so silent, so resolute... so relieved?

Eric couldn't stop himself now, the tirade bubbling inside him, taking a hideous shape.

Since she had gotten home she had been distant. Since she got home to her family, she had been happy.

Content.

Maybe she didn't want to be bothered by some guys who couldn't catch a hint, two guys who were so stupid that they couldn't see the writing on the wall. Because she was done. Fucking done. She had wiped her hands of them and thrown them away. Because she—

"Do you just not care?" Eric had asked her, cutting Mark off to address his other lover. "Does none of this matter to you? Do—do *we* not matter to you anymore, Nicole?"

Nicole had been trying to process everything Mark was saying while keeping her face as inexpressive as possible. She had left the house when she saw the number on her phone, unable to stop herself from smiling. She went outside but couldn't go much further—her husband had run to the store and she was home with the kids. At 7:00 p.m. on a comfortable summer night her kids were doing what every other child in the neighborhood was doing... playing outside. There were several kids in the backyard with her two, some younger ones, about six or seven years old, and some older ones, one probably about 10. Her kids fell squarely in the middle of that range at eight and nine. That meant everyone at the house was entirely too young to be left unsupervised. She had to stay close. She had to pay attention to them even though all she wanted to do in that moment was listen to the voices she heard in her dreams at night.

HAB.

She smiled at the naming convention that popped onto her screen as she answered the phone.

HAB... Hot Asian Boyfriend.

"Hi," Nicole breathed, a mixture of excitement and, well, the other kind of excitement mingling as she spoke, and for a moment, she regretted answering that way. What if someone had taken his phone and was calling to see who the number belonged to? She wouldn't help his argument by breathing into the phone like a sex worker. She tried to fix it, cleared her throat, said hello again using her 'This is how I speak to telemarketers' voice, which wasn't quite 'normal,' was actually a bit clipped and stiff, but it was ten times better than that unbidden sex kitten thing she had used the first time. But then he did the thing that had made her stomach turn flips from the start and brought a beautiful blush to her cheeks.

Mark chuckled.

She could imagine the way he looked when he did it, the way his eyes danced, his lopsided grin. She exhaled into a laugh of her own, feeling a wave of exhilaration at being able to do that again. They had been avoiding this, she knew. Whether it was conscious or unconscious for all of them, whether it had been deliberate at the same time or led by circumstances that none of them knew the whole of, it was true. And now she understood why. Speaking to Mark, just hearing the sound of his laughter over the phone sent electricity through her body. She was buzzing... and that was only after hearing *one* of their voices.

"I'm so happy you—"

“Mom!? Can we have like 20 garbage bags?”

Nicole’s son’s voice pulled her from the edge of the hole she had been ready and willing to jump into. She asked Mark to hold on and inquired why they needed so many. Apparently a makeshift slip ‘n slide was about to be constructed on the hill in their backyard, and the supply list was just being formed. Their contribution included garbage bags, duct tape, and oddly, hangers.

“Please,” Nicole said into the phone, knowing she sounded desperate but not caring, “Please hang on. Just... please don’t hang up.”

“I won’t,” Mark replied, emotion welling up in his throat from out of nowhere. “I promise.”

He brought Eric on the line, and they listened to the conversation happening on Nicole’s end in amicable silence. She approved the garbage bags, vetoed the hangers, and rooted around in what they presumed was the garage for the duct tape, mumbling about how she could have sworn there was a relatively new roll in there somewhere. Eric said hello to Nicole as she rummaged around, things clattering and banging so loudly on her end that he wasn’t sure she had heard him. But then she hummed and issued a girlish ‘hi’ that made him feel like he was back in high school being noticed by the cutest boy in school.

The kids asked what they could use to stabilize the slide and Nicole told them to think about it a little and see what they came up with. When she whispered conspiratorially to Mark and Eric that she needed to run inside and find the string they would be asking for in about a minute, Mark’s heart nearly burst with love.

Mark loved listening to every second of Nicole’s domesticity. He wished desperately that he were there to see it with his own eyes.

"I'm sorry," Nicole said a little out of breath. "Nothing is ever where you think it is."

"I know the feeling," was all Mark could muster. He needed to recover; he had been indulging in a fantasy where Nicole was addressing all of their kids, reminding the older ones to watch out for the younger ones, and Eric was emerging from the basement with the lost roll of duct tape and ice pops for all. In this fantasy Mark was sitting on the deck overlooking the whole affair, smiling that same lopsided grin Nicole and Eric loved as he brought a bottle of beer to his lips. It made him feel good, that fantasy, and hearing Nicole's voice so sweetly in his ear as he thought about it made him wonder if he could actually have it, that maybe he was just calling from the supermarket where he had gone to replace the garbage bags they used up or to get more dish soap for a faster slide. Maybe, just maybe he would turn around and see Eric holding out beer number two.

Mark sniffed, inhaling air briskly to clear his head and fight back the sob that wanted to work its way out of his mouth. If Nicole knew what was going on she didn't say so; she didn't say anything right away. The call was as welcome as it was awkward. They hadn't been talking. They were too afraid to for so many reasons.

What had changed?

Nicole started, wanting to say something but not knowing how to without falling right back into all the things she had been trying to keep at bay as she stood outside watching the children, the 'I miss yous' and 'I love yous' right on the tip of her tongue, begging to be voiced.

But still, the silence wasn't helpful. She was filling it with images of Mark's smiling face on the other end of the phone, Eric's hands, Mark's legs crossed at the knees, Eric's attentive eyes... not good. Her mind needed focus to keep the conversation where it needed to be.

"What made... why..." She didn't know how to finish her sentence without sounding unhappy that Mark had been brave enough to pick up the phone. She couldn't figure out what else to say to fix it and remove the foot already firmly lodged in her mouth. If she kept talking she would sound like even more of a jerk. Her mouth gaped and she closed it silently, bewildered.

"I—I know we haven't been doing... this..." Mark said, also unsure how this should go. They had been avoiding phone calls but never really talked about why. He wanted to talk to them, needed it, but yet they hadn't.

But why?

"I don't know why we haven't, but...," he continued, trying to make sense of it and failing.

"It's just that..." Eric started, then stopped, not know where he was going with the thought.

"I feel like I—Mommy's on the phone, honey," Nicole broke off. "You guys can figure this out without me though, I know you can. All you need now is some water and maybe a little dish soap, right?"

"I love this," Eric said to Mark honestly. "Listening to her like this is everything."

Mark couldn't have agreed more.

"I'm so sorry," Nicole said, coming back to the conversation. "I've moved to the other side of the house. Maybe if they can't see me they won't be inclined to ask me so many questions."

"It's ok," Mark and Eric said in tandem, and they all laughed.

"Just like always," Nicole said, remarking on how they spoke at the same time the way they did so often during their night together.

The laughter died, and suddenly Mark knew.

He couldn't talk to them like this or in text or at all anymore, couldn't keep playing at only being friends, not if he wanted to keep his sanity. He wanted them too much to only have them in this superficial way.

"I don't know," Mark started, and both Nicole and Eric's hearts dropped. He sounded different than he had just a minute before. Nicole knew he sounded different than he had when she picked up the phone. Whatever was going on in his head right then was new, but at the same time, they understood that it had been there all along.

"I don't think I can keep... This is killing me," Mark said finally. He wasn't alone at home; he hadn't thought the idea of calling them through at all before he picked up the phone. Nothing had happened to make him reach out to them in that moment except that he always wanted to reach out to them. He always wanted to hear their voices and talk about what they were doing. He always, always wanted them. And it was driving him crazy.

They had kept the texts down to a minimum, deciding that was probably best even without discussing it. Mark assumed they had their reasons, just like he did. It wasn't that he thought being with them had been a mistake. Even though he had compromised his life for that one day, there was more to it, and he knew it. They meant everything to him, and he didn't understand how that could be possible. He only wanted to be with them, and he didn't understand why. He didn't understand anything except that he couldn't do this half in/half out thing, this unfulfilling tease. And that's what it needed to be because he had children. Nicole had children. They had spouses. They had lives that had been built on those identities. They weren't truly available right now. And Eric deserved to have someone in his life who *could* be available to him, someone who could give him the future he wanted. Mark knew these things were true, yet he still kept going, pining after them, reaching out when he couldn't take it anymore, and now this. But it couldn't go on. He didn't know that until he heard their laughter, all of them together as harmonious as before. He couldn't string them on like this—it was wrong to. So, with his wife in the family room, he called them from his home office and spoke of things that could ruin the life he had worked so hard to build and would most definitely destroy a part of his soul.

"We have... we have to stop." Mark wasn't sure if he had said it out loud or not. Most of him hoped he hadn't and he could forget all about the idea. Because, god, he wasn't ready. He wasn't ready for it to end... he never wanted it to end.

"Stop what?" Eric said, his mind choosing to show anger instead of the pain that threatened to spill over. "We're not doing anything."

"You know, this... this thing is so much more than..."

"Then why?" Eric said, not letting Mark finish. He felt like his head might explode. "Why do we have to change things? Why can't we just...why can't we..."

"Because it isn't right," Mark answered the unfinished question. "It's not fair to any of us. Nicole has young children depending upon her and you, Eric, you have a blank slate to create whatever kind of future you want. It isn't fair to have you tethered to something that isn't—"

"Do you just not care?" Eric spat, cutting Mark off to draw Nicole into the conversation. "Does none of this matter to you? Do—do *we* not matter to you anymore, Nicole?"

"I...," Nicole started, tears stinging her eyes. She had wobbled a bit when Mark said what he said and found that she didn't have the desire to stand anymore. She sat down on the ground as calmly as she could just in case one of the kids spotted her, but down she went, nonetheless. She felt like the wind had been knocked out of her.

"Of course I care," she whispered weakly. "I—I feel sick."

Mark was right. He was. But she wasn't ready to let go. Not really. Not forever.

"Do you think I'm wrong?" Mark asked, unable to strip the hopeful edge out of his voice. "Could we really keep this up? The texting, the longing, the dancing around each other —is that really something you're prepared to do? And for how long?"

"Forever," Eric said, his voice having lost its edge as the sadness overtook him. "I want forever."

"At a distance?" Nicole asked, sniffling, feeling the weight of reality so heavy on her shoulders that she was slumped over under it. "Would that be enough?"

The question was as much for her as it was for them, and she pondered it in the silence that hung in the air afterward, stifling them. Would she be satisfied talking with them in text, not ending what they had but not actually having each other either? Living in some purgatory, some mental waystation—their love existing in a perpetual state of limbo? Could she be a part of their lives knowing how she felt about them... knowing what she wanted from them? Could she push everything they had under the rug? Then her questions changed tack, turning more introspective. Could she leave her husband? If she had to choose between her husband and her happiness, the family unit they had created or the loves of her life, who would win? Nicole looked at her children sliding down the hill with their friends and wondered if she could uproot them, take all of this away from them, change their lives so drastically. They might hate her. Sure, kids were resilient, but changing their lives like this, introducing them to a reality that she didn't even understand yet, would be a lot for anyone to take. But still Nicole wondered. Maybe they would grow to accept it. Her son would love Mark—Nicole imagined she might have to drag them away from the television for dinner during football season. And Eric and her daughter would be two peas in a pod, their interest in theater being only one of the things that bonded them together. It could be good. There would be questions about how it all worked, but it could actually be good... if she had the guts to try it.

But did she?

"C-could we—" Nicole started but Eric cut her off, his voice sounding defeated.

"They'd hate me," Eric sighed, beaten down by stark reality.

"Eric—" Mark started, but Eric stopped him before he could get started. He didn't think he could stand hearing the placating tone that was sneaking into Mark's voice.

"Your children would hate me, Nicole. They would blame me for making their dad go away... me *and* Mark. And your sons, Mark—those jocks of yours—babe, they'd look at your theater-loving gay boyfriend and blame me for making their dad queer. Maybe not right away, but they'll definitely get there at some point, whether their friends teased them about it first or they came up with it on their own. Either way it all boils down to them hating me."

Mark and Nicole wanted to protest, but they didn't know if they had a leg to stand on against Eric's argument. They listened to the sounds of the city passing behind him—he had been walking to the train when Mark called—and tried to think of something to say to take the pain out of his voice, but they couldn't.

"And then... I mean, there's three of us. *Three.*" Eric chuckled mirthlessly. "In what world is that considered normal?"

"We can't get married," Mark said. "It's not legal—" Mark cut off his own thought in disbelief. In moments like these, when he was forced to really think about what he was doing, Mark couldn't believe the picture his life painted now. Instead of using words like trustworthy, husband, and father to describe him, one could use adulterer, bisexual, and polygamist just as easily. But then he thought of Eric's smile and little boy charm; he thought of Nicole's laughter and charisma, and the only word he could think of to describe them was love.

"You deserve to be married if you want to be," Mark finished quietly. The tears came, damn them, just like he knew they would.

"I can't have any more children," Nicole said, surprising herself. She'd had her tubes tied before closing up after her last c-section at her doctor's insistence, something about scar tissue and viability mumbled in a distant past... another lifetime. She hadn't thought about that for years—hadn't allowed herself to—but in light of the facts this conversation was bringing to the table, even though speaking the words felt as painful now as they did way back then, Nicole thought it was important they knew.

"If that is something you want, I can't... I can't give that to you."

"Four is enough," Eric said wistfully, daring to imagine a future where they were all together and their kids were his too, trying not to lose himself in fantasies of birthday parties, princess dresses, driving lessons, and video game tournaments. It was dangerous there in that fantasy-like black hole. It might suck him in forever.

"And," Eric said, pulling himself out of the abyss, "I don't need a piece of paper to tell me I'm in a committed relationship."

Eric sobbed, losing the control he'd struggled to maintain. He leaned against the streetlight on the corner of 51st and 8th Ave. and he could see the subway station on 50th—it was literally right across the street from where he was standing. If he had just gotten to it before the phone rang, he'd have hopped on the E train and made his way out to Penn Station never having heard his phone ring. He might have gotten onto the PATH and made it all the way out to Jersey before noticing the voicemail they might have left, maybe even all the way home. Maybe they would have changed their minds before he called them back. Maybe they would have decided not to break each other's hearts.

Mark cried openly in his desk chair as the sun moved in the sky, creating long shadows on the ground. His boys were at a friend's house so at least he didn't have to worry about them overhearing the heart-wrenching sound of his grief, but his wife was on the same floor as he was. What would he say if she heard him and came in to ask what was wrong?

Would he tell her everything? Tell her that he had met two people who he knew, without a shadow of a doubt, were his soulmates but that he was saying goodbye to them? He was saying *goodbye* to them... forever. If she asked, he would tell her that. It would have to be enough.

Nicole's hand fluttered to her mouth just before a wet gasp escaped her lips. She had been crying silently, her mouth opened in a grimace that might have looked like laughing from far enough away. At least that's what she hoped. It was over. The thing they had been avoiding—the elephant in the room that she saw even before leaving that morning—had finally broken its restraints and leveled everything around it.

They had no future.

"I want you to be happy," Mark whispered through his tears.

"I want *us* to be happy," Eric said, knowing there was no 'us' anymore.

"I want *us*," Nicole said and then gasped clear as a bell, startled.

"Oh my god," she said as she swiped at her eyes frantically, trying to will herself to calm down, knowing she must look suspicious as hell, but unable to stop herself.

"My husband—he just pulled into the driveway, right next to me," Nicole said, her voice quavering.

"Baby," Mark said, wishing he could be there with her to help her get through this moment, whichever way she wanted to... even if it meant having to listen to her deny his existence.

"It's ok. You're ok," Eric said as he tried to remember the name of the town in Virginia that Nicole lived in. He lived closer to her than Mark did, but even if he were on the moon, he would get to her as fast as he could if she needed him.

"Just let me know if you need—"

They could hear a man talking in the background, asking why she was sitting next to the driveway. She sniffled, and before she could answer, that same male voice asked her if she was ok, sounding alarmed. She said it was allergies, something in the air that must have pushed past her while she was sitting in the grass, or maybe even the grass itself—she didn't know. Whatever it was , it was gone, she promised even as she sniffled again. The man was placated. Mark and Eric were subjected to the sound of lips meeting skin, an audible *smack* making them both feel as if their souls were detaching from their bodies.

'I got your favorite,' the man said.

Each man in Nicole's life either thought or spoke 'rum raisin' in perfect unison.

Nicole's appreciative giggle didn't hit the mark. It sounded more disingenuous than anything. She covered it by a barrage of sniffles and more eye rubbing, eliciting an empathetic hum from the man.

'Come inside for a while,' the man said. 'We can see the kids from the window.'

Nicole agreed. Mark and Eric wondered what the man—her husband, presumably—made of the reluctance in her voice.

Nicole called out to the kids, to tell them she would be going inside but could see them from the sunroom.

"I love you," she yelled and was met with a groan from her oldest who was mortified by his mother's admission stated so loudly outside, of all places, and in front of his friends to top it off, but at that moment Mark and Eric knew that she wasn't talking to the kids. She was talking to them.

She was saying goodbye.

But that was then, and this was now.

Eric didn't want to think about that day, about the words they said to each other then, because it hurt so much. Even as happy as he was that they had found their way back to each other months and months later, unable to take the separation anymore, it still bothered him. Probably because their lives hadn't changed. They had each had a birthday; Eric had grown his hair out a little for a new role; Nicole had gotten a promotion at her job, and Mark had bought a new car, but they—who they were to each other, what they felt, the constraints they had—were still the same. That meant they could find themselves back in that horrible place where goodbye seemed like the only option again, and Eric didn't know if he would be able to pick up the pieces next time.

"Hello," an elderly man said to him. "Are you Mr. Smith?"

"Yes, sir," Eric said, standing briskly. He had almost forgotten the name he gave when setting the whole thing up. It wasn't that he was a big celebrity or anything, but if a person enjoyed theater enough to make the rounds, they might have seen him on stage. If they saw him on stage and liked his performance, they knew his name—his real name. If they just happened to be in K-Town at the same time, saw him and recognized that he was there with two other people —two people he seemed very close to... well, Eric didn't want to risk a picture or social media chatter. That would be a hell of a way for Mark's wife and Nicole's husband to find out.

Eric and the quiet older man rode the elevator in relative

silence, only exchanging pleasantries, but that was fine. Eric was too eager to get started and didn't want to learn anything before the others anyway.

When he knocked on the door he was almost unable to contain his excitement. Eric stepped behind the man and waited for Mark to open it, smiling broadly.

"Hello?" Mark said as he opened the door to see an older Asian man standing in front of him and the ecstatic look on Eric's face behind.

"Annyeonghaseyo," the older man said and bowed toward Mark.

A confused smile spread over Mark's face, and Eric returned it over the man's shoulder. The older man placed a hand on Mark's own shoulder, guiding him into a reciprocal bow, and nodded as they stood.

Mark stepped to the side to allow room for the man and Eric to enter, his face amused. Nicole emerged from the dining room wearing a smile of her own as they entered the room. Because it was perfect. It was exactly what she and Eric had hoped for when they planned the trip to Koreatown. The man, who would soon be drinking omija tea with Mark and talking about the North Gyeongsang Province from which they both hailed at least based on the limited information they had been able to glean from what Mark knew, was a teacher at a local school. During the week he taught Korean American students about Korean history and customs. On the weekend he did the same for adults. Nicole and Eric decided to garner the man's services after a video call between the three of them revealed the toll that being disconnected from a part of himself had taken on Mark; even though he tried to downplay it, the pain was written all over his face. Eric would say that it was that girl that laughed at Mark in college that did it for him—he had tried to speak to her using Korean he had cobbled together from study guides, adding honorifics where they weren't needed, lacking inflection where it was required, and she laughed at him. Fucking *laughed.* Mark said after that he went back to what he knew: his white-bread, American pie upbringing.

For Nicole it was something different. Mark said there was nothing in his adoption papers about his birth mother and father. There was really nothing at all in there except the name of the village where he was from, one that was so small he could never find it on any maps. It was supposedly near Taegu, which he *could* find, and that had to be good enough. There was that and a name. The story his parents told him was that the nurse who had taken care of him during the first days of his life had given Mark her brother's name because he reminded her of him. They never called him by it even though they tried to honor it as best they could with an English equivalent, nor did they put it on his official documentation, but it was important to Mark.

Man-seok.

What set Nicole in motion was the fact that Mark couldn't pronounce the name he had been given.

It broke her heart.

With a blush of embarrassment creeping up his neck, Mark had quipped, "Hi. I'm Mark. Sometimes I eat ramen, but don't read too much into that."

Whatever their reasons were, Nicole and Eric were in sync about the trip. They booked a sprawling hotel suite in the center of Koreatown, or K-Town as Eric insisted upon calling it, one that they didn't intend to leave very often. Part of it was because they were skittish about being out and about—they hadn't left Mark's state... hadn't even left his county. And while it was unlikely that someone would recognize him there, none of them wanted to take that chance. And then there was Eric to consider. He had worked in LA, had some memorable performances. They didn't want to risk him being spotted and with whom.

The other part was that they wanted to spend as much time wrapped in each other's arms as possible.

Nicole and Eric had scheduled a chef to come in and make authentic Korean dishes. The ones she described—bibimbap, japchae, kimchi fried rice, mandu—had their mouths watering. They would go out for Korean fried chicken and beer since that was, apparently a necessary experience, and they also had a table reserved at the best Korean BBQ in town so they could experience bulgogi up close and personal. They had an anime bookstore run planned, traditional Korean spa treatments, and a few language and culture lessons like the one getting started in the other room. Nicole had even picked out a few K-dramas they could enjoy while curled up on the sofa after the day's activities were done.

They were going to learn about Mark's culture together.

They were going to fill the hole inside him with love.

"Junbi doeeossnayo? Are you ready?" the teacher asked after finishing his tea.

"Yes," Mark said, unable to stop smiling.

"Ne," the teacher corrected. "Ne means yes."

"Ne," Mark repeated dutifully.

Nicole and Eric exchanged glances from across the room.

Absolutely perfect.

CHAPTER 31

"His hand fit perfectly between her hip and ribs.

That's what she was thinking about as the train left the Champ de Mars station that Sunday evening, the Eiffel Tower's shimmering lights receding from view. As her head rested on the window, she thought about his hand, his piano fingers, long and lean, perched just above the rise of her hips. She could almost feel his index finger grazing the bottom of her breast, fingers splayed, covering the space with ease. His hand was warm, inviting. She felt safe when he placed it there, cared for in a way that she couldn't explain. She felt its absence profoundly as she sat on the train, her skin tingling as if his fingers ghosted the willing flesh. How was she going to get used to this, the loss of contact—the feeling of being left bare? Even though she had only known him for a moment in time, losing him would mark her forever.

As the train whooshed through the tunnels, tracing its way through Paris then over to London proper, Maggie closed her eyes, shutting out the architecture she had travelled so far to see, thinking only of his lips on her neck, trailing over the hollow of her throat, over her collarbones, to settle into a nip at her shoulder. She thought of his hand resting between her hip and ribs squeezing and releasing, squeezing and releasing, adding pressure with every turn, causing her breath to hitch. She thought of them moving together in time, riding the wave that threatened to carry them away and deposit them in places unknown... willing it to, so they could stay together forever. She thought of him as she moved further away from his embrace with every second."

Even over video they could see the flush in Nicole's cheeks as she read, her voice timid. It was unlike her to be so shy, but this was the first time she had shared any of her writing. With anyone. As soon as she finished writing the segment, she felt the urge to show them, to tell them what she had done. Nicole hadn't even edited the work yet, and she found herself tripping over misspellings and forgotten punctuation. But still, there was nothing else she wanted to be doing in that moment than sharing her first real paragraphs with her loves. Writing had always been something she wanted to do—a dream—and now it was coming true. *They* were a dream come true. But now, after finishing the last word, she felt like she couldn't look at them.

When Nicole covered her mouth with her hand after finishing, neither Mark nor Eric could stop the smile that spread across their faces.

It was a Tuesday night, not their usual once a month video call, but Nicole couldn't wait a week for that to come around. She had texted them asking if they were free and the way she did it made Eric and Mark clear their schedules right away. She hadn't sounded like she was in a panic nor did she seem upset about anything, but they could tell that whatever was on her mind was important to her, and if it was important to her, it was important to them.

They weren't where they usually were during their calls, the short notice not allowing them to get in position as they would have liked, but that was ok. Nicole needed to talk so there they were.

"Are you still at the theater?" Nicole asked spotting the bricked backdrop and planked floor.

"Yep. We just finished practicing the fight scene again. We still have some work to do to make it look good, but at least I'm not worried about getting punched in the gut anymore," Eric said with a laugh that wasn't exactly jovial. Being punched in the gut on stage was still a real possibility, especially if the actor opposite him couldn't figure out how to feint left, but he didn't want to worry them. Once he had come onto their monthly call with a black eye courtesy of a faulty prop, and he had to stop Nicole from driving up to make sure he was ok. He would have welcomed the chance to see her—in-person visits were too rare for his liking—but coming up with a viable reason for her to suddenly need to be away for 24 hours was virtually impossible. Her husband would have seen right through it, would have at least been skeptical, and Eric knew that Nicole wasn't ready for the conversation that could have spawned from that.

"Where are you, babe?" she asked Mark. The red wall and abstract painting that they could only see the bottom of was unfamiliar.

"A coffee shop near work," Mark said, then held up his cold brew. "I was just leaving the office."

"Late," Eric commented, noticing that it was just turning 10 p.m. in New York, so it was 7 p.m. on the west coast. Mark had been working late a lot recently because a new product was launching. That meant travel, and that could be a good thing for them, but with the show coming up and school concert season coming around, well, time was of the essence. Scheduling wasn't as easy as it used to be. Mark's boys had made the varsity teams for football and baseball. They also played on travel teams. That meant Mark was always either going to or coming from one game or another. They were 15 now and as tall as he was, athletic, strong, and smart. With their sports and academic clubs, Mark had his hands full. Nicole's children had come into their own as well as they navigated middle school. Her son played basketball on a travel team, and her daughter was getting into track. She was pretty good too—ran a 200m in 26 seconds. So that meant Nicole had entered the world of parent as chauffer almost every day of the week, carting the kids off to one activity after another. For Eric's part, he was working all the time, rolling from one project to the next without much of a break in between. He still played in Toronto and probably would always carve out time for a short-term project there, but he had also done shows in Paris and Prague and Rome.

Life had gotten busy, yet after four years, they were still there.

Mark loosened his tie and unbuttoned his collar, and Eric and Nicole felt something. It wasn't often that they got the chance to see him dressed in his presentation clothes—usually he came onto their video chats in jeans and a T-shirt, which was more than fine to them. But seeing him dressed to impress a client, wearing a suit that looked tailor-made to accent his chest, hug his biceps just so, taper perfectly to show off his form... Eric bit his lip as his eyes wandered, and Nicole smiled ever so slightly.

Mark noticed. It made him feel good that he could still fluster them after all that time.

"Yeah," Mark sighed, smirking a bit at the sight of the two of them trying to get themselves together. "The planning for this thing is bigger than any of us expected."

"It's like 7 there," Nicole said, surprised.

Mark nodded, and they instantly knew what that meant. He was late getting home. Dinner might be waiting, maybe not for dinner around the table together—those days had become few and far between the older the boys got, but his family was surely waiting in one way or the other.

Nicole looked away, her expression unreadable.

"Baby," Eric said, coaxing her back, "that was *really* good."

Nicole covered her mouth again and looked at the two men who had stolen her heart.

"So, so good," Mark emphasized.

Her smile was so wide that her eyes closed, and Mark and Eric laughed, laughed like they did in the beginning, like they always did.

"You really have a way with words. The way you described how he kissed her and the train whooshing through the tunnel... I could really envision it," Eric recalled.

"Yeah, and the way you used my name. Very clever, sweetheart."

Nicole cocked her head to the side in confusion before she asked, "Used your name?"

"Yeah," Mark said. "You said losing him would *mark* her forever. I loved it."

"That's not your name—it's just a word," Eric said, feeling fresh laughter welling up in his chest.

"Don't be jealous, baby. She loves you too."

Mark's eyes were dancing.

Nicole was laughing so hard that she made no sound at all.

Mark and Eric went on about lame jokes and who rated higher, and all manner of silliness that was so reflective of their connection, their relationship... so very much *them* that Nicole didn't bat an eye anymore. It was music to her ears, and she knew then, as she had figured out a long time ago, that she could listen to their back and forth all day long. She was glad that her husband and kids were upstairs in bed and that she was writing in the sitting room that, more often than not, doubled as her office space so that she could laugh as much as she wanted to.

"It wasn't enough to have one fool—I had to go and get two," Nicole said and shook her head as the moment wound down. "But seriously," she continued, "It isn't over the top?"

"It flows," Eric said, considering the question.

"It's melodic—like poetry," Mark added. He wanted to tell her that was how he felt, like he couldn't be without them, like he was the one on that train she wrote about, going crazy as he drew further and further apart from them, but he didn't.

But Eric did.

"It sounds familiar," Eric said quietly and looked down at his hands.

All three of them grew silent then, measuring Eric's words, thinking similar ones of their own.

What were they doing?

Eric couldn't help but wonder what they thought they were doing, where they thought they were going with their relationship. He didn't even know what *he* thought was going on with them. All he knew was that he loved them, wanted to be with them, wanted everything that there was to have with them.

Was that enough?

Eric knew they weren't going to leave their families. It wasn't a matter of changing their lives for him... it wasn't even *about* him. He didn't wonder if they truly loved him or anything like that because he knew the truth. He could feel that they really did love him, that it wasn't just lip service. But they weren't going to change their children's realities on a whim. And even though they had been doing whatever they were doing for several years, it *did* seem like a whim to them sometimes, whether they wanted to admit it or not. Their love and the way it manifested so strongly and so incredibly fast, felt unreal to all of them. It was hard not to think that they were having one hell of a dream and they were going to wake up and find that their lives were the way they used to be. Eric knew they weren't going to turn the kids' lives upside down, and if he was being honest, he loved them all the more for it.

But still...

"It is," Nicole said quietly, peeking at them through downturned eyes. "Familiar."

"Can we..." Eric blurted out, but then stopped himself. He told himself he wouldn't ask anymore, that he would see what happened and then decide if he was going to participate. He told himself sometimes, when he missed them so much he ached, that maybe it was time to stop this for good, that maybe they had been right when they had tried to break if off before. They had started and stopped many times over the years, one of them having the courage to say what all of them had been thinking. It was almost like they had taken turns throwing in the towel, each of them laying out the facts about why their thing wouldn't work—*couldn't* work—but it never stuck. None of them could pull away from each other for long… none of them were strong enough.

The last time had been right after they had gotten back from St. Thomas. Three blissful days in paradise. They had rented a vacation home with a private pool and beach access, had eaten grilled lobster on the beach in the moonlight, had gone sailing to wile the afternoon away. It had been wonderful. They could almost imagine that they belonged to each other completely, that they never had to leave the fantasy and come back to a reality that did not include them together. But then it was over and they had to say goodbye to the turquoise water, the white sand beaches, and the comfort of each other's arms. And then, almost 24 hours from the moment they had kissed goodbye, whispering promises of forever into each other's skin, they watched as the island that had hosted their celebration of love was nearly wiped off the face of the earth. The news showed the street they had travelled to get to the farmers market where they bought guava and passionfruit and mangos and coconuts. It had been washed out, boats going aground as though they had been lifted out of the water and placed on the road by God himself. Their rental home and all the homes on that street were leveled. They could have been there—had they stayed another day like they wanted to, they might have found themselves stranded there on an island they had no business being on, a place that was hundreds of miles away from where Nicole and Mark said they would be… or worse. It felt too close to an omen for any of their liking.

They tried to stop then. They didn't say anything about ending things, didn't make any grand announcements about it, but they backed away from each other, quietly spooked. It was the lack of control that shone a light on their reality, illuminating the shadows with its harsh beam. What they were doing was secret. What they were doing was wrong. And if it had been revealed like that, some force of nature removing choice from their hands, what they were doing would have hurt everyone who mattered.

They tried to leave each other softly, but it didn't last—it never did. They were drawn to each other in ways they couldn't define.

But still...

They didn't talk about it—not the backing away nor the coming back together. They couldn't. None of them could believe that everything they had been hoping for in the future, the fantasy they had nurtured would happen when their children were in college and old enough to understand, wasn't possible, but that fact kept rearing its ugly head. Eric didn't want to acknowledge it, to speak the words out loud and have them become real. He didn't know what he would do if they agreed, corroborated what he was feeling as fact: that even though he had been a devoted lover, staying true to the unspoken promise of commitment when they hadn't—couldn't; even though Eric had waited for them, they might never be able to commit to him. Eric didn't know if his heart could handle the realization that what he thought would be forever was never really going to happen.

Then he met Glenn.

Being with Glenn—it felt like waking up, like being set free from some invisible cuff around his neck that he didn't know was squeezing him, tightening like a boa constrictor, killing him. The way one screams their way out of sleep paralysis, Eric felt like falling into Glenn had pulled him from the void, away from something dark and murky. It was like Glenn had turned on the light to drive the shadows away. Eric had resisted in the beginning, pushing Glenn away first for his sake, and then for his own, then keeping him at arm's length. But then one day, when his reasons for saying no seemed hollow, Eric finally let Glenn in. And it was good. Glenn was good to him and good *for* him. But it wasn't the same as being with Nicole and Mark and somewhere deep inside himself, Eric knew nothing ever would be.

He still wanted what he knew he could never have.

"I just..."

Eric rubbed the back of his neck and frowned. He wished he wasn't so weak for them, but his heart needed them. His very soul did.

"I don't know what's happening with this project," Mark started. "If I can—"

Nicole chimed in, cutting Mark off. "The regional meet is coming up and I—"

"No, I understand," Eric said hurriedly. And he did understand. But that didn't stop it from hurting like hell. "I guess... it's just that the show will be opening soon and I know I won't be able to... to... but I get it."

Eric hated seeing the guilty looks on Nicole and Mark's faces because he had put them there, but he didn't know how to fix it.

"It's ok," Eric said again, feeling the need to fill the silence. He smiled, but it never reached his eyes, and they could tell.

The looks on Nicole and Mark's faces were making Eric feel sick. He needed this conversation to be over now, even though he wanted to stay on the phone with them for as long as possible.

"Keep writing, babe. I can't wait for the next installment," Eric said and he meant it, but it was obviously a segue into ending the conversation.

"I'm gonna call it a night," he continued, trying to ignore the melancholy tone of his own voice. "We're making progress, but I had to dodge more than a few punches. I'm a little tired, and it's a long way back home, you know?"

No, he thought, *they* didn't *know. They didn't know because they had never been to his house. This wasn't a normal relationship so they had never been to his house, seen his neighborhood, enjoyed a meal at his favorite restaurant, the one right around the corner from his place... and they probably never would.*

Glenn had been to his house.

"Ok. Ok, baby," Mark said, trying for upbeat but missing the mark.

"Ok. I'll—" Nicole stopped talking abruptly and looked offscreen, staying so still it almost looked like her image had frozen.

Eric shook his head slightly and instantly regretted letting his frustration show. But damn it.

"Ok," Eric said feeling the dejection deep inside him.

"Are we still on for next week?" Mark said, hoping the answer was yes.

Nicole didn't respond—she was listening to or for something.

Eric gave a noncommittal hum in reply.

"Ok," Mark said, not knowing what else to do. Something had changed. The shift had been quick, but it was real, and he had no idea how to put things back on track.

"I... I wanna say... but she's, you know..." Mark stuttered through his reason for not saying 'I love you' to end the call.

It would have been unusual anyway—they were careful not to say things that, if overheard, could be cause for question. They had to be—earbuds were out of the question for Nicole and Mark. If they put them in, effectively removing the conversation from listening ears, they might slip into a sense of security that didn't really exist. They might laugh louder, speak more fondly, say things that couldn't be explained away. They might be snuck up on and witnessed, their guards dropped so profoundly that they were unaware of anyone else's presence. It could be a catastrophe. So, when they talked they stuck to the basics—work, social life, things happening in the world, keeping their friendship strong until they could be with each other again to nurture the physical aspect of their love.

Friends.

They were good at that.

Eric was starting to wonder if that was the only thing they were good at, when all was said and done.

"Yeah, I know," Eric said, eager to get off the phone with them for the first time ever. "Same."

"O-ok," Mark said, perceiving the coldness but not knowing how to address it.

Eric looked at them for a moment, Mark unsure and Nicole preoccupied. He sighed audibly. Then he said,

"Ok, then. Goodnight."

He closed the call before Nicole could come back to the conversation, before Mark could say goodnight back.

Eric,

I debated whether or not I would tell you this. I definitely didn't think I would start here, but here

we are. I don't know what good it will do, especially now, but one of the things that bothers me most about what happened is that you might feel responsible and as much as I understand why your mind might try to convince you of that, it just isn't true.

I already knew. Before you ever said a word about him, I knew.

There was something different in your eyes, in the way you looked at us. I never hated the fact that we could only see each on video more than when I saw how your eyes were changing. They were imploring but distant all at the same time. It's like you were looking for something, waiting for one of us to say something that would make all the difference in the world—would change everything. I couldn't figure out what that was, and I tried, Eric. I tried so hard.. Sometimes I thought you wanted us to tell you we loved you more often, to prove it somehow, and even though I couldn't be with you the way I wanted to, I tried to make sure you knew how I felt. I tripped over myself trying to show you —I felt sure you and Nicole noticed and thought I was being more ridiculous than usual. That was ok —looking like a fool in front of you two was not ever a problem as long as you understood how much you meant to me.

But then it seemed like you wanted us to choose. You or our families. And it crushed me. It made me see that there was a difference, a delineation between the two. There was what we had and then there were our other lives. Our separate lives. I hated that you made me see it. I had gone for so long not seeing it, ignoring it, accepting that this was us—that I was living two lives, both rich and full in their own ways... that I had two families, both of which I loved very much.

Eric, you are my family. You and Nicole are not just some people I keep on the side to satisfy my appetite when I feel the urge. I love you. I love Nicole. I love us. But I understand that isn't enough.

There is a ceiling for us, isn't there? The glass above our heads has been kept clean to let the sunlight in, let us gaze at the stars at night and think we're among them, but we're not free. We can never move past the glass, break the glass, do away with it. It is our destiny to peer out at the world from behind it, wishing it gone but feeling its permanence on our souls.

Wow. I haven't strung words together like that in a long time, so much like prose. I leave all that to Nicole—she's the one who writes so beautifully, who thinks in terms of metaphor and symbolism, but it just came out that way. The last time I came up with something so lyrical was the day I met you and Nicole. I guess that makes sense, then, since this is the last moment we will ever share.

I love you, Eric. God, I always have, even before I knew your name, before I saw your face, before you sat down at my table in that obscure little coffee shop. I think I was always meant to love you and Nicole. But not everything is meant to be.

I'd like to tell you that my being in London when your play opened was a coincidence, but it wasn't and you'd see through that anyway. Something about that last breakup had a permanence to it that the others hadn't possessed. I couldn't put my finger on it, but I knew something was different this time, that even though we'd want to, none of us were coming back. I wonder if Nicole recognized it too. I never spoke with her about it and I regret that now. I'd didn't think she'd answer the phone if she saw my name come up, but still I wish I had tried. The truth is some part of me figured I would never hear either of your voices again but thinking something and knowing it for sure are entirely different. I wish I hadn't been such a coward. Through it all, I wish I could change that most of all.

I saw you. You are magnificent onstage, Eric. I was captivated by your performance. You show such passion for your craft, honestly, you embodied that role so completely that for those few hours I didn't know where the character ended and where the real Eric began. You told us what that was one day, you used some term to explain it. I remember you talking about it as we lay tangled with each other on the sheets of some hotel room. Was it in Dallas that time we were able to coordinate layovers and squeeze out a few hours together? Was it in Miami? I can't remember. But I do recall you talking about it with such passion while you stroked my hair. I remember Nicole's foot tracing a path along my calf. And then I don't remember much else. I'm sorry, please don't mistake my forgetfulness for disinterest. It's just that you and Nicole have always been able to distract me with the slightest of touches.

That night you owned the stage. The lead role in a show on the West End, just like you always wanted. I was so proud of you. I still am. You were you, pulling all the emotions out of me that you always did, but at the same time you were someone else entirely—someone I had never seen before, and I laughed and cried with the rest of the audience as you did what you do. You had us mesmerized. I loved every minute of it. Eric, you are something to behold, and I mean that sincerely.

I didn't mean for you to see me that night but I lingered too long. I always linger too long when it comes to you and Nicole. That's why everything has been so hard over these past few years. As much as

I loved being with you, sharing this thing we have, it was so incredibly hard to maintain. Hard because I wanted more. I always wanted more—I wanted everything and I knew I couldn't have it. I was never supposed to have it, if I'm being honest, baby. And that made me feel so empty sometimes, I didn't know what to do.

I didn't mean for you to see me there. I had been sitting on the park bench across from you for at least ten minutes before your boyfriend first looked at me. There was space between us, lots of it, and people walked on the path there, blocking my view sometimes. I thought that was good, thought they would hide me while I looked, cover me while I suffered. Because watching you with him was the hardest thing I've ever done, Eric. I didn't think I'd be able to go on afterwards.

You were so happy. So... whole. It seemed like you didn't have a care in the world, not a single thing to weigh on your mind. It wasn't anything blatant that you did—I could just tell. Anyone could if they watched you and him for a minute or two. Turned in to each other, making a table between you as you ate lunch, talking easily, gesturing smiling, laughing. It was your laugh that did me in, what forced the sound that he heard out of me, making him search for its source. I couldn't help it. Everything about you was so right in that moment that I saw all the things I had kept from you with my selfishness, imagined all the ways I had constricted Nicole's movements too. I was already suffering, the tears starting to fall from my eyes in an embarrassing torrent that I couldn't seem to slow or stop. But it was your laughter—the rich and open quality of it... the sound that I would know from anywhere and under any circumstances—that laughter turned me inside out. I gasped in an effort to both catch my breath and stop myself from vomiting.

And then he looked at me. He looked right at me, and for a moment I wondered if he knew who I was. I stared back, not in defiance or in challenge but out of curiosity. Had you told him about me? About Nicole? About the love we shared? Did you telling him about us mean you still loved us, still wanted us, however we came? I allowed myself to hope for just a minute, even though I had no right to—you deserve a life without being tethered to people who couldn't be who you needed them to be. You deserved to be able to sit with your lover, touch them, kiss them out in public. You deserve a real life, not some fantasy nursed under the cover of darkness in snatches and secrets. I knew all those things but still, when I saw real life unfurling before my very eyes, it almost killed me.

Nice looking. About your height, thin build,

blond hair. And he made you laugh that beautiful laugh that I love so much.

When you turned to see what he was looking at, I froze. You saw, you knew right away that it was me, and I froze. I couldn't look you in the face. I couldn't not look. You were so handsome that day, the clean shave you sported for your new role really suited you. I felt like I had invaded your privacy—I know I did, yet still, I couldn't make myself get up and walk away... at least not yet. Not until I was sure you understood.

Did you understand?

Did you see what I was trying to tell you from across the way in those few seconds where we dared to hold each other's gaze? I think you did. I think you would have looked at me longer were it not for your lover's eyes turning toward your own, him saying something that required a response. I imagine that we would have walked toward each other if we had been alone, maybe talked for a while. We might have even embraced there in that park, let our hands trail down each other's arms as we released our grips, memorizing the way it felt. I imagine we might have stuttered around the words we really wanted to say and filled the awkward silence with meaningful stares, ones that we would have had to pull ourselves out of before we drew attention. But what then? Would we have decided to talk over dinner, catch up in some pub with a forgettable name? Would we have a nightcap together in one or the other's rooms? Would we have said we were sorry, said we'd made a mistake, awoken Nicole from her sleep to beg her to start again with us because we needed each other like we needed air to breathe? Who knows? What does it matter now? None of our 'what ifs' were meant to be.

You turned to answer him, and I made myself snap out of it. I left. I shouldn't have been there in the first place. I walked briskly, wanting to disappear, wanting a hole to open in the ground in front of me and suck me in. I was fast but not fast enough to miss you turning toward me again. From the corner of my eye your expression was unreadable. I didn't have the courage to face you head on to see it clearly.

There are lots of things I didn't have the courage to do over the past five years, Eric. Lots of situations I didn't know how to handle—lots of times when I was confused and didn't know what to do. But I know what to do now.

I would quote something from Shakespeare if I could think anything that worked for us, but I can't right now. I'd get it wrong anyway, and you'd laugh the way you always did. Maybe that would be ok though, me making you laugh just one more time.

I guess I only have one thing left to say and it's everything I feel wrapped up in a package and topped with a bow. After everything, whether I have the right to or not, I love you. I love you the way Sade talked about in that moody song she released in the late 80s. I hope you look to find out which one, Eric, and when you realize how well this song fits us, I hope you laugh out loud.

Forever yours,

Mark

Nicole,

Did you know that I couldn't breathe when I saw you? I don't think I ever told you how you took my breath away. Your eyes were so captivating, and your smile curved its way into my heart instantly. I couldn't look away from you and Eric trying to recover from bumping into each other. I couldn't look away from you no matter how hard I tried.

I have never felt more self-conscious than the moment you sat down next to me. It was as if I could feel everything, every inch of my skin, the hair on my forearms, every single one of my cells. And all of it, everything in me, reached toward you. I felt hot and cold at the same time; I felt acutely aware and distinctly numb. I remember wondering if something was wrong with me, wondering why I was having this weird reaction, and then I remember not caring if I was sick or losing my mind—literally not caring at all. Because you were there, sitting next to me, smelling wonderful, looking like an angel. Seriously. I know how ridiculous it sounds, but I have never seen a woman as beautiful as you, and it knocked me off my feet.

You know this part; I've never hidden how stunning you are to me. But did you know that the moment I saw you I knew I needed more? It was like finding out that you need to breathe air to live; I couldn't not take you in... if I didn't, I felt like I might die. This is still true. Dramatic, I know, but Nicole if you could feel the truth in it—if you could just jump inside me for a minute and feel how intensely I feel these words, it would blow your mind.

All of that makes it sound like I fell in love with your looks—like that's where it started and ended, but that couldn't be further from the truth. There is an honesty in you that has always appealed to me. Something so pure that no matter what was happening in our lives, it always shone through. It lit the way on some of our darkest days, like a beacon guiding us back to where we belonged. Back home to each other. You have always represented home to me, and I want to thank you for that.

You impress me, Nicole. More than anyone I

have ever known. I can imagine how prettily the color has risen to your cheeks at me writing that, but it's the truth. When we first met, you had embarked on a new career after years and years of doing something you didn't like. That took courage—a strength that not many people have. I know I don't have it. You sacrificed the equity you had built up over the years—the seniority, reputation, money—and decided to do the thing you wanted to do... the thing that made you happy. What if you hadn't? What if you had stayed in the old job, working long hours and hating every minute of it? What if you had decided that the money was more important? But no, not you... you wouldn't have. Even though you might not think this is true, you are one of those people who goes after what they want. Thank God you did, baby. If you hadn't, we might never have met.

I never felt more honored to be loved by you than when your book was published. Your words filling page after page, telling the story you had imagined beautifully—I am filled with pride just thinking about it again. I remember the three of us celebrating over the phone when you got the deal, us reading lines from it out loud to make sure it flowed the way you wanted it to, then laughing at ourselves when we tried to act out the parts. I remember seeing it in the bookstore and taking a picture to send to you. I remember hearing you read from one of my favorite sections in front of an audience of people who listened with rapt attention.

'The winds blow, flow like the river, dance like the stars in the still night, twinkling so subtly that you wonder if you ever saw them move at all. She moved like that all day, every day, but no one noticed. The one who would see wasn't looking anymore. The one who would see wasn't there at all.'

It's like poetry, honey. So beautiful, so eloquent, but still so accessible. I love the way you write. It was amazing listening to you address the crowd that day—all those people crammed into the back of the bookstore in San Jose to listen to you, meet you, take pictures with you. I wanted to get in line with my books in hand—a new one to buy from the store that day and my first one, the dog-eared one with the battered cover, the one I had read over and over again. I wanted you to sign it 'Love, Nicole' and I would know that message was just for me. I got there early but a line had already formed. I found myself stuck in the darkened hallway leading to the more obscure books on topics like alchemy and root vegetables—I know you think I'm kidding, but I'm not. I had time to leaf through a couple of them before you stood at the podium. I have never been more excited to be crammed in with a slew of strangers at the end of a line. They were all there to see you because you moved them in some way. I couldn't have been happier for you because you were getting the chance to live your dream. I was happy for myself because I was able to see it happen. And I guess things happen for a reason. Because I was pushed to the back, you didn't see me. That meant you didn't blush while you were reading, you didn't get uncomfortable about us meeting in front of so many people, and your children never saw anything at all.

When I saw them, a beautiful young girl who looked just like you and a handsome young man trying to navigate his early teens gracefully, I didn't know what to feel. I had so many emotions rolling around inside me, I don't know how I remained standing. I was thankful, so very thankful that so many people wanted to get a good seat to hear you speak and had gotten there so early that I was stuck in the shadowy overflow space because it would have been difficult to hide the love, the pride, the excitement of being there with you. I wouldn't have been able to hide the fear I was feeling about being there with them. I wasn't entirely sure the fear wasn't already showing on my face. So, I stayed back.

I was sad that I wouldn't be able to talk to you, tell you how amazing you were, have dinner with you that night—just be with you. I had been looking forward to seeing the look on your face when you noticed me. I couldn't wait to see your eyes light up. But then, as I stood inhaling the aftershave of a man who didn't know what moderation was, I knew all the things I had looked forward to wouldn't happen—absolutely shouldn't happen. I couldn't let you see me.

If you reacted, the kids would see it. They might not understand what was going on, but that didn't mean it wouldn't raise questions... questions that would be difficult to answer. I wanted you to be happy on your day, not sad, frustrated, or perhaps worse, scared. So, I hunkered down and leaned against the closest bookshelf, getting low enough that you couldn't make out any features if you noticed me at all.

And I listened.

You talked about how you and the kids were going to Alcatraz after the signing, and your son quipped about leaving his sister there. He's funny, just like his mom. I wish I could have known him.

I wish so many things and sometimes those desires seem possible—like they aren't fantasies, like they really could happen if we just tried. And we did try. We made it work as best we could; we did everything possible to hang on, to make it last even though it didn't seem like it would happen. Even *now I know that if I had called you or Eric and said the right things we would be back together again, in love the way we always have been. I'm not being over-confident—there is no pride in that statement at all. It's just the way we are, isn't it? We were always meant to be what we were. But I didn't. As much as I wish I had, I didn't. Something inside me knew I wouldn't, and that is the worst of all.*

I wish we had met earlier, when we didn't have people who depended upon us... when we were free to love each other. The problem is that the time I'm talking about—that my body aches for—never existed, did it? When I got married neither one of you were even legal. Hell, Eric was a kid. If we had met after our children were grown and too busy living their own lives to worry about what we did and how it might impact them, I'd be too old to enjoy what we have to the fullest extent. There was never a right time, never any time better than when it happened. Yet, it was the perfect time.

Do you remember our trip to St. Thomas? We made so many beautiful memories there, but one of my favorites probably won't come to mind for you at all. You were sitting on the balcony off the bedroom, reading. It was late afternoon. I don't know how long you had been out there, but the sun was low in the sky by the time I saw you, giving you a magnif-

icent backlight of orangy gold. The white balustrades stood out against the turquoise water in the distance, and that was beautiful enough, but it was the wild outcropping of that tree with the red blossoms—I think they called it Flamboyant Poinciana, over by the gates that brought it all together. It haloed your hair, seemed to radiate from you, the bright red flowers arranged in service of you. It was idyllic, perfect in ways I had never seen before. You didn't notice—you were engrossed in your book, and it was that perfect time of day, the time when the breeze reached the upper floor and pushed your hair from your forehead like gentle fingers. But I noticed. I don't think I've ever seen you look quite as lovely. I've carried that memory with me since that day.

I learned something when we got home, something for you, something that you might always remember. It's nothing, really. Most people wouldn't think it was anything special at all, but you will understand. After what you and Eric did for me, you will know how important it was to me to learn this for you. How important it was to get it right.

I wanted to say the words out loud to you, wanted you to hear my inflection when I did so you could understand the meaning fully... so you could understand me completely, but life had other plans for us. I almost blurted it out on that last day, *almost said it and begged you to stay even though I knew the decision to stop was all of ours to make. In the end I kept quiet, promised myself that if I were ever given the chance to say it again, I wouldn't hesitate. That chance never came, so writing it will have to do.*

Nonun aluum dahwo, jagiya. Saranghe.

It's better when you hear it, but I guess this will have to be ok. It means 'You are beautiful, baby. I love you.'

I've thought a lot about what could have been if circumstances were different. What if you had grown up on the west coast instead of me? What if I had been a truck driver, always on the road? What if Eric had been married with children instead of us? You can put whatever variable you want in place, but I think it would have always ended up the same way. Whether in a coffee shop outside Toronto or a convenience store somewhere in Nevada, we would have met. We would have seen each other waiting in line or by the gas pumps—are you envisioning Eric in a plaid work shirt and jeans, taking beef jerky off one of those hooks right now, because I am!—and it would have been the same. I would have been as dumbstruck as I was the moment I saw you, would have been stricken mute just like I was the moment you sat down next to me.

You will always be the woman of my dreams, baby. It was always and forever you.

Infinitely yours,

Mark

CHAPTER 32

The phone rang again just as she was closing the front door, the beep of the second call disrupting the flow of her words. If this was another work call—somebody else just wanting to 'let her know' about the delay, just wanting her to 'be aware' that the project might slip because the person who was supposed to be keeping track of all the moving parts had missed one—she might scream. OK. She understood. Whatever. She wasn't the kind of executive who wanted to be told about every little thing that was going on. She had put people in place to handle the coordination, the minutia, the detail. She liked the ideation, the roundtables, the brainstorming. Seeing all the concepts that had danced around in her head come to fruition in the final product was what Nicole looked forward to. All those little steps between inception and completion were reminiscent of a job she had left in her past, and like a loud, opinionated relative, she didn't exactly jump up and down when it came by to visit.

It was Saturday morning, 9 a.m. She had three birthday parties to get the kids to before 5 p.m., none of which did they have presents for. She had to get her son a haircut, too, and her daughter's heel was riding off the back of her flip flops, so she guessed she might as well take care of that as well. How long had that been going on, she had wondered when she noticed it the night before. Warm weather had been in full swing for at least two weeks already, but she hadn't noticed that the child's foot was about to start connecting with the ground with her every step if she didn't get into some new shoes. Nicole was thankful that the school year was over because she was sure her son would be in high waters were it not for shorts season. He was almost looking her in her eyes when he stood up.

It was Saturday morning.

Nicole had things to do.

“Hang on, Sherri, somebody's on my other line,” Nicole said, trying to hide the exasperation she felt but failing.

Nicole walked down her walkway, looking at the butterflies playing around the potentilla bushes she put in a few years ago. It had grown so much since then, the little yellow rose-like flowers cropping up on all sides of the bushes, so many more than the few that showed themselves that first year. She was proud of them, proud of herself for not killing them. He said it would be fine, talked about zones and light and other things that made her head hurt. He said she could do it, even though her thumb was more black than green. That had sent him to rivulets of laughter. Black thumb—the irony. Mark hadn't stopped laughing for at least three minutes.

Nicole took pictures in front of it, staging the kids just right so you could see the flowers prominently in the background, or capturing the house for their family scrapbook when the bushes were in bloom. She always took a picture of herself in front of it too, just her alone. Sometimes she was sitting in front of the bushes, sometimes she was in profile, smelling one of the flowers that looked so healthy. That picture didn't get posted on Facebook or make it into the scrapbook like the other ones did. Only two other people in the world ever saw those.

She hadn't taken a picture yet this year. She wasn't sure she should.

Untrue.

She knew she shouldn't. But still...

Nicole looked at her phone as she switched to the new call, smiling involuntarily when she saw the name.

MP.

Maybe Pink.

Changed from Pinky years before because Maybe Pink reminded her of their first night together and the way his champagne hair looked in the dim lighting of the restaurant, the way it felt against her cheek as he kissed her neck, the way it felt in her hands as she raked her fingers through it.

The phone rang again, and Nicole touched the smile that had spread across her lips. What timing... but then, it had always been that way with them.

"Hi," she said, her excitement betraying her. Nicole had wanted to keep calm, be aloof even, if ever they spoke again. They had said it was over, had called it quits for once and for all, and while none of them really wanted it to be that way, it was the only way that made sense.

Nicole had promised herself that she wouldn't call, and she hadn't. She had promised herself that she wouldn't try to see them, and she hadn't done that either, though not for a lack of trying. Sometimes she was thankful that she hadn't caught up with Mark when he was on the east coast for the Field Classic Tournament because that was really neither the time nor the place for them to see each other again. But sometimes—most times—she wished she hadn't been late getting there even though it might have meant she'd have to hide, to watch him from afar so his sons didn't see. She wished she had found out about the event sooner and gotten there before they hit maximum occupancy and started turning people away.

Nicole had told herself that she wouldn't look them up, wouldn't keep up with them... would just let it die, but she couldn't do that. That's how she found out about the Field Classic Tournament in the first place—Mark's youngest son had been featured in an article about their team making the cut. As luck would have it, there was a picture of him in there, too. Nicole wagered that there weren't a lot of Asian males with the last name Lewis, so she assumed he was Mark's son. That, and his smile, lopsided like his father's, gave it away.

And Eric, she had looked him up more than once also. After creeping on Mark's son—Nicole definitely felt like a stalker, but she had to do it—she looked to see what Eric was up to. Eric was getting a fair amount of press for his stage work, and every time Nicole read something new about him, her heart filled with pride. He deserved the attention, the praise, for people to see how amazing the man she loved was, even if they only got a glimpse. She wanted to see a show, actually went to New York with a friend who wanted to see The Blue Man Group in the hopes that she could get tickets to Eric's show and see it later, with or without her, but he wasn't there. He was in Australia doing a show in Melbourne they said, and he wouldn't be back for months.

Australia.

A world away.

Nicole remembered how her heart hurt hearing those words, but wow, how quickly the pain was chased away by the pleasure that only being happy for someone else getting their just due can elicit. Eric had made it, and she was ecstatic. That, and so very proud of him.

She tried to act like seeing Eric's name pop up on her phone hadn't excited her, like her skin wasn't thrumming with electricity, like the wall she had built and reinforced time and time again hadn't just evaporated, disappearing like a mirage, but it was no use.

He had her in the palm of his hand. and he hadn't even said a word.

"I—I was just thinking about..."

"Ba...baby, some—something..."

"W-what's wrong?"

The giddiness that had taken over her body moments before was rapidly being replaced by trepidation... trepidation that was approaching stark fear at an alarming rate.

"Eric... baby, what happened?"

"I don't... I don't really know, I..."

Eric took a deep breath. He had scared the hell out of Nicole. He was scaring the hell out of himself. He needed to calm down so he could explain.

"I'm not... I'm not making any sense. I'm sorry, baby. I know I'm not making any sense. But I just read the letter and I don't... Nicole... I don't know what it means. I don't understand what he's... he couldn't have... do you think he would—"

"Wha-what are you... Eric... what..."

Nicole had walked down to the mailbox, following the trajectory her body had already been on when she had walked out of the house. She had intended to grab the mail then get in the car and start the errands. Even as distracted as she had been, she still found herself in front of the mailbox, autopilot guiding her steps, but she no longer wanted to be there. She didn't want to open it. Suddenly it seemed like poison.

"Do you think he's ok? I can't even be sure that something actually happened, the way he wrote it was so... oh my god, baby, I don't know..."

Nicole opened her mailbox while Eric spoke in fragments, trying to keep himself from going off the deep end. There were several thin envelopes inside—likely bills. There was a flyer, a coupon circular, the gas readout after they filled the tank the night before. But there was something else, a thicker envelope. Nondescript, white, sealed. She couldn't see the handwriting nor the return address, but she didn't have to. Eric's worry had taken a turn towards panic in her ear, raising his voice an octave and speeding it up to an almost indecipherable pace, as if in confirmation.

The envelope seemed to glow in the darkened mailbox.

Nicole was afraid of it.

Nicole was afraid.

"We should c-call," Nicole said, not recognizing her own voice. She took a step away from the mailbox, letting the door flop open.

"Yeah. Yeah," Eric said, sounding happy to have a task to do. "I'll conference him in. Then he can explain all this shit he wrote. He—" Eric eclipsed his own words as he broke off to call Mark.

Silent.

Nicole could hear herself breathing, could see her chest heaving at the bottom of her line of sight. She could see the open mailbox, the gaping maw that it was, the bitch that it was, holding a letter she never wanted, didn't ask for, would rather pluck her eyes out than read. With every second that she waited for Eric to merge the calls, her chest heaved faster.

One second.

Two.

Three.

Four—

Eric's voice didn't sound right. He sounded far away, like his mind had detached itself from the sinking ship it was on and had left his emotions to handle whatever came next.

"He didn't..."

"Baby... tell me," Nicole begged, a mantra forming in a whisper. "Tell me, baby... please... tell me..."

Nicole didn't see the woman waving at her as the she drove by, eyes curious as to why she was standing so far away from her mailbox... almost properly in the road. Nicole didn't hear the garage door opening or see her daughter duck under it, arms held out on either side of herself, shoulders raised, eyebrows furrowed—the universal sign for confusion on display. The blackness of the inside of the mailbox seemed alive, seemed to swirl and writhe, like oil heating up in a pan.

"Eric!"

Direct.

Shrill.

She didn't mean to.

She didn't mean to.

She didn't mean—

"It went straight to voicemail," he said, his voice small. "I—I didn't leave one. We can't leave one—"

"M-Maybe he's asleep. It's early there, right? Like 6 a.m. He's asleep, that's all. And maybe, maybe he keeps his phone on his desk. Didn't he say that? He keeps it on his desk, so if he is in bed, he wouldn't hear it ring, so he just doesn't know we called, that's all. Eric. That's all. He doesn't know we called because... and why would he think we would call? He wouldn't be expecting us to call so he wouldn't keep his phone close because we said wouldn't because there's no... no...... we said...we—"

She was thankful Eric cut her off because she felt like she would have kept talking until she couldn't speak anymore.

"It never rang," Eric said, recovering for her more so than for himself. They were taking turns at panic, it seemed, and now it was her turn to go over the edge.

"It didn't ring, baby. It went straight to voicemail, like it does when the phone is dead."

Dead.

Nicole almost dropped her phone at the sound of the word.

Eric gasped after it came out of his mouth.

Dead.

Dead?

"Baby, please don't. W-we don't know anything yet, please Nicole, don't..."

Nicole heard the slow whine but hadn't realized she was the one making it. She sobbed, the effort to stop her own fear from taking over resulting in the most gut-wrenching sound she could remember herself making since... since they had said goodbye.

"No," Nicole said unbidden. "Eric, no, this can't be—"

"I love you. Baby, I love you," Eric needed to say the words, needed her to hear them, wanted to say them to Mark... was afraid he wouldn't ever get the chance to again.

"He's asleep. He's asleep. He has to be. Baby... oh god, Eric. He's gotta be al—"

The horn blared in the garage, setting Nicole's very teeth on edge.

"Nicole, baby, listen to me," Eric said frantically, his tone changing to something more commanding. If he knew her at all, he was sure that her temper had flared before her mind was able to catch up and she was about to snap at the kids. misplacing her emotions and probably shocking the hell out them.

"Oh my god, what're you—" Nicole hissed.

Eric was right. Nicole's voice was angry but laced with so much fear that Eric's heart hurt.

"They don't know this is happening," Eric said as calmly as he could. "You aren't angry with them at all, baby. Please, just... calm down before you respond."

Nicole broke then. Eric had reached through the phone to caress her check and settle her in a way that no one else ever had. Even after everything, their connection was so strong, it was staggering.

"We can't go just yet," she heard herself saying, her voice strangled through her tears. She had turned her back to the house so they couldn't see that she was crying, but she was. She couldn't stop herself. She was afraid, so very afraid.

Eric could hear the kids' protests over the phone. He whispered to Nicole as she spoke to the kids, telling her that it was ok, that she was ok. He counted it a win that she never raised her voice, but her voice was raw... she was barely holding on to any semblance of calm. It broke his heart that he couldn't take her in his arms, be there for her in any way that she needed.

"Eric," Nicole said, her voice recovering just enough to keep the wobble at bay. "It can't... this can't..."

"I'm afraid to look, but we have to. We'll never know if we don't."

Nicole emitted a fresh sob that nearly ripped Eric apart.

"He can't be..."

"I have to know," Eric said resolutely.

Nicole had made her way back into the house, grabbing her laptop off the kitchen counter and sequestering herself in the sitting room. Someone had left it on when they closed the top, and she had never been more thankful that one of her rules had been broken. They set off to their work silently, both searching for something they never expected to look for, something they didn't want to find. It didn't take as long as they wanted it to—there was no need for keywords and elaborate search strings. Just his name. Technology was both a blessing and a curse.

The tribute page was filled with comments about how wonderful a man Mark was, how helpful and genuinely kind. There were posts from his colleagues talking about how good he was at his job; comments from college buddies remembering the good old days. People from his neighborhood talked about how charitable Mark was. Parents whose kids were teammates of his sons talked about how sorely his absence would be felt at the games and tailgates. Nicole vowed to read every one of them one day; she wanted to read the notes that people left about Mark; she needed to. But not now. She couldn't process it now, couldn't understand that all those people knew one of the men she loved with everything she had was dead and she hadn't had a clue. Shouldn't she have known, felt something break in her soul? How could life be so cruel that someone she felt inextricably tied to could leave this earth while she carried on blissfully unaware? Nicole was bewildered, so lost she didn't know if she would ever find her way back.

Eric's tears blurred his vision every time he tried to read the words. His mind wouldn't allow him to process anything more than the first sentence of the obituary describing his love as a distant thing, someone else, someone at arm's length. When he found the funeral home hosting Mark's funeral, when he saw Mark's picture on their recent obituaries page, Eric didn't understand. It wasn't that he was confused by what he saw, wasn't that he couldn't put two and two together—it was just that he loved Mark so he *couldn't* be dead. He couldn't be dead because they were all going to get back together again at some point. Eventually. Later. Even if they had to wait until Nicole's children went to college, they were going to do it. They had said they wouldn't, but those were just words, and they all knew it. They had tried to turn their hearts away from each other enough times to know it was all bullshit and that they would be back together when the time was right. They had to be. They were meant to be.

Right?

So how could the obituary be about Mark?

His Mark?

Their Mark?

How could all of those people be talking about Mark, his love, one of their three? It wasn't right—it couldn't be right. But there he was. The picture they had chosen was stunning. Mark was standing on the deck of a boat, the wind blowing his hair around his head. The sun had kissed his skin to a beautiful gold, and his eyes were squinted against the wind, one them partially obscured by his windswept brown hair. He had facial hair instead of the clean shave Eric was used to, a scruffy mustache and mouche beard framing a relaxed smile. Eric felt fresh tears spilling over his eyelids to wet his cheeks. The picture... whoever had captured Mark in that moment, whoever had chosen it for this final page of his book, knew him. That person knew Mark every bit as well as he and Nicole did, knew what he looked like when he was at his happiest, his most peaceful. That person might have shared moments like that with him, been able to bask in them as he and Nicole had, loving every second and hoping for more. Perhaps they'd *had* more moments like that with Mark than them. Perhaps they'd had all the moments, and it was Eric and Nicole who were left on the outside yearning, craving, wanting more.

"Mark," Eric groaned low from somewhere deep inside himself. "Oh god."

"It's Monday," Nicole said in response. "M-Monday."

She sounded like she was choking on the words as they got stuck in her throat, unwilling to come out.

Eric closed his eyes at her words, feeling a sense of bitter loss wash over him. When he opened them again, Eric's eyes floated up to the dates beneath Mark's name, and a sob wrenched free from his throat.

He died two days ago.

Two whole days.

Days he couldn't remember. Days where he lived as if everything was normal, as if all were right in the world. But it wasn't. It wasn't all right. The world had ended, and Mark was dead, and he and Nicole were left with memories of his smile and his touch and they never said goodbye.

Two whole days.

"Mon-Monday? Oh... I..."

One of his loves was dead.

Much Ado About Nothing opened at Shakespeare in the Park on Monday.

He just paid for the furniture for the place on The Vineyard.

Mark was dead.

Mark was dead.

Fuck.

Mark was dead.

Two days.

Mark was dead for two days, and he had breathed and smiled and laughed about nothing, about stupid, stupid unimportant things while Mark lay cold.

Mark was dead.

We are dead.

Mark.

"G-getting a flight n-n-n-..." he stuttered.

Inner Eric had taken over and his hands had complied, opening his usual travel website so he could look for the earliest flight into LAX.

Nothing.

Not until Monday, when it would be too late.

"I found one. I'll be there tomorrow night. I don't—I don't know how I'll explain..." Nicole said, rambling.

Mark is dead.

"No flights," Eric said, his voice louder than he intended. "How can there not be any fucking flights?"

'To where?'

Nicole heard the voice through the phone and jumped, startled. Eric inhaled sharply, surprised as well.

'Where're we going?'

The voice was playful, happy go lucky.

Male.

Nicole hated him instantly.

"N-nowhere. Look, let me do this and—"

Nicole was hot. Angry as hell. It was irrational, hypocritical in so many ways, and she knew it was, but she couldn't stop it. She was not going to listen to Eric talking to his new lover while Mark lay dead. She didn't think she could stomach another second of it.

"It's fine, Eric. Go ahead and talk to him. We're done here." Nicole's words were laced with venom, and she hated herself for it.

"Wait... Wait, Ni—"

"Careful! Don't say my name and spill your dirty little secret!" she chastised mirthlessly.

"Nicole, don't do this. We need—"

"There is no *we*, Eric. There wasn't before this call and," her own words felt like they were ripping her to shreds as they poured out of her mouth, "there damn sure isn't now."

Eric was panting. He felt like he couldn't breathe.

"I n-need... you..."

She wanted to tell him how much she needed him too, that she was sorry, so sorry for lashing out, that she was so upset about Mark, about them, about everything that she didn't know what she was saying. She started to, to stop running down the path that took her further away from him and jumping onto the one that led to his embrace, but then his new lover asked him if he was ok, his voice full of concern. Eric must have looked awful. She imagined tears streaking his face, his eyes bloodshot. She had seen him look like that only one time and hoped she would never witness that again. But she wasn't *witnessing* it, not really. Eric was on the other side of the phone and Mark was gone and the whole world had turned upside down.

"Please, baby..." Eric said through a sniffle, and Nicole's heart broke, but then the man that had Eric's heart now spoke again, more urgently this time, closer. He told Eric it was ok, that whatever it was, they would get through it together. A sob broke free from Nicole's mouth, sounding loud to her own ears.

Nicole was happy that someone was there to comfort Eric now, when he needed it most. But she couldn't bear to hear it.

Even though she didn't want to, even though she felt like she was forming words into knives and stabbing out with them, drawing blood with every thrust, she said irrevocably,

"Goodbye, Eric."

Nicole heard Eric call her name, but she followed through, disconnecting the call without hesitating. She closed her eyes to find Mark and Eric waiting there for her, only they were smiling as they so often were when they were together. Smiling as if they were happier than they had ever been. Smiling as if they had all the time in the world to do so.

When she opened her eyes the sun had shifted in the sky, drawing short shadows out from everything it touched. Whether from a separation in the clouds or God's own finger of judgment, the sun illuminated the mailbox like a spotlight.

CHAPTER 33

Eric turned the corner faster than he intended to, but that was ok. Most of the people approaching the funeral home were coming from the other direction, where the restaurants and specialty shops lined the cross street. The street he was on led deeper into a quaint little neighborhood that appeared untouched by the modern covetousness that marred newer communities.

Mark had lived in this neighborhood.

Eric figured that he'd had to live close by. He couldn't imagine the woman Mark had described—homegrown, shy, domestic in a way that felt retro rather than new age—going all the way across town, not if services were nearby, so Eric figured he was close to the place where Mark had laid his head every night, the place he shared with his family. He drove to the funeral home early to get his bearings, then put Mark's address into the GPS.

Bingo.

It was a cute little suburban community with brick sidewalks and trees old enough to have overhanging branches that met in the middle, shading the street with a heart-shaped arch. A throwback to a time when you shared a cup of sugar with a neighbor and waved hello to everyone who walked by. It was the kind of neighborhood where you could walk to the market for your groceries every day or to the movies at the single screen theater on Saturday nights. Eric smiled as he took it in. It was the kind of place that would have suited Mark to a tee, convenient in that it had everything he would ever need at his fingertips—a barber with an authentic pole, even; a post office; a hardware store, restaurants... a funeral home—and quaint in that it appeared to house nothing of import on its sleepy streets, all the bright lights and neon signs reserved for some other place, one interested in the attention those things brought with them. Eric wasn't the slightest bit surprised to find that Mark's house wasn't even a mile away from where he stood.

Did Nicole know that too?

Was she planning to walk in front of it, to fantasize that if she rang the doorbell, Mark would answer and sweep her into his arms... the same way he himself had imagined it? Eric hoped she wouldn't go to the house. He didn't want her to feel the pain he had felt when he drove by and looked at the modest Cape Cod with its meticulously manicured lawn that Eric knew Mark ended up having to pay a landscaping company to maintain after numerous failed attempts at doing it himself. Eric didn't want Nicole to think about how it might feel to stand in front of the house and contemplate what flowers would look nice among the hostas that had finally taken root to border the bushes or wonder what it would be like to sit in the backyard and drink iced tea with Mark. There would never be magenta azaleas for Mark to prune, would never be posies for Mark to pick for her because Nicole wanted some color in the dining room. Because there would never be any more Mark.

Nicole *had* walked in the direction of Mark's house; Eric caught a glimpse of her making the turn in that direction from the steps as he came out of the funeral home. Eric had parked on the other side so he could avoid going by Mark's house again even though he knew he had to do it, had to see the place where Mark smiled, laughed, lived a life Eric was not a part of one last time. But now Nicole was going that way, and he wouldn't let her do it alone. He couldn't.

But they shouldn't be together now. Not there, so close to where Mark used to lay his head. There were too many people around, too many neighbors that used to share stories with him by their mailboxes or on each other's decks in the summer, too many people who had been to enough of Mark's impromptu get-togethers to recognize the people in his inner circle and realize that they had never seen his nor Nicole's faces even once. It was more than probable that somebody would notice there were two people milling around that shouldn't be there, two outsiders who didn't belong even if they felt like they did, two people who...

She had looked at him.

Mark's wife had looked at him when he was leaving the room.

She had probably been looking at him the whole time he was standing at Mark's casket, absently at first, but then with a pointed intention that would have made him shrink away had he noticed it. Because it was wrong. It was all wrong. Eric shouldn't have been there. He had no right to be there, no right to encroach that space, no right to see them and be seen by them.

But Eric had to say goodbye.

He had to touch Mark one more time.

He had to.

He knew he couldn't let anyone see, but he couldn't not be there.

Eric had been calm about it, well, as calm as one could be when someone they loved lay dead in a casket surrounded by white lilies and potted gardenias that had glossy waxen leaves so green, the color didn't seem real, like an artist had painted them on. He tempered his tears when they threatened to spill over onto his cheeks, steadied his legs when all they wanted to do was buckle beneath him. He didn't allow himself to react, not even when he could feel Nicole trembling beside him, her body rippling with emotion as she too struggled to keep it together, to not wail out the pain so sharp it felt like her flesh was being cut with a rusty knife, to not press her lips against Mark's to share her warmth, to share her life—to not scream loud enough to break the stained glass half rounds atop the Tuscany windows that lined the wall.

Curious those... the Tuscany windows being there, in that place. Eric remembered Nicole opening the Tuscany windows that overlooked the marina in Delray one early morning, the sun catching her hair and kissing her skin. And then Mark was kissing her, following the sunlight's path as it trailed down her cheek, the line of her jaw, the angle of her neck. Mark's hand rested on hers and coaxed it away from the ornate knob, a bejeweled thing done in antique copper, and interlaced their fingers effortlessly, like he had done it a thousand times. Like he was *made* to do it.

Eric tried to ignore, tried not to feel how hard Mark's hand was now.

How cold.

Eric bit back a sob, felt his chest heave with the effort.

Goodbye, my love.

As Eric followed Nicole's path out of the door, he realized that what they had not been was quick. He wondered if Mark's family had studied them as they mourned, wondering who they were, what they were doing there, why two people who were strangers to them were having such a reaction. Did they know enough to be concerned, to look at them with a careful eye, to run at them from behind with balled fists and words that would cut like knives? Or were they apathetic, waiting for the chance to be alone, anxious for it but reluctant at the same time? Because being alone with Mark now would mean they were that much closer to having to say goodbye forever. Eric felt more than knew the answer lay somewhere in the middle.

Eric gave the family the center aisle as he left the room just as Nicole had, his heart screaming as if being pulled apart while his legs carried him to the door with brisk strides. He made sure he looked away so as not to be remembered, didn't even offer a kind word to the family as he retreated because he didn't trust his voice not to quaver. He felt rude and embarrassed and disappointed in himself for such behavior, but there was nothing to be done about it. How could he ever explain his tears? How could he hide how much he loved Mark, how much he had always loved him, how the thought of being without him was driving him mad?

Eric opened the door not two minutes after Nicole had left the room where they were forced to leave one of their three behind. He had almost escaped the room and walked into the foyer without incident, would have made it were it not for the slow-closing door, but fate was cruel in more ways than Eric could count.

He caught Mark's wife's eye.

She was staring at him.

Eric's first thought was that Mark had been right. His wife was a beautiful woman. His second thought was that this beautiful woman, the one who had lived with Mark, loved him, had him in ways that he and Nicole could only dream of, was sharing space with him now... *seeing* him.

Did she notice anything as she looked upon Eric's face? Did she wonder who he was, wonder why she couldn't remember him from anywhere?

Did it make her nervous that she couldn't?

Eric was sure, as Mark's wife leveled her eyes squarely on him, the answer was yes.

Questions swam in her eyes, but he would not be there to answer any of them, and there would be no way to find him once he walked out of that funeral home. This goodbye was final.

Eric left. He turned the corner fast and found Nicole moving in his direction, a sudden fright coloring her cheeks.

Eric stopped short to avoid colliding with her.

"It's ok," Eric said as quietly as he could even thought there was hardly anyone around.

A half smile spread across Nicole's lips, and she looked away but was immediately sorry for it. Nicole stared at the ground, Eric at her profile. Neither was sure of what to say when the only words they could think of were 'I love you,' but they somehow didn't seem enough. They took turns wanting to touch, leaning toward each other, hands twitching at their sides, desperate to connect, to soothe and be soothed, but they didn't allow themselves the comfort—

they didn't allow themselves to help each other mourn. And there were reasons. Of course they had reasons to stay away, reasons to keep their distance, but none of them would have mattered if one of them would have just given in. Maybe that was why neither of them did. To do it now like it was easy, simple, the most logical thing ever, would be to spit on Mark's grave.

After what seemed like forever, Nicole took her cell phone out of her purse and opened the Uber app. Eric watched as she arranged for a ride stiffly, fingers moving of their own volition, mind struggling to remain present. Even though he knew he should, Eric couldn't take his eyes off her. She was right there, just out of his reach. But as he watched her on the phone planning her next step, she seemed so far away.

Eric leaned against the fence. What else could he do? He didn't know where he should go or what he should do in that moment. Leaving meant saying goodbye to Mark, his sweetheart with the warmest eyes and the most endearing wit... forever. Even though he knew he couldn't go back inside, would never be in Mark's presence again, Eric felt rooted in place, stuck by the weight of his sadness. He wasn't ready to leave Mark forever, even if there were eyes boring holes into his back.

And Nicole. He wasn't ready to be away from her either. He would gladly have stayed with her, mourned with her, been together for once and for all, but suddenly, even as he thought it, even as the words formed in his head, the idea of Eric being with Nicole now, brought together by grief to make it work properly this time... it just left him cold. Mark would have wanted them to do it; he knew without a shadow of a doubt that Mark would have loved it if they found themselves together after all was said and done. But would they be enough? Could they ever do enough, laugh enough, love enough to fill the empty space Mark had left between them or would they always, through every second of their time together, be staring into the black hole, wondering if it might be better if they jumped in?

An older couple dressed in black walked up the sidewalk, covering the ground between them slowly.

That made two more people who saw them together.

A young girl ran up the block ahead of her parents who were barely just rounding the corner on the sidewalk down the hill from where they stood.

Foot traffic was starting to get heavy.

Eric looked at his phone to check the time, the heavy weight of loss pressing on his chest, on his mind, on his soul. Fifteen minutes before the hour. The service was about to begin. He couldn't stop the wet gasp that escaped his lips.

The little girl stopped between them at the sound of her mother's voice admonishing her to stop running, don't go too far ahead, telling her to wait for them. Her black lace dress swished around her short legs clad in white tights. She liked the way it moved so she spun on the chunky heels of her black patent leather shoes, watching as the lace made intricate shadows on the ground as the sun poked through the clouds to shine down on her. She was dressed up that day, wearing black instead of pink or yellow as was her usual—her favorite—but she didn't know why. She was completely unaware of the color's significance, its intention, or meaning. She knew only the exhilaration of a twirl in the breeze, noticed only that even though the dress moved the same way her others did, this color sucked up the light, consumed it like food. She only knew that she matched her mommy that day like on Mommy and Me day at school. And that the lace made pretty patterns on the ground.

Eric looked beyond her at Nicole, whose eyes had begun to tear again—had they ever really stopped?—and whose bottom lip was caught between her teeth.

A nondescript car pulled up and idled, waiting.

Neither Nicole nor Eric would have noticed it if the little girl's voice hadn't pulled them out of their fugue.

"Ok, Mommy," she said exasperatedly. "I'll wait."

Nicole's eyes darted toward the car and then to her cell phone. When her eyes returned to Eric's, they were even sadder than they had been before.

The little girl dropped to her knees and picked up a rock that called to her, opening a hole in her tights, and starting a run that her mother would be angry about when she saw it.

Eric took a deep breath and let it out through his nose, dipping his chin once in acknowledgement... only once. They couldn't risk more than that.

"Don't get dirty," the mother said, her voice elevated to compensate for the distance and punctuated by the effort of trying to get up the hill and to her daughter quickly.

"Ok," the little girl responded knowing that dirty is what she had already gotten and there was nothing to be done about that now.

Nicole's mouth dropped open as she pondered the moment... their very last moment. She looked at Eric and then at the façade of the funeral home behind him, felt a wave of despair hit so hard she nearly gasped. It was over. Finished. Done.

Done.

Pure laughter, happiness, joy?

Done.

Future, the potential for a release from fear, an acceptance of the reality that had unceremoniously knocked them all on their backsides in the most amazing of ways?

Done.

Mark was gone.

Eric, for all intents and purposes, was too, though as she looked into his eyes she realized that he didn't know it yet.

They were done.

Water under the bridge.

Their love?

Dust in the wind.

Nicole wanted an ever after with Eric and Mark so badly, had made the mistake of thinking she could have it—she might have been old by the time she got it... it might only be for a season, but she wanted it, nonetheless. She reminded herself of the stories that filled the books, the great love stories that talked of years passing between kisses, lifetimes spent before lovers could embrace. And hadn't it been that way for them already? Hadn't they had to wait to be together, coordinating, scheming, plotting just to eke out a few hours? What had seemed like fantasy, the product of some lonely heart's imagination, had been their reality.

Nicole had sold herself on the idea that she would have Eric and Mark again, would have them body and soul, without restriction, without a care. Someday.

Had she become too brazen? Had she settled into the thought of an expected future too securely and not seen what was right in front of her eyes? Mark was dead by his own hand. Eric had moved on. It seemed Nicole was waiting by herself for a future that was never meant to be.

Icarus.

Every time.

Would they have taken her back if she had asked for their forgiveness? Would they have listened if she admitted she had taken them, this thing they had, for granted? Would Eric accept her apology for being jealous, being mean, being dismissive now? Would Mark have allowed her to show him how much she wanted him in her life... how much she needed him to stay? Would they forgive her distractions, her prioritizations, the cold shoulder that she so often gave when reality hit her hard? Would they have still wanted her if they knew how she told herself to forget about them, set them aside, cast them out like demons if that's what it took? Would they have loved her as much if they knew how she tried to replace their faces with her husband's, tried to replace their love with his?

Nicole felt a chill cross her, raising gooseflesh on her skin as she thought things she never wanted to under one of her lovers' unsuspecting gazes. She wanted to turn her mind off, wanted to beg for it to stop, to show mercy, but still the questions came, ones with no answers—at least not ones she could bear to face.

Would they have wiped away her tears, embraced her, surrounded her with love if they knew how she tried to curse their names, tried to ruin the memories of them by finding fault and casting judgment even though each and every one she ascribed to them applied to her as well?

When she spoke their names in her sleep, awoke with the feeling of their kisses on her lips, when she daydreamed a memory they shared, reaching for them before realizing where she was and what she was doing... when she longed for them, cried for them bitterly, wouldn't get out of bed sometimes because another day without them seemed intolerable—would that have been enough to turn their heads, to make them come back, to make them love her again?

Would they have stayed if they knew that no matter what she tried, it was always them?

Nicole bit her lip to stave off the tears that threatened to blur her vision and let her eyes take in Eric once more.

Her Eric.

Her love.

Together they stood in a place where they never belonged to say goodbye to their third, their love, their future.

Nothing to be done about that now. No, not anymore. Because it was over.

They were over.

The little girl waited, fidgeting, skipping, spinning in her black lace dress, while her parents hurried up the hill... while Eric watched his love walk toward the Uber, open the door, and drive away.

CHAPTER 34

Ryan watched as Eric and Nicole stood outside of the funeral home, their faces distorted by the stained textured glass. He stepped forward to get a better view of Nicole, who faced the funeral home most directly, and was disappointed by what he saw. Disappointed and curious. Her face was a battlefield of emotions. She showed a quiet defeat most clearly, but that was for Eric's benefit, he knew. What intrigued Ryan most was what lay beneath the surface, the emotions that either Eric couldn't see or wouldn't allow himself to understand.

Pain, loss, despair—those were apparent. They worked together to create the mask she wore that might look like a resignation to the casual observer and generalized empathy to the passerby. Ryan was pleased with that—he had worked hard to create that response to the deaths that persisted, and he was happy to see it called up appropriately. But the confusion that lingered just beneath—the uncertainty about what was going on... the uncertainty about her own reaction was what baffled Ryan. Like a mixed breed dog, one designed to protect and the other to attack, Nicole's mind continued to confuse her. The mixed signals threw Nicole so far off track that, though she always struggled to make her way back, she never quite got back on her path.

And Mark.

What was reflected in his eyes troubled Ryan greatly. It made him refocus, almost made him hit pause before things had even gotten started. Because it was still there, after so many world restructures, so many reboots. It was still fucking there.

With a sigh, he acknowledged that Nicole's response wasn't the only thing that had remained in place from previous runs this latest iteration. Regardless of what they had done to change the scenario, intensify the risk, amplify the loss, the outcome kept finding its way to this point.

He had tried new scripts, environment immersions, hypnotic implantation, identity subversions, tissue regeneration. He had switched their roles, added backstories the likes of which horror authors could only imagine, played God in so many ways, he had lost count. But still they ended up here.

At Mark's funeral.

It wasn't always only Mark laying in a casket in the funeral home, but he was always among the dead. Sometimes Eric was in his own casket across town, two states over from where Nicole and Mark were, on another continent—wherever he ended up. When that happened Nicole was rendered just as useless as they were—her head wasn't together enough to attend either of their funerals when they both died... she was usually too far gone, despondent, irretrievable within the play. And that was good, Ryan supposed. He was sure that if the higher ups were watching, if they could get Nicole alone, they would pull the plug on her, destroy the specimen's native psyche so badly that Ryan couldn't reuse it. And after so much effort to get it right, after he had done so much work on her cognitive suite, that would be a catastrophe.

One could argue that he hadn't done enough, and they would be right. He didn't have an answer for why she couldn't do the one thing she was supposed to... why she *never* could.

One could argue that he had failed with Mark too, and he would add an enthusiastic 'hell yeah' to that assessment as well, if push came to shove. Mark's behavior wouldn't deviate at all. He was always the one to throw a wrench in the plans, always the one to burn the house down at the first glimmer of trouble. No. Not trouble. It was insight, and Ryan might as well acknowledge it for what it was. It pissed Ryan off to no end, but still it was an amazing phenomenon. Mark always guessed right. And the others were always swayed by him.

Curious, indeed.

Eric played his role just fine, he always did; Ryan was beginning to think that some of his programming had been a little too on the nose with him. He was as sympathetic as Ryan wanted him to be—that his temperament vacillated somewhere between Nicole's and Mark's was actually a good thing, at least it would be if Nicole did what she was supposed to do.

Ryan surveyed Nicole and Eric's postures outside the funeral home. They had not moved—the Uber was in place, the child still played between them, the parents were still en route. No other mourners had entered the space. Nicole had a clear shot—she wouldn't even hit the kid this time if she did it fast. But she didn't even have a gun on her, Ryan knew —she had never taken it out of the drawer in the island in her kitchen this time around. Not even once.

And again, Mark lay dead in the casket behind him.

"It happened again," Maureen said, scratching at her forehead under the veil before finally taking it and the fascinator it was attached to off, wishing she had talked Ryan into adding more character profiles into the run instead of dressing the part of the grieving family each and every time.

'Authenticity,' he had told her early on when she protested some costume or another... perhaps the Madonna-esque '80s one, replete with big bows and fingerless gloves.

'It will help them stay present if real elements are scattered throughout,' he had continued.

Authenticity my ass, she thought. She was sure that he secretly liked torturing them... or was it that he enjoyed the view?

Ryan hummed noncommittally.

"Something's faulty in the simulator code," Jason said, the glee in his voice so thinly veiled, Ryan was sure Maureen heard it as clearly as he did.

"It's not the simulator code," Ryan snapped, barely keeping his temper in check. But he'd better. If he wanted to get out of this without watching years of work go down the drain, he'd better hold his tongue.

"Well, *something's* faulty..."

Ryan could hear the smirk in his brother's voice without having to see it. Jason was always ready with a reply, a jeer, some sarcastic comeback, and it didn't help that this project had given him ample opportunities to take shots. Ryan shook his head and bit back his first response. It was full of expletives anyway, and if Jason had taken the high ground, using his big boy words instead of the base language Ryan knew he had in his arsenal, Ryan might have slugged him. In front of Maureen. And that would have been bad.

He locked eyes with Jason.

Jason was almost brimming over with self-righteousness.

His brother was an asshole.

"It isn't the simulator," Ryan started but was interrupted this time by Maureen. She had walked over to Mark's casket and was peering down at the CGI.

"No, it isn't the simulator, Ryan; you are right about that."

She got close, almost nose to nose with the image of Mark laying in the casket.

"Such attention to detail," she marveled, her voice almost a whisper. "Seems like you should be able to just reach out and," Maureen reached out her hand to cup Mark's cheek and bit her bottom lip when her palm passed through his face.

"Truly amazing work," Maureen said, staring at the flower on Mark's lapel, the muted golden hint of the pinstripe in his jacket. She regarded the hands, the manicured fingernails with neat cuticles, for god's sake... mind-blowing. She breathed her appreciation—just a puff of breath, but it spoke volumes—before standing to face Ryan. "No one could ever challenge your skill, Ryan—"

Jason had to bite his tongue. All that fawning over a product that didn't work turned his stomach. Pretty wasn't enough.

"There are a few kinks to work out with the emotion

grid," Ryan said, ignoring the praise in favor of spewing out anything and everything he could to make his case. He was running out of road, and he knew it.

"It— I just need more time to sort out the different scenarios."

"You've had *years* to work with them... yet Mark keeps killing himself." She looked back at Mark's visage in the casket, the Christmas tree box that it was in reality, once more before walking toward Ryan. "I almost don't care why anymore."

"But we *should* care," Ryan said, hating the desperate quality sneaking its way into his voice. "Why he's doing it and why Nicole reacts to it the way she does are all that matters."

Ryan turned to watch as Nicole got into the Uber, leaving Eric on the sidewalk abandoned... again. He sighed, realizing there was nothing left to learn from this attempt, silently hoping that he would be able to start another one—this time observational only. Because maybe the introduction of live variables *did* change the simulation. Maybe it was some kind of parallel realism effect that created a kind of cognitive distortion—something that altered free will and fed upon the assumptions of the sample group. It could be that they were responding to the stimuli unwittingly introduced by Maureen and Jason and even his own biases and that none of this had been free will at all. Ryan almost got excited about the prospect, even felt his eyebrows unfurl and a smile begin to creep across his lips until his mind doused the flame, trotting out the memory of Mark lying at Nicole's feet, the sword from the mantle of a lover's retreat nestled in the Appalachian mountains lying beside him. The rusted blade, stained with blood almost to the hilt, told the story of how Mark had lunged for it, wrenched it off the hooks that held it in place, and raked it jaggedly across his throat. Ryan had been so shocked that he tried to staunch the bleeding, dropping to his hands and knees and pressing his hands to Mark's neck before his hands hit the floor, going through the visual, distorting it, disrupting it like dust floating in a beam of light. He had been caught off guard, sent into a panic, applying a real-life reaction to a made-up situation. In all of his pre-go live calculations, Ryan hadn't considered the possibility of suicide. Overpowering Nicole, maybe an informal alliance between Nicole and Eric where they conspired to kill Mark—he'd written code to prepare for these scenarios. But suicide... by *sword*?

Who does that?

The pain Mark must have felt was inconceivable to Ryan because he'd had to saw at himself to find purchase because the blade had been so damaged... Ryan almost wished he hadn't included realistic response to their packages, but he'd had to—it was the only way to get sustainable results. But that meant he'd had to witness the pulling of the skin to expose tendons and ligaments, the blood spurting in time with the beating of his heart, Mark's kneecaps shattering as they hit the cold, hard stone. Ryan had to see it, but Mark had endured it—all of it and the pain that came with it—but why? So that Nicole didn't have to be the one to do it? So she didn't have to inflict such pain on him? So she wouldn't feel the guilt? Ryan didn't know. After all the years and all the simulations, he still didn't know what drove Mark to it every time. And sometimes, when he interacted in the scene and got Mark's attention, he could almost tell that Mark knew... and he was laughing at him.

"—nd, but it might be time to—"

"I just need to see what's going on—" Ryan cut in, unsure at first who he was speaking over. He had been stuck in his head again. He couldn't afford to do that right now, to wallow—the stakes were too high.

"More observation?" Jason said incredulously, and Ryan instantly regretted not punching him in the mouth before. He leveled his eyes on his brother, a silent warning passing between them.

"I need to understand the dynamic. Nicole can't kill them—neither of them. She can kill any other adversary—she's taken out everyone we've ever thrown at her—but she can't kill them. Not when they're her siblings, not when they're her sworn enemies, not—"

"Not when they're her lovers either, apparently," Jason added, looking out at Eric himself, watching him give into tears on the sidewalk.

"This one was touching, I'll give you that. Fit for the Romance of the Month Book Club, if you're into kinky."

The smug smile on Jason's face was making Ryan's blood boil.

"You know Ryan didn't write it that way," Maureen said, sensing the tension growing between them. "The characters do what they're compelled to do, you know that as much as I do, Jason. It's why this project is so ingenious—the intuitive nature of choice."

Jason shrugged slightly, hardly enough to be noticeable. Ryan took it as a win anyway.

"I'll need to modify the algorithms, maybe try identity reassignment—"

"Changing their names won't cut it," Jason scoffed.

"Not their just names... it's more than that. I just... I just need to figure out how *much* more."

Jason sighed; his brow furrowed. When he spoke again, the words came from low in his throat.

"This is not what the Galactic Collaborative wants. It's not what they paid for."

Maureen's downcast eyes served as the only response.

Eric was sitting on the retaining wall, his back leaning against the wrought iron fence. He was crying openly now, all attempts at restraint gone. If Ryan had decided to cue rain clouds, darken the skies, and command a slow, steady storm to soak Eric's suit and mix with his tears, no one would have been surprised.

But he didn't.

He turned it all off, doing away with the small California town and the quaint little funeral home, to look at Nicole, Eric, and Mark as they lay in their pods.

Sterile.

Antiseptic.

Impersonal.

Hadn't Mark said something about that?

Ryan made a mental note to review Mark's earlier transcripts to find out.

There was a low hum from the console station.

Unforgiving fluorescents lit the room, everything bright, too bright.

They all needed haircuts.

Mark's gray was starting to come in.

Ryan sighed. This last run had gone too long.

"It's time," Maureen said as she measured Ryan, gauging him for a response. "Maybe for good."

"Not yet," Ryan replied and Jason shook his head, leaving the room without another word. "We can still learn more from them," Ryan implored, though the argument had not teeth.

Ryan moved to the control panel and turned off their focal stimulators, sending them into the insentient sleep their bodies so desperately needed after being engaged for so long.

Maureen touched another button, one that Ryan had been avoiding since the first failed simulation, the one he wished he could cover up, disconnect, remove from the panel all together. With compassion in her voice she said,

"Not anymore."

CHAPTER 35

The letter was a surprise. Ryan had taken time away from work to rethink the project, consider anthropological transmogrification from a phrenic perspective rather than the somatic nature of muscle memory that he had favored first, which all amounted to him throwing spitballs at the wall to see which ones stuck. The truth was that Ryan needed time away from all of it, the faults in the code, the way Jason's lip curled when he got the upper hand, how easy he was making it for Jason to laugh himself to sleep. But those weren't even the real reasons that Ryan hadn't set foot in the lab since the night the simulation went off the rails again... since the last time Mark had killed himself. The truth was that Ryan needed time to recover from losing them.

Nicole, Eric, and Mark had become a part of his life, a part of who he was. He sat up nights trying to figure out why they weren't working out as expected, trying to pinpoint the anomaly. He wrote and rewrote lines of code, planned enhancements, tweaked and discarded and reformed, like a sculptor working with a mound of clay, but nothing had worked. And now they were gone. Ryan took it like one would experiencing a death. And perhaps it was.

But then the letter came. Emailed from Mark while in the last simulation to show up in the inboxes he monitored. No surprise there—it was part of the design, should the subjects choose to communicate in that way—but the content knocked him off his feet. It was so raw, so authentic... so *them*. Ryan had considered just deleting it, cutting the cord and moving on, told himself he would do well to let Mark stay in the grave he dug for himself for once and for all since he seemed to want to be there so much. But he couldn't. He had to know what Mark thought important enough to tell them after his death. He wanted to know why Mark, without fail, removed himself from the equation, changing everything Ryan had planned with the swipe of his hand.

And blade, Ryan thought as a chill not unlike an icy finger touched the nape of his neck.

Ryan was continually impressed by the behavior the subjects displayed, each action completely of their own volition in response to the conditions he had put in place. This response was real, but he only admitted it to himself. Ryan felt quite a lot like God, setting up elaborate scenarios, talking snakes and ruby red apples, mayhem for all to see if they dared chance a glance. He was a puppeteer, Doc from *Back to the Future*, and the whole thing was *The Truman Show* on steroids. Sometimes he went down that path, blamed everything on an adolescent infatuation with late 20th century movies, but it never truly stuck. Ryan wasn't just playing around with time travel—indeed, he had never intended to get involved with time travel at all.

He was trying to weaponize living human tissue, to equip it with logical thought and intuitive conduct—quick, crafty, and clean. Ryan was trying to create the most skilled soldier to date, one that would never be detected in a crowd; one that would be clean and efficient. He'd added a lot of elements to the configuration. He had purposefully left out empathetic sensitivity, either inherent or transferred.

But it hadn't worked.

Ryan had considered Mark's email, giving the idea of simply ignoring it real, honest thought. To deny himself this last communication, this marvel in and of itself, seemed silly. In fact, reading it might help him understand how to make sure the next set avoided the pitfalls that plagued these doomed three. If there was to ever be a next set... Still, Ryan almost felt like he was intruding by reading it, eavesdropping on personal matters that didn't involve him.

He grappled with that for days. But read it, he did.

My loves,

It must be so weird to get a letter from me now. I scheduled it for two weeks after, thinking that it might be ok by then—that you might actually be able to take in what I want to say instead of... I knew sending this too early would be a mistake—the sentiment would get lost in the grief and all there would be was sadness. I don't know if two weeks was long enough to wait, but I was afraid to send it any later than this. Too long might reopen the wound that had started to heal, and I don't want to cause you any more pain than I already have.

I need to say some things now so that you never forget them. I need to make sure of that. I need you to know, without a shadow of a doubt, that this was not a hallucination or some elaborate dream. We were real. Our love was real. I have never been more certain of anything in my entire life. We were meant to be together.

I love you. I really do. I've never felt this way about anyone else, and it scared the hell out of me sometimes. It is insane, this feeling. There in the coffee shop, I knew I needed the two of you more than I needed air to breathe. That sounds so romantic, like something out of one of your books, Nicole, but I really do feel that way. I feel like something inside me finally woke up when it saw you two, Eric with those gorgeous blue eyes and Nicole with the most appealing smile—you two changed my whole world in an instant. I was nervous, unsure of myself, flustered in a way that I had never been before. And I had only been in your presence for a minute. I knew I needed to know you. In fact, I felt like I couldn't live without getting to know you, even then. That feeling never went away. And when we gave ourselves to each other it felt more right than anything ever had.

We shared something that most people can only dream of. It was all-encompassing but not cloying, multi-faceted but not smothering. I always wanted more of you—more trips, more kisses, more love, more time. You were my drug, and I was addicted. Yes, that is corny, but it is the truth. I couldn't have stopped loving you if I tried. And, God help me, I did *try.*

After our second year I told myself that it had to end. Told myself that what I was doing was wrong and that I was some kind of horrible person for continuing on like this. And much of that was true. I can't claim that what we did was right. I had a family—a wife who treated me well and two boys I was over the moon about. I had no reason to compromise everything I had, to be so goddamned reckless—my life was fine before I met you. But I did. And I had decided it was time to stop. I gave myself a pass, gave into the idea that I had been bored and you guys represented excitement and, I don't know... something new. I tried to tell myself that I'd had my fun but playtime was over. That ok, I'd had some good sex, the best sex I'd ever had in my life, if I'm being honest, but enough was enough and I needed to cut you both loose and get back to being the man I knew myself to be. But I couldn't. Even as I formed the words in my head I knew I couldn't stop. Even as I got angry with myself for being weak, for throwing everything I had worked so hard for away and ruining the life I built, I knew it held no water. Because us getting together was not some fluke. No other woman has ever turned my head, and I have never been interested in a man before or since. I also never had a crisis of conscience—I know in my heart that we weren't random. We weren't wrong. The circumstances were, but not us. *We were meant to be—I know that's true as well as I know my name. It was more than just sex. It was more than finding something new to occupy myself with. It was love. True love. And you were my destiny.*

Baltimore. Do you remember? That little place on the water, just before you left the restaurant district and entered the part of town where they shot The Wire. *Eric, you drove down from New York and Nicole, you came up from Virginia to meet me there for lunch before my flight during the summer of, I want to say it was our third year. We were getting used to meeting in places that were off the beaten path but this one took the cake. Eric, you said you knew some people from an acting company in the area who spoke highly of it, so off we went, ignoring the boarded-up units we could see out of the corners of our eyes without so much as craning our necks. It didn't matter anyway, just as long as we were together.*

I had never eaten blue crab before so we thought we'd spend the afternoon by the water doing that. Crabs and beer. Laughing with my loves. It was the perfect way to spend a day. I never forgot how it felt to be fed by you, Nicole. I was struggling with the crab, pulverizing it with that stupid mallet they gave us, cracking the claws overzealously, breaking apart the meat. You had a much easier time getting the meat out of the shell than I did and instead of letting me starve, you started holding out pieces for me to eat. I couldn't resist missing a few of them and licking your fingers instead or nipping them just a little as I sucked the offered meat into my mouth; I know you knew that. You were in control the whole time. I thought I was teasing you, but it was really you who was teasing me, and we were both teasing Eric, giving him a show. None of us had a chance. The way we kissed that day has stayed in my mind forever—lazily, comfortably, passionately but content to stay right where we were. Sometimes I wake up to it at night and feel myself responding as if I had just tasted your lips. Sometimes I forget we're not together and I reach for you there in the dark so that we can finish what we started.

My memories are filled with moments like that—the times when I laughed so hard that my stomach hurt and I couldn't catch my breath, or the times when I was so proud of you both that I couldn't stop beaming. The times when I felt so adored that I didn't know what to do with myself. The times when all I wanted to do was show you how much you meant to me.

Nicole and Eric... your names are like a song to me, the only one I ever wanted to sing.

I have to say this part too and there's no way to ease into it. I want to put it off, don't want to talk about it at all, but I have to. It's hard. I know it is, and I am so, so sorry.

So... If you try to find out what happened to me, you will hear that I had a brain tumor. That's the story I've created to explain why I've done this to my wife. Believe me, I know how horrible that is. She and I had a discussion years ago about whether or not we would want to be on life support or have heroic efforts performed to sustain life if something terrible happened to us. I said I didn't want to live if it was going to be like that, so while my decision will hurt her, it falls in line with what I have always maintained, and she will believe it. I left her a letter too, dropping hints about this mystery illness, implying that much of my travel was related to secret doctor visits and things like that, my changing moods were because of this thing growing inside me. Sounds realistic, at least I hope it does. I begged her not to have an autopsy performed, and I know she will do everything she can to honor my wishes because her religion frowns on autopsies anyway. If I know her, she will deny receipt of the results if they perform one without her consent, so I am not worried that my family will find out that my body was healthy and that this had nothing to do with illness. If I'm wrong... god help me, I hope I am not wrong about that. I had to protect my family from the burden of thinking they were somehow to blame, so I did the best I could. They'll never find the doctors they might decide to go looking for, and they will be frustrated by that, but that too will serve its purpose. It will help them to focus on something other than my death, and then, when they come up empty, maybe they will be able to move on properly. I have to believe this is the way it will go. If not, I'm a different kind of monster than I ever suspected.

I know all of that was morbid, but I had to make sure you knew the truth. We were on purpose. Even though I felt things that I never once expected to, did things you could never have convinced me that I would do just 10 minutes before we met, it was real. Me being with you, loving you, those were not the actions of someone who was no longer in their right mind. We were kismet. And for me, we always will be.

I don't know what else to say.

I know I've said it already, but I want to say it again, I want to say it over and over again because maybe it will change things, alter reality. I love you, Nicole. I love you, Eric. I love what we have and who I am with you. I feel like I finally saw the real me reflected in your eyes. I want that again. I want that always. I want us, even though I have no right to ask for it. I know you can't give that to me, and I guess I always have. Our happiness was only out on loan and had to be repaid at some point. But my god, do I wish it were possible. I wish that forever was us.

But I know it isn't. Right now you're probably making things worse by telling yourself that it could have been different, maybe even that it should have been, but please don't do that. Please don't assume blame where none belongs. We were all caught in a terrible cycle that would never have ended, not really. We started and stopped so many times, trying to do what some moral code engrained in us dictated one moment, then falling back on what our hearts demanded the next. It would have been that way until we were old and gray because we never would have had the chance to live together as partners and make a true home. Think about it—be honest with yourselves right now and think about what would have really happened, not what you wanted to happen or what you hoped would. Even outside of the worries we would have had about the kids—if they resented us for breaking up their homes or whether they thought that everything they knew about their lives and who we were was a lie—we would have worried about how things looked to the world. It's one thing to be in a relationship, same sex or opposite. But to have three people like us—three people who loved each other so obviously that it couldn't be denied... when was the last time you saw anything like that? They exist, I looked it up and some of them call themselves throuples or triads... I'm just glad we never decided to use one of those terms to describe us, that's all I'm saying... except the second one is kinda funny. Like we're in some kind of gang... 'we're the triads—what's good?' Anyway, these relationships are out there, but they're under wraps. They hide away, for the most part only feeling free to enjoy each other when they're sure no one is looking. How would we have navigated that? I am in love with a stage actor whose popularity is skyrocketing and an author who is gaining more recognition every day. After our kids had left home, we would have that to contend with. Sure, we would have made it work, but not in the way that we all wanted—a flat in London or a villa in the Caribbean. We would never have had the peace we so desperately wanted, that freedom to love each other and not care who saw us. And we would have tried so hard to have it, I know we would have, and that it would have remained just out of our grasps would have crushed a little bit of each of our souls, because we would have failed. We would have loved each other so much that we'd have each waited our time, waiting out the buzz, waited for the moment to be right, and we would have done it without resentment, no, none at all—there would have been nothing but genuine happiness for each other, and I know that for a fact. But the right time would never, ever have come. So, maybe it's good that I see it now. Maybe it's good that I recognize the truth for what it is.

I'm rambling now. The problem is I know that when I stop I will become a part of your past. You might wonder why now. Why not wait and see what happens? There isn't an easy answer to that. The fact is that I knew after that last time we said goodbye that there wouldn't be another run for us. We were going to stick to our collective guns and really stay away this time. Because this time we weren't being selfish about it. We were doing it because it was the right thing to do for the other two—we were being more selfless than we had ever been. Us being over... that left a hole that I couldn't fill with anything. I tried forgetting about you, forgetting about what we had, but the memories played like movies in my head. I tried living on the sidelines of your lives, celebrating your wins from a distance, but I saw more than I ever should have and got my feelings hurt more times than I could count. Social media is a bitch. Being able to see you but not touch you, watch a live but not be recognized, read something you wrote but not comment—it made staying away harder. You were right there—so close, but yet so far. Forbidden fruit. Nothing I tried took away the feeling of missing a part of myself. That must say something about me, and if it does, so be it. I couldn't bear it.

There was no sound the day we stopped. It was like I had survived something the world had succumbed to, and I was left there alone. The house was empty, and there were no birds chirping, no dogs barking, no cars driving by. I remember looking at the closed blinds—between the slats I could see that it was dull and drab outside, but I was afraid to open them fully and look out. And it was so very still. Do you remember that Twilight Zone *episode where the guy realizes he is the only person left in that little town—maybe even in the whole world? The silence... the stillness was like that—it was everything and nothing at the same time. And then all of a sudden a sound came from behind me, a clicking that sounded like a light switch turning on next to my head. Color poured back into the world from above like spilled paint over a ledge and suddenly I knew how important you were to me, suddenly I knew you were gone, gone for real this time. Suddenly I knew that without you in my life I wasn't truly alive.*

When you were both lost to me—utterly gone—only the heady feeling of desire mixed with the most poignant wistfulness remained, as torturous and base as that might be. I lived the life of a man who was someone different, someone other than who I really was—who I used to be—and that was harder to do than I thought it would be. I take issue with whoever came up with that saying, 'it's better to have loved and lost than never to have loved at all.' I was blissfully ignorant of what love could be before I found you. Having enjoyed it and then lost it undid me in more ways that I care to recount.

I wasn't rash; please don't worry that I was just sad one night and did something that I couldn't take back. I didn't rush. Some part of me knew I was going to do this months ago—maybe even a year ago. Not long after our goodbye. I could have done it in the spring but that would have put a stain on what we had. The memory of the day we met should be a happy one for you forever, so I waited to be sure this didn't coincide with that. I also couldn't bear to go without hearing your voices again, and I waited as long as it took to make that happen. There's no way you can remember the last time we spoke—you didn't even know it was me on the line. Nicole, you were easier to reach—all I had to do was call your office number to find you, so I called you last. In fact, I called you today. Eric, you've been travelling so much it was hard to pin you down. I finally spoke with someone who thought I was calling about a promotion they were running in your home theater—the one where the cast would answer the phones for a few days to hype up the next show. I guess they were trying to pack the amphitheater for the summer, but with you in the cast they won't need any gimmicks. You are on fire right now, and it is so well-deserved, my love. Anyway, they gave me the schedule, and you were going to be answering calls on the fifth day, so I called. And called. And called. I kept getting a busy signal, kept wondering who was calling so much—the blue hairs interested in the matinee? I kept at it for what seemed like hours, and then I finally got you. I thought at first that it was a recording because you sounded fresher than I thought you would after having been on the phone all day. You said hello, said who you were, asked if I was coming to see the show... what was it again... Much Ado About Nothing, *I think. I stayed quiet, waiting for you to say something else. In the silence, you chuckled, and my heart stopped in my chest. You asked if I was still there, and I hung up. I didn't want to say anything because if I started talking, I wouldn't stop. All I wanted to do was talk to you, tell you how much I love you, tell you how sorry I was for making you put your life on hold. I didn't want you to hear my voice because you might have said you loved me too and then we'd call Nicole and we'd start again and the cycle would be reset until the next time. And no matter how much I wanted that to happen—no matter how much I wanted to touch you, to hold you, to kiss you both again, it would have been irresponsible to ask you to compromise your life away. We were done with that. Both of you deserve more than that.*

Nicole, you answered the phone so fast, I didn't have time to think. They transferred me to your desk, and you picked up before I was ready. You were all business, affecting a tone that you have never used with us, so I was a little taken aback. You didn't say much, just thanked me for calling and told me who you were, but boy, was it impressive. Your tone was formal but open. Just like with Eric, I wanted to tell you that I love you and that this was nonsense... that we were meant to be together. But that isn't what I called for... it wouldn't have been the right thing to do even if it was the only thing I wanted to do. So I said nothing. You said 'Hello?' beckoning me to reply, and I just listened. Just before hanging up, you uttered the tiniest humming sound, as if you were perplexed. It made my breath hitch in my throat, it was so real, so you. And then you were gone.

For some time afterward I thought about what I was about to do, how it would affect you both. I know that you will be sad and hurt that this happened, that I didn't come to you about it before doing such a drastic thing. I also know that you won't have any way to express those feelings because the people around you don't know what is going on. You will only have each other, and I hope that you realize that early instead of suffering alone. I hope you come together to get through this moment in time because only the two of you know what the other is feeling—only the two of you understand.

You might think I took the easy way out of this strange existence we've been embroiled in, and I don't know that I blame you for that. I will already be gone by the time you find out, won't have to see the tears or live through the aftermath. The whole thing feels cowardly even as I write this, please know that. But I didn't do this because I couldn't hack it. I didn't cut and run because I was afraid or weak or had given up. I did it because as long as I'm here, we don't move on, we don't grow, we don't exist. It took me a long time to realize that, to truly understand what it meant, but I can see it now. We come from three different worlds and were brought together by an amazing stroke of fate. We had what we could during our time, little bits, little moments, never enough. But whatever else we can get, whatever else could be in our next chapter, is unattainable the way we are now.

So, what does that mean?

I wish I could answer that intelligently, but I can't really go beyond saying that I want to know. I have *to know. If the next chapter is the two of you together at last, if you are experiencing that now, reading this letter together as you remember me, then I will find peace in that. But if there is something else to us, if there is more... I know we can't find it doing the same thing we've always done.*

And so, now we're here.

I guess I should stop now, I've gone on long enough. There aren't enough pages for me to say everything I want to say anyway, not enough words to use to make clear how I feel about you. You two are the best things that ever happened to me. You showed me love, accepted me for who I really am because you saw the real me—the one I didn't know existed—probably from that very first moment. For that, I thank you. For that, I was in love with you, so deeply in love that I didn't know where I ended and where you began. I hope you remember the way it felt to be in each other's arms, the way it sounded when we laughed together. I hope you remember the way we were forever. Our love ordered my steps and changed me for the better. I was never happier than when I was with you. Thank you for showing me what love really is.

Nicole and Eric, I adore you.

If God is kind, maybe you'll tell me about all the plays and books that I missed when we meet again.

Until then,
Mark

With a sigh, Ryan turned on the light in the laboratory where they lay in stasis.

Then he pressed the button.

About the Author

L. Marie Wood is a Bram Stoker®, Golden Stake Award, and International Impact Award-winning author. She is also a MICO Award-winning screenwriter, a Rhysling and Elgin nominated poet, an accomplished essayist, and a playwright. Wood has won over 50 national and international screenplay and film awards. She has been published in groundbreaking works, including the anthologies *Sycorax';s Daughters* and *Slay: Stories of the Vampire Noire*, as well as industry staples such as the Magazine of Fantasy & Science Fiction and Nightmare Magazine and in multiple languages. Her nonfiction has been published in academic textbooks such as the cross-curricular, *Conjuring Worlds: An Afrofuturist Textbook.* She is also part of the 2022 Bookfest Book Award-winning poetry anthology, Under Her Skin, as well as Bram Stoker Award® and Shirley Jackson Award Nominee anthologies *Shakespeare Unleashed* and *Mooncalves.* Her papers are archived as part of University of Pittsburgh's Horror Studies Collection. Wood is the Vice President of the Horror Writers Association, the founder of the Speculative Fiction Academy, an English and Creative Writing professor, a horror scholar with a Ph.D. in Creative Writing and an MFA in Speculative Fiction, and a frequent contributor to the conversation around the evolution of genre fiction. Learn more about L. Marie Wood at

www.lmariewood.com.

MORE FROM L. MARIE WOOD

Patrick thought he knew what awaited him in the afterlife. He's learning the hard way that he was dead wrong. He is hunted by a race of giant beasts, the likes of which have never been seen by living eyes, and he is surrounded by the newly-dead from worlds beyond knowing. In this Realm, nothing and no one can be trusted.

Patrick's choices will create echoes in the world of the living. He may be the key to salvation in this Hell known as The Realm, but it may come at the cost of his family.

With his legacy on the line, can he make the right choice?

https://www.mochamemoirspress.com

About Mocha Memoirs Press

Established in July 2010, Mocha Memoirs Press's mission is to amplify marginalized voices in speculative fiction genres (science fiction, fantasy, horror). We publish bold, fearless fiction that pushes boundaries and smashes gatekeepers.

We invite you to review our catalog to review the diversity in our stories. You can access the catalog at https://www.mochamemoirspress.com. Join our newsletter **here.**

You can also find us online:

Instagram - @mochamemoirspress
TikTok-@mochamemoirspress
BlueSky-@mochamemoirspress.com
Facebook facebook.com/MochaMemoirsPress

www.ingramcontent.com/pod-product-compliance
Lightning Source LLC
LaVergne TN
LVHW030908080826
845145LV00010B/2815

* 9 7 8 1 9 6 2 3 5 3 3 1 1 *